THE INFLUENCER

MIRANDA RIJKS

Miranda Rijks

INKUBATOR
BOOKS

PROLOGUE

I see them in my mind's eye. All jolly as they climb into the small airplane; a nerve-tingling excitement fizzes through them, even if they've done this a hundred times before. Because it would, wouldn't it? Flying in a metal container with just acrylic and aluminium to protect you isn't normal. Humans aren't meant to fly.

The plane will take off and rise quickly, the patch-work of green fields and darker splodges of woodland shrinking in size, pinhead cars meandering along ribbons of roads. Perhaps they'll be chatting amongst themselves, or maybe they won't, the brutal noise of the engine too loud, allowing only their thoughts to keep them company. Perhaps they'll be planning the weekend ahead, imagining selecting seafood from an extensive menu at a fancy restaurant, or sensing how the salty sea air will prickle their nostrils as they take a leisurely walk along the seashore.

I don't know how long it will take for my plan to take effect. I don't even know if it's going to work. But if it does, they'll begin to feel sleepy, a bit nauseous probably. I expect it takes hold quicker on women than men, because they're smaller. Or perhaps it doesn't. Maybe they'll all doze off at the same time, their heads lolling from side to side, their hands flopping down on their laps. And then the airplane will start doing its own thing. Because machines need to be controlled. I expect a disembodied voice from air traffic control will come through the radio, the tone becoming increasingly urgent as the controller on the other end gets no response. And then the engine will start whirring and whining, and the nose of the plane will dip downwards, tilting heavily towards the grey sea far below. Maybe one of them will wake suddenly, fear coursing through them as they realise that the plane is toppling out of the sky and there is absolutely nothing they can do about it. Or perhaps they will all stay asleep, knowing and feeling nothing as they hurtle through the air.

And me, I will be the master of the plan, yet no one will ever know. All those people who think they know me. They make assumptions, but you should never judge anyone. Never. But we all do, don't we? We look at the way someone dresses, the colour of their skin, how they talk, where they grew up, what education they had, and we presume they are going to be a certain type. And the more outspoken the person is, the more we think we know them. I learned that early on. Never, ever judge, because nine times out of ten, you will be horribly wrong.

And so, back to my plan. I know all about carbon monoxide poisoning. I read the air accident report from the tragic death of that world-famous Italian model, the one who commissioned a private plane to take her on a middle-of-the-night flight to the house of her lover. 'Deeply unconscious at impact' is how the report described the pilot and passenger. It's all in the public domain if you dig hard enough. And so it is that I discovered most privately owned small planes are not fitted with carbon monoxide alarms. And that there is a V-band clamp around the exhaust, which allows gasses to leak into the heater muff when the cabin heating is turned on. It's cold up there in the skies, so the heating will be turned on. Carbon monoxide is scentless, a fatal killer and such a useful tool.

I wonder if I will feel guilty for snuffing out life. I wonder if, when one has successfully killed once, that rush of excitement, that feeling of power becomes addictive. I expect it does. Because we all like to have things our own way, don't we? But only someone who has destroyed the life of another human being knows that you never need to accept *no* as an answer. It *is* possible to always get your own way. Always. You just need to be brave and sufficiently singled-minded, and if you have to destroy life to achieve your goals, so be it.

1

NATHAN - NOW

I feel my shoulders relax as I steer the car into our driveway. Clusters of daffodils are poking their heads through the grass-covered ground, and I smile as I glance up at the house. It has been home for nearly a decade, a decade during which I have experienced the full gamut of human emotion. Not that I like to think about such things. Instead, I focus on the welcoming lantern that glows with an orange hue over the front porch, even though it isn't fully dark yet. I park the car next to Sacha's. And then I kick myself. It's Marie's car now, and it's about time I buy her a new one.

How lucky we are to live here. It's a traditional Sussex farmhouse, with what estate agents call "tile-hung elevations" and stone roof tiles. Red-coloured tiles line the upper portion of the house, and two twisted chimney stacks give the old property a surprising grandeur. When we stumbled across the house, it was a derelict wreck, and because it wasn't listed, the developers were ready to raze it to the ground. Now it is the perfect family home, with four bedrooms and three bathrooms.

What makes it particularly special is the location. A house like this is more typically found in the country-side. We're just a ten-minute walk from the centre of Horsham, at the end of a residential street. The only compromise is the small garden.

It's the kitchen we all love the most, with its impressive oak beams, gleaming black Aga and large island unit. I recall the first time I showed Marie the Aga. She stared at it, a frown creasing her brow, her teeth gently biting her lower lip.

'I'm sorry, *Monsieur*,' she said in faltering English, 'but I never see such an oven before.'

What a difference three and a half years make. Now, her English is faultless, although that Valaisan accent is still prominent, and no one bakes as good a cake in an Aga as Marie.

I put my key in the front door and shout, 'I'm home!'

'Hello, Dad!' Chloe grins as she lopes down the stairs, her violin case over her shoulder. She's still wearing her royal blue school uniform. Chloe looks like her mum, with wavy strawberry blonde hair and big blue eyes. Her older sister, Isla, has my darker hair and pale skin.

'Have you finished practising?' I ask as I deposit my bag on the hall bench.

She rolls her eyes at me. I am sure she shouldn't be so good at that contemptuous expression at thirteen years old. 'Yes. Marie's already given me grief. I don't need it from you, too.' She lisps slightly, thanks to her newly applied braces supplied by our dentist for an extortionate fee. My two loving daughters have meta-morphosed into sarcastic adolescents. They have had to grow up too quickly. I suppose that's what happens when you lose your mother at such a young age.

Marie walks into the hall, a tea towel over her arm. Her big blue eyes, clear skin and dark, pixie-cut hair make her look younger than her thirty-two years. She stands on tiptoes to give me a kiss, and I pull her into my arms, inhaling her scent, which is so very different to Sacha's, and still takes me by surprise.

Isla stomps down the stairs. Two years older than Chloe, she has borne the brunt of our suffering and acts as if she's eighteen.

'Gross,' she mutters. 'Get a room.'

I ignore her. I'm careful which battles I choose to fight.

'How was your day?' Marie asks, clasping my hand as we walk together into the kitchen.

'It was good, actually. I think we're making progress.'

I sink into a kitchen chair. Marie pours half a glass of red wine and hands it to me. Within the first couple of months of her arriving at our home, it became abundantly clear that Marie knew far more about wine than I did. Her father owns a vineyard on the slopes above Sion in the Rhône Valley, an exceptionally sunny spot of south-western Switzerland. These days, all wine selection and purchasing decisions are made by her. I think one of her greatest disappointments in me is that I drink so little. I enjoy the taste and the relaxing effects; unfortunately, my stomach doesn't.

'Something smells good,' I say as I flick through the post.

'Chicken à l'orange,' Marie says.

'Do you need any help?'

Marie roars with laughter. 'Only if you want to get

food poisoning! It'll be ready in five minutes, so I'll go and get the girls.'

These days, we eat as soon as I get home so the girls get a proper meal with us. I like to know how their days have gone, what's new at school. Sometimes I wonder why we bother, because with Isla in particular, it's almost impossible to get a coherent response to my questions. Her latest ploy to keep her life private is to say that she doesn't like talking when she's eating. Apparently, she needs to count how many times she chews a mouthful so she can fully savour the food; talking disrupts that. Marie thinks it's funny. I try hard not to be annoyed. At least both the girls enjoy Marie's meals. We are very lucky that she is an outstanding cook.

Ten minutes later, we're all seated around the kitchen table, and Marie is spooning the chicken à l'orange onto our plates.

'I've got some news that might interest you girls,' I say. 'I was on my way out of the office when Ash shouted that we've been approached by some Instagram star's PR. She wants to support the charity.'

'That's good, isn't it?' Marie asks as she passes me a plate.

'I think so. Ash and the team seemed excited. She's called Skye. What is it with musicians and Gen-Z stars who think they don't need surnames?'

'What did you say about Skye?' Isla asks. When the conversation interests her, concentrating on food quickly gets forgotten.

'Sacha's Sanctuary have been asked if we'd like someone called Skye to be our figurehead.'

'Oh my god, Dad! Do you realise who she is? She's, like, a megastar. Surely even you have heard of her.' Isla shakes her head as if she can't believe I'm so out of touch.

'Nope,' I say as I slice a Brussel sprout. There is a clatter as both girls drop their cutlery on their plates, their mouths agape. They stare at each other, and then both look at me.

'You must have heard of Skye, Dad!' Isla says.

'Can we meet her?' Chloe's eyes are bright. 'I love Skye! She's the best.'

'What is she famous for?' Marie asks. The girls roll their eyes at each other. I'm relieved I'm not the only one who hasn't got a clue who Skye is.

'She's got, like, millions of followers on YouTube, TikTok and Instagram. Everyone loves her. She's awesome,' Chloe says.

'Okay, so we've established that she's famous, but what for?'

Isla takes a sip of water. 'She was homeless. She had a really crap childhood. Everyone she knew got into drugs and stuff, but she decided she wanted a different life. She talks about healthy living and being true to yourself.'

'Fair enough, but what's she actually famous for? Is she a singer, an actor or what?'

'You don't have to be good at something to be a social media celebrity. You just need to be authentic.'

Marie smirks at me, and I realise that this is another of those times when the age gap between us is apparent. I have to bite my tongue to stop myself from telling the girls that hard work is the only thing that really matters; recognition will follow if it is merited.

'I suppose she's beautiful,' Marie comments.

'You're both so cynical,' Isla groans. 'I'll show you her Instagram account and YouTube channel.' She scrapes her chair backwards.

'After supper,' I say. 'Finish your food first.' I can't keep the girls off their phones, but I do insist on phone-free mealtimes.

'Can we meet her?' Chloe asks.

'Maybe.'

'Oh my god!' Chloe does a little jiggle of excitement, and even Isla is grinning.

'What's she going to do for Sacha's Sanctuary?' Marie asks. I notice how the words slip off her tongue these days. She used to hesitate before saying Sacha's name.

'According to Ash, Skye wants to discuss fronting some fundraising campaigns for us. Obviously, I need to meet her and make sure that she's not just a pretty face. I can't have some B-lister celebrity who leads a drug-fuelled lavish lifestyle be a patron of our charity for the homeless.'

'She's not like that,' Isla says, scowling at me. 'She's a really good person. She promotes a healthy lifestyle; she's seriously into caring for the planet and helping people out. You're so cynical.'

'Well, if it works out, that will be marvellous,' Marie says.

SACHA, my beloved wife and the girls' mother, died four years ago. Sacha and I had a commercial catering company that did well, really well, actually. We managed all the in-house catering for large companies such as law firms and banks based in London and the south-east, but when Sacha was diagnosed with terminal cancer, all I wanted to do was to be there for her and the girls. I had no time to think about work, so when one of our competitors made an offer for the business, I grabbed it and sold up. It meant that I could dedicate my time to Sacha during those final months of her life, knowing that there was enough money in the bank to keep the girls and me going for a few years.

Whilst I was lucky in business and in wealth, we were unlucky in life. My heart exploded into smithereens when Sacha died. She and I were childhood sweethearts. We split up briefly during our early twenties, and later agreed that those couple of years apart were utterly miserable. Of course, it's easy to filter out the difficult times and the negatives of a relationship when all one has is memories, but I'm confident Sacha and I had a good marriage and truly loved each other. If I hadn't had the girls, I would probably have gone completely off the rails after her death. Perhaps I would have ended up like one of my homeless clients.

It was some months later that I realised I was doing a lousy job at everything. My cooking was dire; the girls were frequently late for school, wearing clothes that were too small, dirty or full of holes; and I felt utterly futile, struggling to get through each day. It was my brother, Simon, who told me I needed to get my act together, in the way that only close family members can do. *Get some counselling. Go back to work,* he said. *Do something meaningful.* He got me thinking.

Back in the days when we ran the catering business, despite trying to keep waste to the minimum, we always had leftover food. We donated all surplus to a couple of soup kitchens. But if I'm honest, our motivation was to look good to our customers rather than wanting to make a real difference. During those dark months after Sacha's death, I had too much time to think, and I realised that the catering business was no great legacy. It was the difference we made to the people who frequented the soup kitchens that really mattered. I decided to set up a homeless charity, in Sacha's name, a not-for-profit with big ambitions, ultimately to banish homelessness in the south-east.

It quickly became apparent that although my mojo was slowly returning, and the girls no longer wore clothes that were too small, I couldn't be their primary carer and run the charity. I got in touch with an agency, and Marie came into our lives. I know it's a cliché, falling in love with the au pair, and it didn't happen overnight. It's been a slow-burning, deep realisation that I love her and simply can't imagine life without her. Unsurprisingly, the adjustment from au pair to step-mother has been challenging for the girls and Marie herself. But Marie is very careful not to trample on Sacha's memory, and I think – and hope – that we have achieved a fine balance.

As SOON AS we have finished supper, Isla jumps up and, rather surprisingly, piles up the dirty plates with a clatter and carries them over to the island unit. It is very rare she helps out without being asked. She then grabs her phone and walks back to the table.

'Look, Dad, this is Skye.'

She leans over me as she shows me a video of a woman, who I assume is mid to late twenties.

'This is Skye yesterday. It's a behind-the-scenes of one of her photoshoots.' The footage zooms in on video-graphers, photographers and rails of designer clothes. Girls with jutting shoulder blades and stick-thin thighs are running around holding notebooks and clothes hangers, and then the camera rotates so that it focuses on the woman behind the lens. 'Remember, if I can reach for the sky, you can too. Be true to you. Until next time, my lovelies!'

'That's her catchline,' Chloe says. 'She's so pretty, isn't she?'

I nod. Yes, she's pretty in an artificial, too-much-make-up kind of way, with big blue eyes and fake lashes and golden tresses and teeth that are so white they're in danger of burning your eyes with their glare.

'Can I see?' Marie asks. Isla slides the phone across the table and returns to her chair.

'Skye used to date that film star, I can't remember his name, but now she's with a professional sportsman,' Isla says.

'How do you know all about her private life?' I ask.

Isla gives me the eye-rolling treatment again. 'Because it's not private!'

'Right.'

I'm beginning to wonder why on earth Skye wants to have anything to do with my charity. It sounds like she's in the big league, with millions of fans across the world.

'The thing that I like about Skye is that she hasn't had any plastic surgery, and she promotes natural brands. Some of the social influencers are like porn stars,' Isla says before yawning. 'And she's had a tough life. Her best friend died in some tragic accident, she was brought up in children's homes, she lived on the streets, she hasn't got any qualifications, but she's a multimillionaire and goes out of her way to help others.'

'How do you know all of this?' I ask. 'You can't believe everything you read or see on social media.'

'For god's sake, Dad, what do you take us for?' Isla shakes her head. 'You'll see when you meet her. Tell her me and my friends all think she's great.'

· · ·

TWENTY MINUTES LATER, Marie is washing the dishes and I'm drying. The girls are upstairs, supposedly doing their homework, but most likely on their phones.

'The wedding invitations are coming back from the printers on Friday,' Marie says. 'Can you have another look through the guest list?'

'Of course.' I put the tea towel down on the counter and put my arms around her waist, pulling her towards me.

'I'm all soapy!' She laughs, dripping washing-up suds onto the floor and shaking the rubber washing-up gloves at me.

'I love you,' I say as I plant my lips over hers. 'And I can't wait for us to be married.'

And it's true. I am looking forward to Marie becoming my wife. I want to banish those feelings of guilt that I've moved on, forgotten my first love too quickly. And I'm hoping that formalising our relationship will make that just a little bit easier. I had thought that Marie would want to get married in her native Switzerland, have a church wedding and all the ceremony, but she said her life is here now. So we're having a registry office wedding, followed by a reception for sixty guests in a local hotel. It will be an early summer wedding, so very different from my first time around when Sacha and I got married in December with a heavy frost on the ground. In the autumn, we will go to Switzerland and have a party there, hosted in a fabulous barn next to her parents' vineyard. According to Marie, September is the best month of the year, and she intends to put us all to work harvesting grapes.

'The girls have their bridesmaid dress fittings on Saturday,' Marie says, pulling away from me. 'I hope it will go well.'

I hope so too. I can't help but recall the evening we told them that we were getting married. Isla ran out of the room and refused to talk to us for forty-eight hours. Chloe wept. Their tears may have dried, but their hearts have not healed. Perhaps they never will.

2

I can't sleep. There's a streetlight outside my window that glows orange through the ill-fitting blind. It throws a weird glow across the room, a bit like the sun trying to shine through heavy smoke. The bed is hard, but I've slept in much worse. The room smells of disinfectant, and there are scuff marks everywhere: on the walls, the wardrobe, the desk. I suppose it's a bit like a down-market hotel, not that I've ever been inside a hotel, so what would I know? The difference between here and all the other houses I've lived in is that this place is sterile. In the children's homes and in foster care, the houses were full of stuff; sometimes chaotic, but always lived-in. This is the very first time in my life that I have a room that is just mine. And other than the furniture, it's empty. Paint has peeled off the walls where previous occupants have torn away posters, and a single light bulb hangs from the centre of the ceiling.

There are five of us living in this flat, each with our own bedroom and en-suite shower room and a communal kitchen and living room. There are staff who live next door, apparently. Not that I've seen anyone yet, except the skinny man with pockmarked skin who showed me around yesterday.

There's an almighty crash. Shouts.

I sit bolt upright in bed. I've heard all of this sort of thing before, obviously. Male voices and the sound of breaking furniture. I'm about to swing my legs out of bed to double-check the chair is properly wedged up under the door handle, when there is the sound of splintering wood, and my bedroom door crashes open. Two boys stumble inside. One of them shines his mobile phone light directly into my eyes, blinding me. I fumble and switch on the bedside lamp, then bring my knees up to my chest and hug the duvet around me, praying they're not going to try anything on.

'You're gonna do a job for us.' It's Kyle. He's got tattoos running up his neck and the left side of his face. His hair is shaven off. I noticed yesterday that he bites his nails so badly, they're bloodied. I reckon he's not as tough as he pretends to be.

'Piss off,' I say.

He takes a step nearer to the bed. I glare at him, hoping that my trembling doesn't show.

'No one lives here without chipping in,' the other boy says. Pike, I think his name is. He looks younger, probably seventeen, like me.

'You can start off small, with this.' Kyle opens his fingers and reveals a stash of white pills in the centre of his palm. 'Sell the Molly for fifteen quid each. Best place is outside the sixth-form college on Turnstile Street. You can keep one quid for every Molly sold, alright?'

'No, it's not fucking alright. Just piss off out of here.' My voice sounds strong, but my nails are digging painfully into the flesh on my thighs.

'No one tells me to fuck off!' Kyle's eyes narrow as

he steps closer to the bed. 'Playing hard to get. Wanna a bit of action, do yeh?' He thrusts his groin forwards just inches from my face, and I can't stop myself from flinching.

'Just leave them on the table and fuck off out of here,' I say.

Kyle hesitates.

'Come on, bruv, she's butters,' Pike says.

He turns away to look at his friend. 'Yeah, you're right.'

Arseholes. They think my body is attractive, but my face isn't.

Kyle steps away from the bed and drops the pills on the desk. I'll take their insults if they just get out of my room.

'Tomorrow,' he says as he stands in the doorway. He points two fingers at his eyes and then at me, turns around and slams the door shut behind him. It isn't until I hear their voices in the corridor that I let out the breath I didn't know I was holding.

I can't stay here.

I've known since I was small that I've got two options. Take the easy route and follow my screwed-up mum's example, starting off on weed, moving to ecstasy and then onto heroin, quickly sinking to the scum of society, or staying well clear of all drugs and having a chance at life, however small that chance might be. I've sworn to myself I'll do the latter. Give it a shot to stay clean, at least. But I don't know how strong-willed I am. Maybe I've got the addict's gene, and if I'm dragged into that world, I may never get out. For all I know, my dad, whoever he was, was a junkie too.

I wait a long time until there's silence. It's nearly 4 a.m., but I'm sure they're all asleep now. I shove my meagre belongings into my rucksack, get dressed and carefully open the bedroom door. The light is on in the hall and the living room. Kyle is passed out on the sofa, snoring loudly with his mouth wide open, and the place is a mess. It stinks of beer and weed. Pike is nowhere to be seen. A wodge of banknotes is on the coffee table, held down by an empty bottle of vodka. I grab the notes and stuff them in my jeans pocket, and then I'm out of there, tiptoeing along the corridor, undoing the latch to the front door and sprinting along the pavement.

The light is grey, and there's no one around. I glance over my shoulder. A car passes me, and I hang back inside a doorway and then remind myself I'm free. I'm allowed to be out here in the grey, early light. I've done nothing wrong other than nicking Kyle's drug-pushing money. I suppose he might come looking for me, but I'll be long gone before he wakes up.

The problem is, I've got nowhere to go. No one who gives a toss about me except my social worker Sandra, who pretends to care. I don't think she does really. I'm just a number to her, a job. She's got her own family: a husband, two children and a couple of foster kids.

I walk briskly, past the boarded-up shops towards the school that I attended when I felt like it. These London streets are familiar. Wilma, the foster mum I've just left, lives half a mile away, which is why the authorities put me in supported accommodation in this borough. I walk towards her semi-detached five-bedroom house, which I've called home for the past eighteen months. She's one of the better foster mothers: a big, black lady with a bellowing laugh and endless amounts of patience. She's a good cook, too, and made it her mission to feed us all up. I told Wilma and Sandra that I wanted to leave when I turned seventeen. I hadn't caused any trouble, so it's not like the relationship broke down. I've learned how to play things. Keep your head down, eat the food, don't cause trouble. I just wanted some independence and not to be around little kids anymore.

I wait until 6.30 a.m. Wilma will be up and preparing breakfast. I walk up the steps to the primrose yellow door and press the silver bell.

It takes a while, but eventually I hear shuffling, and the front door is opened.

'My little Skye, what the heck are you doing here? I only just got rid of you!' Wilma has a twinkle in her eye. She's wearing a bright green-and-white tunic dress over black leggings and has bare feet. Wilma has an impressive collection of massive beaded earrings, and today they're a neon green. Too bright for this early in the morning.

'I can't stay there,' I say quietly.

'Oh, my lovely girl, you know you can't stay here either. Not now.'

'I can't go back. They want me to push.'

'Hey, lovie, you knew it would take a bit of adjustment, and you've only been gone twenty-four hours. The new li'l girl is already here. A sweet thing called Josie, not all grown up like you.'

My face falls.

'Never you mind. Come along in, and we'll have a chat about it over a cuppa. I'll give Sandra a call, and she can sort things out for you.'

'No,' I say. If Wilma calls Sandra, goodness knows where I'll end up next.

'No, what?' Wilma puts her hands on her hips. She's kind but doesn't stand for any nonsense.

'I've got to go,' I say. 'Sorry.' I turn on my heel and run along the pavement.

'Skye!' Wilma shouts after me, but I don't look back.

• • •

RUSH HOUR IS under way when I find myself at Victoria Station. Most of the people are striding in the opposite direction to me, hordes of important-looking people on their way into London. I keep my eyes down as I weave through the hurrying commuters and head towards the massive departure and arrivals board. I've never been to any of the places listed on the signs, but I know I want to go south. To the seaside, ideally. My fingers curl around the wad of notes in my pocket. I'll buy the cheapest ticket I can and wing it for the rest of the journey.

'The 7.55 a.m. train to Bognor Regis and Southampton Central will leave from platform eighteen. This train divides at Horsham. Please ensure you are seated in the correct part of the train.'

I run towards one of the automated ticket machines and fumble around buying a ticket. I select a child's ticket, which isn't too much of a lie, as I look younger than my age, but it's still a bloody rip-off. I consider trying to hop the gates, but the last thing I need is trouble right now. I pay, grab the ticket and sprint for the gates. Bognor Regis sounds good. I'm pretty sure that's where some of the kids went on their holiday to Butlins. Perhaps I can get a job cleaning rooms or showing visitors around.

I hop into the second compartment, which is practically empty, and sink into one of the seats, pulling my hoodie up over my head. At some point, Sandra is going to report me as a missing person. A misper, and then they'll be out looking for me. The borough has parental responsibility for me, which is a joke, but I know how the system works. So long as I keep my head down and don't get picked up by the police, I'm in with a chance. They'll expect me to be in London, not far away in

Bognor Regis, where I know no one and no one knows me.

My bones ache, and my stomach growls. I should have picked up a Coke and a bun before leaving. But when the train starts chugging out of the station, a flicker of excitement catches the back of my throat. This is it. I'm free. Middle finger up to all authorities. I can do whatever I want, go anywhere. It's scary, but fantastic, all at the same time. No one telling me I need to get a job, do some training, tidy up my room or eat what's in front of me. No one telling me I need to sell Molly or snow or smack.

I glance around the compartment to check I'm not being watched, and then pull out the banknotes and count them. Sixty-five quid. I'm disappointed. I thought there'd be more, but all the notes are fivers. I lean my head against the window and watch the world go past. It must be lovely living in one of those houses, watching the trains chug along, imagining what all those people sitting on board are off to do. Work, meeting illicit lovers… perhaps some of them are like me and running away.

The warmth in the carriage and the regular chug-chugging of the train make me doze off for a while, and the next thing I know, we're pulling into Gatwick Airport. For a fleeting moment I wonder if I could get on an airplane and fly off to a foreign country. But I miss the chance. The train is off again. Besides, I don't have a passport, let alone enough money for an air ticket. I'll stick with southern England.

And then we're really in the countryside. Green fields, woods, I even see some cows. I wonder if I could get work on a farm. It's as if I'm entering another reality, a world that I've only seen on the television. The excitement ignites into a full-blown swoop of joy, and if I wasn't sitting on a train, trying to remain unnoticed, I'd stand on the seat and do a dance of joy. This is my new life. I'm on an adventure.

There's an announcement. My heart plummets. What if Sandra has notified the police and they've found me already? And then I tell myself that's ridiculous. Who the hell cares about a stray seventeen-year-old? It's not like I've done anything wrong. I remember Sandra telling me and some of the other kids that they'd send the police after us if we ran away, but I bet that was just to scare us. The police don't have enough resources to tackle crime, let alone runaway kids. Anyway, I'm not a kid anymore. The train slows down as it enters a town.

'Ladies and gentlemen, due to an incident on the line, I am sorry to inform you that this train will terminate at Horsham. I repeat, this train will terminate at Horsham.'

I hear a few groans. I don't care. Perhaps it's fate that I'm being chucked out here. Perhaps this town that I've never heard of will become home. I jump down from the carriage and follow everyone else getting off the train. I jog up the station steps and back down the other side, my rucksack bouncing on my back and nerves tingling with excitement.

I EXIT the station and stand underneath a hanging basket filled with red and pink flowers. I think they're fake, but even so, it's pretty here, as if people take pride in their town. There are big bushes in the roundabout in front of me, and the air smells different, fresher and colder, not like it's been regurgitated by engines and chimneys. I accost a posh-looking woman wearing a camel-coloured coat, her white hair as fine as silk.

'Excuse me, where's the centre of Horsham?'

She looks startled that I've spoken to her and points to the left. I wander along the road, passing a glass-fronted cinema building, crossing over at some traffic lights and eventually find myself in what I assume is Horsham centre. There's a large pedestrianised area with an old-fashioned bandstand. I am tempted to run up the steps and stand in the middle of it and bellow out a tune. Perhaps I would if I could sing, but I can't. Instead, I find a coffee shop that does takeaways and buy myself a cup of hot tea and a bacon sandwich. I take them and sit on the steps of the bandstand and savour every mouthful as I take in my new surroundings. It's so much quieter and more spacious than the south-eastern parts of London where I grew up. The people wear smart coats and hold their heads up high, bags swinging from shoulders with no concern of pick-pockets or worse.

I spend the next few hours wandering around the streets, meandering in and out of shops, and none of the shopkeepers eye me suspiciously, wondering if I'm going to pickpocket anything. I find a little street with candy-coloured houses that look as if they've been lifted from a doll's house in the Middle Ages, and I sit on a bench and stare at them for a while. When I need the loo, I find out where the public toilets are and try to work out where would be the best place to lie down for the night.

In one of those shops that sells outdoor clothes and stuff, I spend the bulk of my money on a purple sleeping bag. It's my favourite colour, and I hope it'll bring me luck. And I steal a black marker pen from WHSmith. In the bins behind the shops, I find a piece of card and write, *I've got nowhere to go. Please spare me some change.*

I saunter back down the main street and spot a

woman wearing a headscarf selling *The Big Issue*. She wasn't there earlier.

'Where are all the other homeless people?' I ask her, but she just shrugs at me. I'm not even sure she speaks English. Eventually, I find a covered alleyway, so I sit down there, propping the piece of card up against my rucksack.

It's dark by 4.30 p.m., and I'm freezing, and no one has given me any money. Literally no one. In fact, people walk past so quickly, their eyes focused anywhere except on me. What seemed like a good idea this morning now seems like a lousy one. If I'd stayed in London, I could have hooked up with other homeless people, and they'd have told me where to find the best cardboard, where's the safest places to bed down, and where the nearest soup kitchens are. In this fancy little town, I doubt they even have a soup kitchen. Everyone walks with a purpose. Somewhere to go; someone to care about them; something to do.

I'm not one to give in to pity, but I sit, my arms around my knees, shivering from the cold, and I wonder what the hell I should do. Perhaps it would be best if I return to London, give Sandra a call. No. I cannot give up after one day; that's pathetic. If this town is no good, tomorrow I'll find another one, or I'll go to Butlins. I just need to take one day and one night at a time. Pins and needles jab and then numb my left foot. I kick my leg forwards, shaking my trainer-clad foot from side to side.

'Bloody hell! Watch what you're doing.'

A girl nearly stumbles, but manages to right herself. She's about the same age as me, but that's where the similarities end. She's wearing a fancy navy parka jacket with fur around the hood and neckline. Her blonde hair bounces down her back, and she hikes a Ted Baker bag over her shoulder. She's wearing jogging pants, but they don't look anything like the cheap ones I get at the market.

'Sorry,' I mutter, pulling my legs back towards my chest. I expect the girl to carry on walking, but she doesn't. She just stands there staring at me. It's really weird the way she's looking at me, as if I've triggered a long-buried memory or she's working out a complex problem.

'What's the matter? Not seen a homeless person before?' I snarl.

'Yes. No. Yes, of course I have. Just wondering if you're alright?'

'I wouldn't be sitting here if I was okay, would I?'

'No, I suppose not.' She takes her bag off her shoulder and places it on the ground. She rummages inside it and removes a gold leather purse. 'Have this,' she says, handing me a fifty-pound note.

'Shit,' I say softly, reaching up to take it from her. I've never held a fifty-quid note before. Perhaps she was working out what fifty quid could buy me or wondering if her daddy will replenish it. 'Are you sure?' I ask.

'Yeah. You need it more than me.'

I nod. 'Is it normal to hand out money like that around here?'

She opens and closes her mouth and looks away for a moment. 'No.'

'Thanks,' I say.

'Everyone has a reason for everything they do,' she says. Then she hoists the bag over her shoulder and, after throwing me a tight smile, walks briskly away.

3

NATHAN – NOW

My meeting with Skye is to be held at the offices of her talent management agency, a firm called So She & All. I have taken the train to London and the tube to South Kensington. Now I'm standing outside their offices on a cobbled street tucked behind the Fulham Road. The low-rise converted mews houses on the cul-de-sac are all different in shape and size. Some have large garage doors painted in pastel colours, others wide windows, blinds or shutters concealing what lies inside, all very tasteful and inconspicuous. So She & All's offices are the exception. Candy-pink-and-white-striped shutters frame either side of the large downstairs window, which is lit by a row of extra-large vanity lights, an enlarged version of the lights that frame a mirror in Isla's bedroom. The words So She & All are written on a gold plaque on the candy-pink front door. It feels as if I'm about to enter a make-up studio; not exactly somewhere I would choose to visit.

I ring the doorbell and am buzzed in immediately. A

blonde girl with overly tanned skin throws me a dazzling smile.

'Good morning and welcome to Social! How can I help you?'

Of course. So She & All said quickly sounds like *social*.

'I'm here to meet with Skye and her agent, Tiana Johnson.' Once again, I wonder what Skye's surname is.

'Please have a seat, and I'll let Tiana know you're here.'

I look around the room, which is furnished with leather-and-chrome chairs and transparent ghost side tables stacked high with glossy magazines. An abstract modern painting in turquoises and pinks, the sort I will never understand, sits above a stone fireplace. On the opposite wall, there are pictures of beautiful young women and men set in black-edged frames, all pouting or posing suggestively. I sit with my back to them, trying not to inhale too much of the air, heavy with cloying floral scent coming from a reed diffuser.

'Can I get you a drink? A freshly squeezed juice, mountain spring water, perhaps?' the receptionist asks, her long pink fingernails tapping her desk.

'A coffee would be nice,' I say.

I see the flicker of a frown.

'Nathan?'

I hadn't heard anyone else enter the room, and I jump slightly.

'I'm Tiana Jackson. It's a pleasure to meet you.'

I stand up and we shake hands. She must be six feet in her heels, because her eyes are level with mine. She is long-limbed and exceptionally beautiful, with brightly painted red lips and afro hair cut so short, it's barely visible. She is wearing a white jumpsuit, her waist tightly cinched in with a wide gold belt. It's a most unlikely outfit for work.

'Skye is already here. We had some things to discuss earlier, so if you'd like to follow me.'

I grab my raincoat and briefcase and follow Tiana up a short staircase. She holds open a door for me, and I walk into a small but bright room that looks out onto the cobbled mews street.

'You must be Nathan Edwards! It's such a pleasure to meet you.'

Skye dashes forwards, and rather than accepting my outstretched hand, she moves straight in to kiss me on either cheek. I am enshrouded by the scent of apple blossom, pleasant enough, if a bit overwhelming. As she stands back, I am surprised how ordinary she looks, particularly in comparison to the model-like looks of Tiana. I had been expecting one of those women with plumped-up lips and a Botox forehead, bronzed skin and clothes that leave little to the imagination. Yes, she's attractive with wide blue eyes and well-contoured cheekbones, but her lips are thin and her chin a little pointy. She sits down and flicks her long blonde hair over her shoulder. I certainly wouldn't have known she was the same woman as in the pictures and videos that Isla showed me.

'Have a seat. We've got so much to talk about.'

I sit on the opposite side of the glass table, while Tiana sits at the head. Both women are drinking some unpleasant-looking green juice in cut-glass tumblers.

'What's your surname, Skye?' I ask as I take my notepad out of my briefcase.

'Skye doesn't use a surname,' Tiana says firmly. That's me put in my place.

'I've been wanting to meet you for ages.' Skye smiles at me, her eyes unblinking. 'Your charity does so much good, and I'd love to help out.' She pushes up the sleeves of her black cashmere V-neck jumper to reveal a Rolex watch on her left wrist and several gold bangles on her right.

'I thought it might be helpful if we start at the beginning,' Tiana says, clearly wanting to control the conversation. 'If I may, I'll do a little introduction to Skye, who is ridiculously modest and never blows her own trumpet. Then, Skye, perhaps you can explain some of your ideas as to how you could help Sacha's Sanctuary.'

We both nod in accord. There is a gentle knock on the door, and the receptionist brings in a cup of coffee, which she places in front of my notebook. I thank her and take a sip. It's disgusting, and I wonder whether it's some sort of coffee substitute.

'Skye came to our attention about two years ago. As I'm sure you know, she's amassed the most amazing following on social media, currently well over three million followers on Instagram, upwards of five million on YouTube, and similar numbers on TikTok, Facebook and Twitter. What makes Skye special is that she's a mega-influencer superstar, but she didn't come to the role as a celebrity. Skye isn't a singer or an actress or a model – although she could have been.' Tiana winks at Skye. 'She's grown her following organically. She became a social media influencer early on, and she's what we call a real-life influencer, someone who is passionate about what she is recommending and someone who facilitates real change, and that's because she engages with her followers, and they engage with her. There is no one more authentic than Skye, and I can't begin to tell you what an honour it is to be her agent. Anyway, I'll give you an example of the Skye effect. Skye is an ambassador for a paper straw company. It's not sexy or exciting, but sustainability and

eliminating plastic is something she believes in passionately. Skye abhors what plastic is doing to our planet,
don't you, darling?' Tiana glances at Skye with a look of
adoration. Skye barely smiles in response. 'Anyway, by
vlogging about paper straws and using them when
drinking her smoothies, she has single-handedly
changed the marketplace.'

I swallow my incredulity over what is patently a
ridiculous claim, but Tiana carries on.

'The thing about Skye is that she is an inspiration to
so many people. It's her authenticity that they adore.'

I glance up at Skye, expecting her to look at least a
little bashful. She is expressionless. I suppose she has
heard this spiel so many times, it washes right over her
head.

'I'm not sure how much you know about Skye's
backstory, but she was in care for the majority of her
childhood, passed from one foster home to another. She
was then on the streets for a while. With barely any
education, at the age of twenty, Skye decided she
wanted a different life. She was destined for drugs,
thieving, prison and an early death. But Skye took
control of her destiny, and look at her now, just eight
years on from being homeless, here she is.'

'Impressive,' I say, wondering what makes her so
unique. There are many people who successfully get off
the streets, although probably not with the affluence and
visibility of Skye. It's what Sacha's Sanctuary does.
Helps people into employment and homes of their own.
It isn't an easy trajectory but is certainly possible. It's as
if Skye can read my mind, because she leans across the
table, looking me directly in the eyes.

'The difference between me and other homeless
people is that I started vlogging about my journey to get
off the streets. I then came up with a ten-point

programme and started helping other people do the same. And the more I talked about my story online, the more people got interested in what I had to say. I moved on from adversity, and now I'm famous for positivity. I've been very lucky. Today, I get paid for promoting brands. This necklace I'm wearing.' She brings her finger to her neck and pushes forwards a simple gold chain with some delicate pendants hanging from it. 'Sales of Duel My Jewel increased by four hundred percent when I posted about them, and they ran out of stock of this necklace within an hour. I really care about all the people who follow me. I thank them for their comments and respond to their questions. It's a full-time job. Brands know that they will get sales when I talk about their products, and they pay me well for it. Very well.'

I shift uncomfortably. My charity is about as far removed from this consumerist world as it's possible to be. I frown, wondering whether I have just wasted a day and a train fare, not to mention having to deal with my girls' disappointment when I tell them they won't be meeting Skye.

'We're not in a position to give you any payment for helping promote Sacha's Sanctuary,' I say.

Skye smiles and leans back in her chair. 'I want to help you, not the other way around.'

'It's win-win for your charity,' Tiana interrupts. 'Although Skye's brand will also benefit from being associated with such a high-profile charity as yours. Her supporters love a do good story.'

I don't buy Tiana's comment. Sacha's Sanctuary is a minor charity. Yes, we've grown massively in the last three years and have won various awards, but we're small fry in comparison to the likes of Crisis or Shelter.

'This is all about you and your charity, Nathan,' Skye

says, smiling widely at me. 'I came from the streets, and I want to give back to those people still on the streets. I was homeless for a matter of months, and they were the worst times of my life. Every day and every night was about survival. The person you're looking at now is nothing like the person I was then. I've worked relentlessly to better myself. Everything from how I speak, to how I act, to what I do to positively impact upon the world. But I'll never forget where I came from. I regularly spend a night on the streets just to remind myself how lucky I am. It's a great leveller.'

I glance at Tiana. She is sitting there, her arms crossed, her head to one side, as if she's the proud parent watching her child protege giving the winning performance in a competition.

'So what I was thinking was it's time that I throw my full support behind a charity that has meaning to me. I want to fundraise for you, to tell the world all about Sacha's Sanctuary. There's nothing I want more than to help every single homeless person get off the streets. I believe our ambitions are aligned.'

'What do you propose to do?' I ask.

'Crowdfunding, fundraising events, vlogging about the charity, delivering brand sponsorship.'

I suppose I look a bit doubtful, not least because I only discovered that vlogging was video blogging thanks to Isla's explanation last night.

'Why don't we put a proposal to you?' Tiana suggests as she shifts in her seat. 'People trust Skye. If she tells them to do something, they'll do it. They relate to her. While people are impressed by actors and musicians, they don't trust or relate to them in the same way as they do social influencers. Skye is someone like them, an ordinary person who hasn't been handed wealth, talent or good looks on a golden spoon. But with her determination and positivity, she's turned her life around. People relate to that. They think "if Skye can do it, I can too". That's why all the leading brands are spending massive chunks of their advertising budgets on social media influencers. There really is nothing for you to lose, Nathan. You'll have Skye as your figurehead and brand ambassador, and thanks to her magic touch, you'll see a massive leap in revenue. Then it's up to you to decide what to do with the money.'

'Although,' Skye interjects, 'as homelessness is so close to my heart, I'd love to have some involvement in the charity.'

'Of course,' I say, wondering if this is where the catch lies. I realise she wants the credibility of having a charity behind her name, but it seems like we're potentially going to get a great deal for very little in return. 'When we receive your proposal, I'll discuss it with my team and board of trustees and will get back to you.'

'Thank you,' Tiana says.

I put my notebook and pen back into my briefcase and shift my chair backwards.

Both the women stand up, and when I step towards the door, Skye reaches up and gives me a kiss on both cheeks. She then clasps my right hand in both of hers. Her hands feel cool but soft.

'I really want to make this happen, Nathan. I've been looking for a charity to throw my full support behind for a while now, and I'm so excited about improving the plight of the homeless.'

I nod, a little out of my depth with these women. I wish I'd brought one of the girls on my team to the meeting, someone who might have more knowledge of social media and who might be able to ask the right probing questions. Let's see what their proposal suggests. We can ask the questions then.

Tiana walks me downstairs.

'Thank you very much for coming. So many exciting opportunities for everyone. I was wondering whether you might like to attend one of Skye's influencer events. She will be at a breakfast meeting at a hotel in Sussex tomorrow morning, not far from your offices, I believe. Would you be free to go? It'll give you the chance to experience the full Skye effect?'

I pause. I don't like making quick decisions without all the facts.

Tiana picks up on my hesitation. 'They'll be no commitment to having a working relationship with Skye. It's simply for you to see how she works.'

'I don't think I have anything in the diary for tomorrow morning. Why don't you email me the details, and I'll confirm with you when I'm back in the office.'

'Sure thing.' Tiana beams at me, and we shake hands.

When I step outside, I'm glad to inhale the cold London air. As I'm walking down the Fulham Road, I go over the conversation, and I can't see any downsides to the charity being linked to Skye. She seems wholesome, natural and genuine. But at the same time, I feel as if I've just walked straight into the sticky fibres of a glittery web.

4

SKYE – THEN

It's started to drizzle now, and I'm getting scared. I've slept in a doorway a handful of times, but then I was with a mate, and there were some older women who took us under their wings. Here I'm totally alone, in a town I don't know. I'm used to nobody giving a toss about me, but not a soul in the world knows that I'm here or, for that matter, gives a damn. If I go back to London, I'll be able to hook up with other people, but it will be dangerous there. Stabbings. Drug fights. Hallucinations. Police. Being hauled in as a missing person. I've seen it all. At least here, I'm not competing for a decent doorway, and although I'm alone, I don't feel that heart-thumping fear that judders through me when I've been alone and sleeping rough in London. I'm just cold and hungry. I'll give it a night or two in Horsham and then take stock.

It's unlikely that anyone is going to nab my doorway, so I leave the bits of cardboard I've collected on the ground and go to Costa Coffee. I order a hot chocolate and a sandwich and warm myself up. But then one of the servers comes over and says they're shutting now, and I have to leave. I saunter back to my doorway. Even though it's only 7 p.m., the town is empty. It's so frigging quiet, it gives me the heebie-jeebies. What is this place, a ghost town? Can't win, can I? Too noisy and frenetic in London, and too silent here. But at least there aren't any coppers hanging around. I haven't seen a single policeman since I arrived in this place nearly twelve hours ago.

I'm laying out my sleeping bag when three blokes approach. I hide my face from them, but it's no good.

'Oi. Why are you sleeping on the ground?'

I ignore them.

'We're talking to you, lassie. Want a beer?'

'No, thanks,' I mutter.

'Suit yourself.'

And then they're gone, laughing, having a good time. I slide into the sleeping bag, take my wallet out of my rucksack, and shove it deep down into my sleeping bag. I use my rucksack as a pillow. The ground is hard, and I can feel every single ridge in the paving stones underneath me. I shiver and pull my old beanie far down over my head. I snuggle right down inside the sleeping bag, curling my legs up underneath me and pulling the top of it over my head, my damp, hot breath giving me a little bit of warmth. But it's so hard lying here, aching and shivering. I hear footsteps and voices and hold my breath as people walk past. Perhaps they can't even see me, on the ground in the shadows.

I suppose I drift off to sleep because I'm suddenly awake. My heart pumping. There's a bloke taking a slash just a foot from my head. If I don't move, I'll be lying in a puddle of urine. I shift as quickly as I can, and he laughs. A cruel, hard laugh.

'Get a roof!' he says as he zips himself up. 'Shit, you're a girl. Like what you saw?' he asks, his words slurring together.

'Fuck off!' I say.

He stares at me, but his eyes shift around, and he wobbles. I relax. If he tries anything on, I'll be okay, because he's too pissed to have any coordination. And then I freeze. There's another voice.

'Kev, are you done? Taxi's here.'

The creep called Kev leers at me, but then turns and walks away, trying to swagger, but he's too drunk, and he weaves from one side of the pavement to the other.

I thought I'd be safe here, in this small town. But I suppose if you're on the streets, nowhere is really safe. But what choice do I have? The streets, back in care in some shithole, or earn money and be able to pay for a flat share. My only real hope is to get a job.

I don't sleep the rest of the night. I daren't. I shift around a lot to keep warm, trying and failing to get comfortable. A fox trots past me, its tail held high. I let out a little yelp, my heart hammering in my chest. It turns, stops and stares at me with amber, gleaming eyes. Why doesn't it run away? Is it going to attack me? Will I get rabies? I thought it was meant to be scared of me, not the other way around. I've seen foxes before in London, but this one terrifies me.

'Go away,' I hiss. He lifts his head up high, as if he's king of the streets, and with a haughty last stare, continues on his journey.

I am so relieved when the sky begins to lighten, when I hear the clatter of a dustbin lorry and a siren in the distance. I don't belong here in this quiet place. At 6.30 a.m., I roll up my sleeping bag. I feel gross, dirty; my stomach is growling and cramping. I go to Starbucks, but nothing in this town opens until 8 a.m. It's not like London, where something is always open. I walk for a while, and at least I get warm, and then, on the dot of 8 a.m., I make my way to yet another coffee shop and waste a few quid on a tea and bun. I sit in the corner for ages, until a man, who is probably the manager, tells me I have to order something else or leave.

I find the library and sit there for a few hours, flicking through books, unable to concentrate on anything. When the cloying, hot atmosphere becomes too much, I wander outside and stand staring at the window of the job centre, but I don't have the energy to go inside. What's the point? I have no skills, no qualifications; I'm good for nothing, really. And looking like this, unwashed, dressed in old clothes, is hardly going to make a good impression. That resolve I had earlier has disappeared. I wander back to where I sat yesterday and prop up my cardboard sign. I doze off.

'Hello again.'

I force my eyes open. It's the girl who gave me the money. She stands there awkwardly.

'How come you're still here?' she asks.

'What business is it of yours whether I'm here or not?'

She winces and drops her chin towards her chest.

'Oi. Sorry. Didn't mean to be rude. It's just I'm cold, hungry and knackered.' Aggression seems to be my default setting these days. It's what comes from looking over your shoulder all the time.

She stares at me for a moment and then absent-mindedly strokes the fur on her collar. I wonder if it's the real stuff.

'Do you want to get a coffee?' she asks. 'There's a Starbucks around the corner.'

'You paying?' I narrow my eyes at her.

'Yes.'

'Alright, then. I'm bloody freezing.' I jump up and grab my bag. Perhaps she'll give me another fifty quid – or if I'm really lucky, one hundred – and then I'll find a hostel or somewhere I can stay the night. This could be my lucky day.

It's busy in the coffee shop, full of happy families and people my age gathered in big groups. How do they have enough money to fritter away on drinks? We stand awkwardly in the queue. When we're about to be served, she turns to me. 'What would you like?'

'A coffee?'

'What sort?'

I shrug.

'A flat white, a latte, a macchiato, a cappuccino?' she says.

'Whatever. I'll have what you're having.'

The barista is a lanky youth with deep-set eyes and pimples around his mouth. 'What can I get you?'

'Two Caramel Cloud Macchiatos and two brownies.'

She doesn't even look at it him when she places our order, and I notice that she doesn't say *please* or *thank you*. I would have thought a posh girl like her would have manners, or perhaps he's too lowly for her. But if that's the case, why is she being nice to me?

A couple of minutes later, she collects our drinks and plates, places them on a tray and carries it to one of the few empty tables near the back of the shop, with me trotting along after her. We both sit down. She passes me a coffee and the plate with the brownies. I can sense her eyes on my face, but I don't look up. I'm wondering what she wants from me.

'What's your name?' she asks. 'I'm Tiffany. Tiffany Larkin.'

I look at her then. 'Skye Walker.'

'That's a nice name. I don't know anyone called Skye.'

Evidently, she's not a *Star Wars* fan. That's a relief. But I can't return the compliment, because I think Tiffany is a weird name.

'How old are you?' she asks.

'Seventeen.'

'Me too. Don't you go to college or anything?'

I shake my head and let out a bitter laugh. 'People like me don't go to college. Why are you being nice to me, anyway?'

She shrugs her shoulders and lets her blonde hair fall over her face. It's a moment before she swipes it away. 'Just fancied making a new friend and doing something nice.'

'Doing something nice!' I laugh. 'So I'm your charity case, am I? Part of a school project.'

'No! Not everyone is out to get something, you know,' Tiffany says, with a harsh edge to her voice. Perhaps not in her cosy little world, but I've never known anybody to do something without thinking what's in it for them.

'So why aren't you with your mates having a good time?' I ask. 'Like that crowd over there.' I glance at the gaggle of youths seated at a large table, laughing raucously.

She reddens. 'My friends don't live around here. I moved to a new school, and it's really different to where I was before. I'm at the local sixth-form college.'

'I'd have thought you'd have loads of friends.' Who wouldn't want to be friends with her, with those fancy clothes and designer bags and hair the colour of pale gold?

We sip our coffees in silence for a while, and I savour the sweetness of the brownie. I let the warmth soak into my bones and relax into the chair. It feels so good.

'Are you totally homeless?' she asks.

'Yeah. I spent my money on a sleeping bag. Your fifty quid wasn't enough for a cheap hotel, and anyway, food is more important. I need to save up so I can eat over the next few days. It's a doorway for me again tonight, or perhaps a hostel if you'll give me some more dosh.'

'Where do you come from?'

I'm annoyed she hasn't taken the bait.

'London. I've lived in children's homes and foster care all my life. I went to college for a while, because they gave me a bursary to stay in full-time education, but I didn't attend much, and then they chucked me out. And then I reckoned it was time to leave foster care, because it's not like I'm a kid or anything, so they put me into some crappy supported-accommodation place thanks to my social worker. I didn't like it there, so I've run away.'

'You've got a social worker?' Tiffany's eyes widen.

'Yeah.' I chuckle. 'Do you even know what a social worker does?'

Tiffany ignores my question. 'Is all your stuff in that bag?' She looks at my old, grubby rucksack that contains everything I own.

'Yup. All my worldly possessions.'

'Have you got any waterproofs and warm clothes?'

'Ergh, no! Some of us don't have rich mummies and daddies, which is why we're in care.' I can't stop myself from being sarcastic, even though I'm not being fair towards this girl, who is only being nice to me.

'I'll buy you some.'

'You'll what?'

'Take you clothes shopping. I'll buy you some things that will keep you warm. You can't sleep outside in that!' She frowns at my thin parka and ripped jeans.

'Why do you want to do that? Are you a pimp or something?' She looks horrified and I laugh. 'Where does all your money come from, anyway?'

'My parents. My dad has his own business. He grows salads.'

'Like lettuce?'

She goes bright red. 'Yes.'

What is it? Why is she embarrassed about her dad's job?

'So he's a gardener, then. He must grow a lot of lettuces to give you enough money to flash the cash.'

'Yes, he does. Come on, let's get out of here. We need to get to the shops before they close.' She stands up and grabs her bag.

FORTY-FIVE MINUTES LATER, Tiffany has bought me two thick sweaters, a fleece, a waterproof parka that cost nearly two hundred quid just by itself, a pair of jeans, a woollen hat and some Doc Martens.

'What else do you need?' she asks as she scrutinises me with narrowed eyes.

'A roof over my head.' We carry on walking up the high street. 'I don't know why you're being so kind.'

I'm just waiting for the punchline. What do I have that this posh girl could want? The warning bells are ringing like sirens in my head. People always want something from you. Always. Nothing is ever free.

'Why don't you get a job?' she asks.

'I will, eventually. It's not as if it's going to be easy with no qualifications and no address. Besides, I only just got here.' We're walking past a shop with an extra-long covered entrance. 'That's the doorway I've earmarked for tonight,' I say. 'I reckon it will be quieter than last night's walkway. Nearly got pissed on and mauled by a fox. I didn't sleep a wink.'

Tiffany stops walking and turns to face me. 'You can't stay here.' She twirls a lock of that golden hair around a finger. 'Look, why don't you come home with me?'

'Really?' I'm not sure about that; I'd rather she give me the money. 'I don't know. It's kind of you and all that, but I'm used to looking after myself.'

'You're really okay with sleeping here? You just told me how horrid it was last night. You might get stabbed or raped or even killed.'

'Does that happen a lot in this town?'

Tiffany shakes her head. 'It's just…'

'If you want to be kind, why don't you give me some cash, and I'll find a hostel or a bed and breakfast.'

'Maybe.' She bites the skin at the side of her nail. They're more of a bloodied mess than mine are. 'But it's better if you just stay at my house. I can't pay for you to stay at a hotel for more than a night or two.'

'And I can stay at yours for longer?'

She shrugs her shoulders. 'Maybe.'

'And they'll be no squaring of things?'

'What do you mean?'

'I won't have to do anything in return?'

'No. Of course not.' She looks affronted.

I think for a long moment, although there's not much to think about. A bed for a few nights or the pavement. 'Okay, then.'

'That's fab!' She claps her hands and does a quick hop, like a small kid. 'You'll have to excuse my parents, and you'll need to tell them that you're a friend from college. You won't say that I found you on the streets, will you?'

'Of course not. I'll tell them whatever you want.' But the alarm bells are deafening inside my head. No one makes an offer like this unless there's something in it for them. I will have to be very, very careful.

5

'Can I come with you to the breakfast meeting with Skye?' Chloe asks as she drops her spoon into her cereal bowl, splattering milk across the table.

'No, you can't. It's work,' I say.

Marie is seated opposite Chloe at the kitchen table, sipping a black coffee. 'I find it funny that it is a breakfast meeting that doesn't start until 9 a.m. I guess the world of influencers works on a different timescale to the rest of us.'

Isla's standing next to the toaster, waiting for it to pop up. 'You're so sarcastic, Marie,' she says.

'Isla!' I rebuke her. I wish she would stop being rude to Marie. As the eldest, Isla has suffered the most. No child should have to watch their mother be ravaged by a cruel disease and then pretend to be strong when she dies. I understand that Isla is resentful towards Marie, but it's not as if Marie has ever tried to take on the maternal role. She has always been my helper, deferring to me in all the major childcare decisions.

Isla discovered that Marie and I were sharing a bed

very early in our relationship. She started having nightmares, and one night she rushed into my room, her eyes wide with terror, beads of sweat on her forehead. I couldn't be sure if the relentless sobs were because another woman was lying in my bed or whether it was the effects of the nightmare. She told Marie that she hated her, and then she hated me. We took everything that she threw at us. But that was two and a half years ago, and I thought she had come to accept that Marie made me happy and life was so much smoother with her around. I suppose her resentment towards Marie is re-emerging due to our forthcoming wedding, and I totally understand. I try to reassure both the girls that I will never forget Sacha; that she was my first love and my love for Marie is different. Special, but different.

Their impending visit to try on their bridesmaid's dresses won't be helping Isla's mood. Chloe is excited; Isla anything but. Both Marie and I have agreed to give Isla space. We know she is still hurting, but it's a fine line between being a pushover and being understanding but firm.

I finish my cup of coffee and place it in the dishwasher.

'Right, I'm off,' I say. 'Have a good day, everyone.'

'You're wearing *that* to meet with Skye?' Isla frowns as she looks me up and down. 'You should be wearing an open-necked shirt and a pair of smart, skinny jeans, not an old suit.'

Marie giggles. 'Your daughter has a point.'

I shrug my shoulders. 'It'll have to do. I haven't got time to change.'

I LISTEN to Radio 4 as I drive through the Sussex countryside towards the luxurious five-star country house hotel just twenty minutes away. It's a pleasant journey, meandering along lanes with overhanging trees and hedgerows with their new spring leaves just beginning to grow. And then I get stuck behind a tractor travelling about ten miles per hour, along a narrow road where passing is impossible. I'm going to be late, not that I suppose it matters.

When eventually I pull into the Three Oaks Country House Hotel, the car park is full of gleaming, luxury cars. I follow a sign to the overflow car park and pull up next to a Bentley. A uniformed chauffeur is sitting in the driver's seat, his eyes lowered. I leave my briefcase in the car, double-check I have some business cards in my wallet, and stride towards the main entrance.

A doorman smiles at me and holds the door open. 'Good morning, sir. Welcome to the Three Oaks Hotel.'

'Good morning. I'm here for the meeting with Dawn Chorus Granola.'

I jump as a flashlight goes off in my face.

'There is a lot of press here today,' the doorman says quietly. 'If you would like to follow me, I will get one of my colleagues to check you in.'

The entrance lobby is panelled in dark oak, and the air is infused with the scent of freshly burning wood, not that I can see an open fire. We walk past the reception desk and down a corridor where the lower half of the walls are in the same oak panelling as in the lobby, but the upper portions are covered in oil paintings, mainly portraits featuring men in hunting pinks and women in ball gowns dripping with jewellery. The noise levels increase, and as we approach the conference room, people are spilling out into the corridor.

'My colleagues will take over,' the porter says, nodding at me deferentially before retreating the way we came.

'Good morning, sir. Can I have your name, please?' The woman is wearing a bright orange T-shirt with the words *Dawn Chorus Granola* in purple lettering that strains across her chest. She stands next to a large table with name tags placed on it in alphabetical order.

'Nathan Edwards.'

'Here you go, Mr Edwards.' She hands me my name badge on a lanyard and then passes me one of the linen bags that everyone seems to be carrying. 'There are samples of all of our products in the bag, along with product information, vouchers for complimentary brands, and an order form. Enjoy!' She turns away from me to welcome the couple standing behind me.

I walk into a very large, bright room that is like an orangery, with glass doors looking out onto the extensive patio and park-like gardens beyond. The room is buzzing with noise, pumping upbeat music that is much too loud for the time of day, and in the centre of the room is what looks like a massive five-foot transparent fishbowl, which appears to be filled with granola. I walk towards it to get a better look. I'm right: It is full of granola, and emerging from the centre is a woman wearing a skimpy bikini. Photographers are gathering around, snapping away as the woman contorts herself for the camera. So much for female emancipation.

As I'm glancing around the room, looking for Skye, a young man comes up to me, holding a tray of juices and cereal bars. I thank him as I help myself to a glass of orange juice – or, at least, I hope it's orange juice. Isla was right, though. I do look out of place. There isn't a single person wearing a business suit, and at forty-four, I am definitely one of the oldest people in the room. The men are all in tightly fitting trousers with highly starched open-neck shirts in an array of colours, and the women fall into two groups: those dressed in revealing outfits, particularly jumpsuits or miniskirts and high heels, or boho in flowing dresses and a profusion of colourful jewellery. The photographers are in jeans and T-shirts.

The thing that strikes me the most is that everyone is taking photographs. Not just the official press photographers, with their large Nikon or Canon cameras, pointing their lenses at the handful of people who I assume are the stars of this morning's show, but almost everyone has their mobile phone clutched in one hand, taking occasional pictures of other people, but mostly of themselves.

'Nathan!'

Skye flings her arms around me. She's wearing a scarlet red wraparound dress that enhances her figure and a gold chain that descends into her cleavage.

'I'm so happy you could make it,' she says as she releases me and immediately slots her arm through mine. 'I want to show you exactly what happens at events like this, and how you could benefit from being with me.'

Her immodesty takes me aback. We are striding quickly across the room. I realise that Skye is almost the only person not carrying anything: no linen bag, no handbag and no phone, perhaps just as well, because she is wearing vertiginously high-heeled boots that make her the same height as me.

'Rosie, darling, you must meet Nathan. He runs the most amazing charity, literally turning people's lives around.'

A very large young woman, dressed in tightly fitted baby pink Lycra that leaves nothing to the imagination, blows Skye a kiss.

'Can't reach you, babe,' she says as she pretends to

stand on tiptoes. 'Hello, Nathan. Do you like the granola?'

'I'm afraid I haven't had the chance to try it yet.'

She guffaws. 'Me neither. But so long as we post good photos of ourselves munching our way through it, we'll be fulfilling our contractual obligations.'

'I'm going to be the figurehead for Nathan's homeless charity,' Skye says.

I try to stop my eyebrows from darting up my forehead.

'There's no cause I'm more passionate about than homelessness.'

'Good for you,' Rosie says before blowing Skye another kiss and wandering away.

Skye pulls me in even closer as she whispers, 'Rosie is also a social influencer. She promotes size inclusivity, and she's fronting campaigns for leading high street fashion retailers.'

A photographer plants himself directly in front of us, forcing us to stop walking. 'Skye, have you been in the granola yet?'

'It's not really my thing,' Skye says, plastering on a wide smile. 'I mean, getting in the granola. I'm happy to eat it. Would you like a photograph of me eating a Dawn Chorus granola bar?'

She unlinks herself from me, grabs a bar from a server carrying a tray laden with them, and poses with the bar just inches from her pouting lips.

'Can you take a bite, love,' the photographer says. Skye does as she's told, striking a highly sexualised pose.

'Thanks, Skye.' The photographer wanders away.

'Don't tell anyone,' Skye says, whispering into my ear, 'but that was gross. I'm planning on bringing out my own range of breakfast foods. They'll be gluten, dairy and sugar free, and all the ingredients will be UK sourced and priced as cheaply as possible. They'll be designed to perk you up whether you've slept in a doorway on cardboard, or on pure linen sheets.'

'Does that mean you're endorsing products that you don't like?' I frown.

'I'm very careful as to what brands I associate myself with. Our ambitions have to align. I like the values of Dawn Chorus Granola, but I think it could be done so much better. I'm happy to endorse it in the meantime, but I'm in discussions with a manufacturer to produce similar products to my own recipes. Watch this space,' she says, drawing her finger along her lips as if to indicate she's zipping them up.

And then we're interrupted by a woman dressed all in black. 'Skye, can we have a quick interview?'

'Do you mind, Nathan?' Skye asks. 'Anya is a really well-connected journalist!'

'No problem,' I say.

'You're welcome to listen in,' Skye suggests.

I follow the women to the far end of the room, where two chairs have been placed in front of a large banner promoting Dawn Chorus Granola. A video camera is set up on a tripod, facing the chairs. The two women sit down. Anya presses the button on a remote control.

'Here we are at the Dawn Chorus Granola launch, and I'm thrilled to be interviewing the one and only Skye. So, Skye, what was it that drew you to Dawn Chorus?'

I frown. This doesn't sound like a *well-connected journalist* interview.

'Healthy eating means everything to me. If you look after your body, you look after your mind and your soul. I resonate with Dawn Chorus's brand values.'

'Take us back, Skye, to when you were living on the streets. What did you eat in those days?'

'Whatever I could get. It's literally a fight for survival when you have no money and no roof over your head. I remember one night when I hadn't eaten for forty-eight hours, I was rummaging in a bin outside a supermarket. A member of staff saw me and gave me some sandwiches that were past their sell-by date that they were going to chuck out. It's the soup kitchens, like the ones run by the charity Sacha's Sanctuary, that keep homeless people going.'

'And acts of random kindness,' Anya prompts.

'Yes, that too.'

'You've talked about your best friend and how she found you on the streets. How—'

'I'm sorry, but I don't talk about her,' Skye interrupts.

'Of course.' The interviewer seems surprisingly unruffled by Skye's put-down, but it piques my curiosity. Who was Skye's best friend, and why did she shut down the question?

'So tell me, what new things are you getting involved in?'

And then I jump. A hand is placed on my shoulder.

'Nathan!'

I swivel around and, to my relief, see Pete Brandine, an old friend who runs a big charitable foundation. I turned to Pete for advice when I first set up Sacha's Sanctuary, and haven't seen him in a while. We walk away from Skye's interview, out of earshot.

'Surprised to see you here,' he says.

'Relieved to see you. I'm out of my depth.' Actually, I feel like I've stepped into an alternate reality.

He laughs. 'Why are you here?'

'Skye wants to endorse Sacha's Sanctuary, and her

agent invited me to this event to see the "Skye effect".' I highlight her name with my fingers.

'Congratulations. Skye is a top-tier influencer. What's she charging you?'

'Nothing.'

'Even bigger congratulations! Social influencers at her level normally charge a fortune.'

'I'm still a bit hesitant about the link-up.'

'Don't be. She'll add legitimacy to your brand, and she could seriously up your fundraising income. If I were you, I'd be welcoming her with open arms.'

'I was worried that these people are all about image and no substance. They're like PRs for brands, and I wonder how our charity can sit easily alongside such consumerism.'

'Seriously, Nathan. Linking up with Skye could propel Sacha's Sanctuary to the big league. If things haven't massively changed for the better this time next year, I'll owe you a magnum of champagne.'

We shake hands, and he pats me on the back. 'Deal,' I say.

I glance over at Skye and am surprised that her gaze is on me. She looks away when she realises I've seen her. Why is it that my brain is telling me that this is the best thing for my charity, yet my heart is screaming *beware*?

6

SKYE – THEN

I walk with Tiffany through the shopping streets and down some steps into Sainsbury's car park, wondering if we are about to do some more shopping, but no. She stands next to a brand-new bright red Mini and presses the key fob. The doors unlock. She walks around to the back of the car and lifts up the boot.

'Well, don't just stand there. Put your bags inside,' she says.

'Is this your car?' I stare at the personalised number plate. T1F ANY

'Yeah! I'm hardly going to be nicking someone else's, am I?'

I bite my tongue. Since when is it normal for seventeen-year-olds to own their own fancy motor? I hesitate. Is this a trap? Perhaps she's a scout for a drug trafficker, and I'm about to be ensnared. Or maybe she works for a pimp.

I make an instant decision. I can't risk this. I grab all the shopping bags and leg it, darting between cars and running towards the entrance of the supermarket. I'll lock myself in the public toilets inside and wait until she's gone.

'Skye! Please don't go!' Tiffany yells after me. I hear her footsteps behind me. 'Skye! Wait!' Her voice catches in a sob. A sob.

I stop still and turn to look at her. A white car hoots at me, and I give the male driver the finger. Tiffany arrives in front of me with tears pouring down her cheeks. What the hell? She wipes her eyes with the back of her hand and sniffs loudly.

'What did I do?' she asks.

'You? Nothing. It's just weird to be inviting me back when you don't know me. You could be a pimp, or you might be luring me into some drugs ring.' Now I'm saying it out loud, it sounds stupid. I doubt there are any seventeen-year-old female pimps with personalised number plates.

'Really?' She smiles through her tears. 'You've led a much more exciting life than me. All I wanted was a friend and to do something nice, but you're probably right. Stupid idea.' She shrugs her shoulders and sniffs again.

And now it's my turn to apologise. I've got to stop being so cynical about people. Perhaps she's just a genuine, poor little rich girl with no friends. I've never met anyone like her before, so who am I to judge?

We stare at each other.

'I'll come back with you if the offer is still open?' I say eventually.

She nods. I pick up the shopping bags and follow her back to the Mini.

TIFFANY TURNS on some loud music I don't recognise, which breaks through the awkward silence in the car. I have absolutely no idea where we are, and I'm beginning to regret getting into this. We drive along dark, narrow country lanes with overhanging trees that throw spooky shadows, until eventually she indicates to the right, and we turn off the road. Her headlights light up a vast pair of iron gates. There is an ornate, lit-up sign saying "Bashfield Manor". Tiffany presses a key fob, and the gates open, silently and steadily.

'What is this, a prison?'

'No, silly. It's my home.'

'You've got electric gates to your home. How do I get out if I want to leave?'

'Press the exit button from the inside. You won't be stuck here.' She laughs.

The driveway is illuminated with up lights so that the trees either side of the drive throw more ghostly patterns across the lawns. And then we're in front of the house.

It's huge.

It's ugly.

And I've never seen anything like it.

'Wow!' I say as I stare at the three enormous concrete cubes built at strange angles, one on top of the other.

'My dad designed the house,' Tiffany says. 'He worked with some leading architect from Los Angeles.'

'How long have you lived here?'

'Five years.'

Tiffany drives around the side of the house, and I see there's another concrete cube at the back of the property, wedged underneath the main house, again at a weird angle. She presses another button on the fob, and a large black garage door lifts up and over. Inside there is a white Rolls Royce and a red Porsche. Tiffany pulls up to the left of the Porsche.

'Mum and Dad are both home,' she says. 'Be careful when you open your door. Can't let it scratch Mum's car.'

We get out of the Mini, and I'm hit by warmth. It's like we're standing inside a house, but this is a garage.

'Why's it so hot in here?' I ask.

'Dad likes a heated garage. It's more comfortable when we start the cars in the morning.'

I try not to show my expression of amazement. We collect our bags, and I follow Tiffany around the side of the cars to a door.

'You will pretend that we're at college together, won't you?' Her eyes are narrowed, and her long nose creased with concern. Strangely, the more uptight she becomes, the more relaxed I am.

I nod. 'Don't worry, I won't let on.'

Tiffany opens a door, and the second she steps into the corridor, lights come on. The floor is a slippery white marble, and my trainers squeak with every footstep. There are vast photographs of greenhouses and factories on the walls. Each to their own, I suppose.

'The swimming pool is that way,' Tiffany says, pointing to the right. 'I'll show you later.'

A swimming pool. She mentions it as if it's normal to have your very own swimming pool. I used to love swimming. I remember when Maggie Barker took me and the other foster kids swimming in the big public pool when I was seven or eight. She paid for us to have six swimming lessons, one a week during the summer holidays. Goodness knows where she got the money from. Unlike the others, I didn't complain. The minute I got in that pool, I loved it. If I'd been born into another life, I'd have become an Olympic swimmer. When I was younger, I used to pretend that Mum was a mermaid who had to abandon me because she couldn't survive on land. If only.

I squelch along the corridor and follow through the door that Tiffany pushes open in front of us. We walk into a vast room with a white ceiling and floor, lined with cupboards and shelves, painted in dark green.

'This is the boot room. You can leave your coat in here and your shoes.' She opens one of the cupboards, exposing a rail stuffed full of coats.

'I'll hang onto my things, thanks,' I say. I'll be damned if I'm going to let all my new clothes out of my sight. What if Tiffany changes her mind and wants them for herself? Or what if they're given to someone else? With the number of coats hanging up, it looks like there are a lot of people living here.

'It's not a choice!' Tiffany says, laughing nervously. 'Dad likes things to be kept in their proper places, so shoes and boots stay down here along with coats. Indoor shoes and clothes can go upstairs into the bedroom wardrobes.'

One of the other things I've learned from my years in care is to pick your battles. Sometimes, however puke-making it is, it's better to follow the rules – in the short term, at least. Reluctantly, I shrug off my parka and hand it to Tiffany. She puts it on a coat hanger and shoves my boots into the cupboard. 'This is my cupboard,' she says, closing the door.

I pull it open again. 'What, you mean all the stuff in here is yours?'

'Yes,' she says, blushing. She hands me a pair of white slippers, and I slip my filthy socked feet into them, sinking into their softness.

'Ready to meet Mum?' she asks, running her fingers through her hair. There's a nervous energy about her now.

'Sure, bring it on.'

She lets out a short, sharp breath and opens another door. I follow her into a kitchen. I've never seen anything like this room before, not even on one of those home makeovers programmes. It is black and huge. All the units are black; the massive island unit is made from black shiny marble; the cupboards handles are gold, as are the taps. The floor is white marble, and gigantic gold pendant lights hang from the ceiling.

'Wow,' I say quietly, swivelling around to take it all in.

'Hi, Mum. I've brought a friend home from college. She's called Skye.'

A tall, very skinny woman with blonde hair pinned up in a casual bun steps towards us. Her cheekbones are high, like rosy apples, and her mouth is broad, with plump lips. She smiles at me with green, feline eyes and extends her hands. Her long, pointed fingernails are painted in pale pink, which matches her pale pink velour tracksuit.

'Well, this is a nice surprise!' she says, smiling at me. She speaks with an accent, one I can't place. 'It's a pleasure to meet you, Skye. My name is Adina Larkin. Will you be joining us for supper?'

'Actually,' Tiffany interrupts, 'I was wondering if Skye could stay for a few nights? She's having some problems at home at the moment.'

'Nothing too bad, I hope?' Adina asks.

I have to think quickly, but I'm used to making up stories. 'It's been a bit tough. I was living with my grandmother, and she's just died, so I was very grateful to Skye when she said I could come here. I don't want to be alone in the house.'

'Good heavens! How terrible. Of course you can stay

here, for as long as you like. It's been such a long time since Tiffany invited a friend over. Tiffany darling, the blue room is made up. Take Skye up there and make her at home. Is there anything you don't eat, Skye?'

'Don't eat?' I ask, frowning.

'Food intolerances,' Tiffany says quickly.

I shake my head.

'The perfect guest. Have you got much homework to do, girls?'

'Not too bad,' Tiffany says, beckoning me. 'Come on, Skye.'

I follow her out of the kitchen and into a massive square hall. I whistle as I stare at the vast crystal chandelier that throws prisms of coloured light onto the white walls, and I take in the sprawling flower arrangement of orange blooms on the circular glass table in the middle of the space. A portrait, which at a guess must be at least eight feet high and six feet wide, hangs on the wall facing the staircase.

'Is that you?' I ask. The portrait is of a couple and their daughter. The girl is probably eleven or twelve years old and bears a faint resemblance to Tiffany.

'Our family portrait. It's hideous, isn't it?'

I say nothing. It's not hideous, just very large and pretentious. As I stand there, my attention shifts to my feet. There's a warmth that seeps through my slippers and worn socks.

'Is the floor hot?' I ask, removing my foot from the slipper and placing it directly on the marble floor. My socks are truly disgusting.

Tiffany smiles. 'It's underfloor heating. Nothing exciting about that. Come on, let's go upstairs.'

The staircase is glass. The steps are glass, and the balustrade is glass, and I get a dizzy, vertiginous feeling if I look down. I concentrate on putting one foot in front of the other. Tiffany turns to the left and walks along a corridor, but the staircase continues spiralling upwards to another floor.

'What's up there?' I ask.

'Mum and Dad's bedroom, bathrooms and dressing rooms. This is my room,' she says, opening the door with her shoulder. Once again, the light miraculously comes on without her having to touch a button.

It's huge and decorated as if it were for a fairy princess. There is a big four-poster bed in the middle of the room, with sheer white frilly curtains coming down from the ceiling. Opposite the bed is a full-height book-case that looks like it belongs in a toyshop. There are so many soft toys and dolls sitting on the shelves, it gives me the shivers. Imagine having all those eyes watching you at night. There is a kidney-shaped dressing table in the corner of the room, covered in pink fabric dotted with little white flowers that match the curtains. Over-sized white fur rugs are on the carpet. This massive palace-like room is designed for a little girl, not a teenager.

'Sorry it looks like this,' Tiffany says. 'You can see why I don't want to bring friends here.'

'Why don't you get rid of the toys and stick up some posters? And get some new curtains. My last foster mum got some at Ikea, and they were really nice.'

'Mum and Dad would have a hissy fit. It's not worth the hassle.'

I nod. Who am I to judge? I don't have any parents.

'At least the bed looks comfy,' I say, 'and your dressing table is cool.' I notice the piles of make-up and curling brushes and hairdryers and so many bottles of perfume it looks like the counter in a department store.

'My dressing room and bathroom are through here.'

I follow her through a doorway. Her dressing room is lined with cupboards, and the en-suite bathroom is in pale pink marble, with a vast white bathtub and walk-in shower.

'Wow. I've never seen anything like this.'

'I'm a bird stuck in a gilded cage,' she mutters.

I don't know what to say.

MY ROOM IS next door to Tiffany's. It's equally ornate and frilly, with floral curtains in shades of blue, and a big, tall bed with a velvet headboard. I also have my own bathroom with a walk-in shower. I could get used to this.

I lean my rucksack against the side of the bed and open the door of a built-in wardrobe. Long dresses covered in fabric bags hang at one end. The shelves are empty.

'Some of Mum's dresses,' Tiffany says. 'We always have supper at 7 p.m. I need to do some homework beforehand, but you can watch telly in here if you want.'

I glance around, looking for a television.

Tiffany presses a button on the wall next to the bedside table, and to my amazement, a television rises from the end of the bed.

'Holy crap!' I say, flopping onto the bed. 'Can I stay here forever?'

Tiffany smiles coyly. 'Come and find me if you need anything; otherwise I'll see you at 7 p.m. Oh, and you might want to change into some of the new clothes we bought.'

AN HOUR LATER, I have had a shower and changed into the pair of new jeans and jumper that Tiffany bought me. The shower was glorious: sparkling clean and so strong it felt as if I were being massaged by thousands of blunt hot needles. I feel clean and refreshed, although after two nights with barely any sleep, I'm exhausted. I doze off watching some stupid soap on the telly and wake with a start when Tiffany comes into my room at five to seven. I follow her downstairs, back into the kitchen.

Adina is bustling in the kitchen. I'm surprised. I thought that people as rich as this family would have staff.

'Come and have a seat at the table,' Adina says. We follow her to a large circular table in a conservatory-like room just off the kitchen, which I hadn't noticed earlier. A big man is seated at the kitchen table, opening a pile of post. He only looks up when Adina speaks.

'This is Skye. A friend of Tiffany's from sixth-form college,' she says, placing manicured fingers on my shoulder.

He gives me a cursory glance, narrows his piggy eyes at me and grunts.

'Hello.' I smile, but he isn't looking.

'My husband is called Jeffrey,' Adina says, although I don't know why he can't tell me that himself. He looks like a complete geezer, wearing a checker white-and-green shirt and a green tie. He's fat, with a triple chin and a wide nose with hair sprouting from his nostrils. Why would a pretty woman like Adina end up with a slob like Jeffrey? Money, I suppose.

Tiffany and I sit down. Adina brings over a green tureen and serves up soup with some hot, crusty bread as a starter. I don't know what it is, but I'm so hungry, I could eat anything. I start shovelling the soup in the second the food is put in front of me. It's delicious.

'What A levels are you taking?' Adina asks as she sits down and breaks through my slurps.

Fortunately, Tiffany answers for me. 'Skye is doing English, history and geography, which is why we didn't meet sooner.'

'Into the arts, are you?' Jeffrey says. So the man talks.

I smile. I used to read a lot, and if I had been bothered to study, I suppose I might have done okay in my GCSEs. As it turns out, I only passed two exams: drama and English.

'Something like that,' I say, using my bread to wipe my bowl clean.

Jeffrey glowers at me, and I'm not sure why.

'Tiffany is going to study engineering at university so she can join my husband in our business,' Adina says. 'What about you?'

'What about me?' I turn to look at Tiffany. Is this some kind of trap?

'Skye hasn't decided what she wants to do after school, have you?'

I shake my head.

'What do your parents do? Jeffrey asks.

'I don't have any parents.' At last, I can tell the truth.

Both Adina and Jeffrey stare at me, matching frowns across their foreheads, although Adina's is barely furrowed, unnatural-looking.

'They're dead,' I say. 'My parents died in a car accident when I was a baby, which is why I was living with my grandmother, and now she's dead, too. I'm waiting to find out what's going to happen next.'

'Gosh, I'm so sorry,' Adina says. 'That's truly shocking.'

I let a tear slip from my eye. It's always been useful to be able to cry on demand. 'I probably won't go to university. I'll just find a job somewhere.'

'It's not like in my day, when a degree didn't matter,' Jeffrey says. 'If you want to get on in life, you need an education. Law or engineering. They're the ones to go for. Tiffany's going to be an engineer, and then she can start in the business. I'd wanted her to do chemistry, so she could have got into the growing side of things, but she didn't do well enough in her chemistry GCSE. A terrible disappointment.'

Tiffany keeps her eyes to the table. She's left an inch of soup in her bowl and has just nibbled at the bread. She bites the side of her thumbnail, gnawing at it until a drop of blood rises to the surface.

'Stop biting your bloody nails!' Jeffrey snaps.

I nearly jump out of my chair, so it's just as well I've finished my soup.

Tiffany scrapes her chair back and collects the dishes, walking towards the kitchen. Adina picks up the soup tureen.

'Can I do anything to help, Mrs Larkin?' I ask, my voice sugary sweet, desperately hoping I won't need to stay sitting at the table alone with this oaf of a man.

'No, dear. It's all under control.'

Jeffrey doesn't look at me, but reaches to the console table behind him and studies his mobile phone. At least it means I don't have to talk to him. In fact, neither Tiffany nor I speak during the rest of the meal. Jeffrey goes on about his business, and I zone out. Who gives a toss about tomato yields or the cost of peat?

'I'M SORRY,' Tiffany says. It's after supper, and we're up in her room, me lying on a white sheepskin rug on the floor, her on the bed.

'What for?'

'My parents.'

'Your dad's a jerk, but your mum seems okay.'

'She's not. She criticises me all the time; she just didn't do it in front of you. It's, Tiffany, we need to put you on a diet, or Tiffany, your hair is all lanky, or Tiffany, if only you tried harder at school, or Tiffany, it's not surprising you haven't got any friends with an attitude like yours. Or Tiffany, if you hadn't been such a fat baby, I could have had other children. You tore my perineum, and I face a lifetime of pain. The PTSD from your birth means I have to have therapy twice a week. And so it goes on.'

'At least you have parents, and you're living surrounded by all of this.' I wave my hands around.

She harrumphs. 'What's it like being an orphan?'

'No one gives a shit about me, and I don't give a shit about anyone. I do whatever I want.'

'I wish I could do whatever I want. I hate my life,' Tiffany says. 'I hate college. I'm crap at all my subjects. I don't want to study engineering, and I don't want to work for Dad.'

'Well, don't,' I say.

'It's not that simple.'

'Yes, it is. If you don't want to go to college, don't go.'

'And what will I do all day?'

'You can hang around with me.'

Tiffany looks at me wide-eyed.

'It's your life. You can do whatever you want with it.' I carry on stroking the sublime soft pile of the rug.

We're both silent for a while, and then I ask, 'If you don't want to work for your dad, what do you want to do?'

'I want to be famous. To have my own YouTube channel showing people how to put on make-up.'

'Really?' I laugh. 'Is that even a job?'

'You can become a millionaire or even a multimillionaire doing that.'

'You're going to inherit millions anyway. Why
bother?'

She stares at me, as if I've uttered the most profound
statement. I chuckle.

7

NATHAN – NOW

It's Monday, three days since the granola launch, and I'm in the office. We have a modest premises that takes up half the second floor of a small shared office block in Horsham. There are five of us working here, and we sit in an open-plan office, although we have two separate rooms that I use for confidential meetings or on the rare occasion I need to make a private phone call. It's been a hectic day, and I'm looking forward to going home to Marie and the girls, slumping in front of the television with a glass of wine.

'Skye's agent is on line one for you,' Ash shouts across the room.

Ash is my number two, and much of the credit for Sacha's Sanctuary's success lies firmly at his feet. He was my first recruit, and with his decade of experience working in both smaller and larger charities, he has stopped me from making some major mistakes. Ash is one of the world's good guys. He combines an excellent head for business with a social conscience, but he doesn't like being a front man. A big bear of a man, with a full reddish beard and moustache, he is verging on gauche and prefers to be the person in the background.

When he shouts his message, the whole team stop what they're doing and turn around to look at me, eyebrows raised.

I pick up the phone.

'Good afternoon, Mr Edwards, this is Tiana Johnson speaking. Skye would like to invite you for dinner so that the two of you can get to know each other better and discuss how your objectives can align. Would tomorrow evening be convenient for you?'

'If you could just hold on for one moment, I'll check.' I don't really need to check, because my only regular evening commitments are on Thursday nights, when I help out at our soup kitchens.

I put the phone on mute. 'She's inviting me for dinner!'

'Go for it!' Ash says.

'Oh my god, that's so exciting!' Sophie does a little wiggle in her chair.

I unmute the phone. 'Thank you, I look forward to that.'

Ash and the girls are buzzing with excitement about the potential agreement with Skye. I still have my doubts, but hopefully those can be laid to rest when I get to know her better. We barely spoke again at the granola launch, as she was pulled from one interview to another. In the end, I just waved at her from across the room. And we're still waiting for the promised proposal from Tiana.

On Tuesday evening, I leave work early to drive to London, taking the car so I don't have to worry about missing the last train home. The restaurant she has chosen is in a residential street in London's Knightsbridge, tucked behind the Old Brompton Road. I find a parking space surprisingly easily and walk around the block to kill time. Nevertheless, I am still ten minutes early when I arrive at La Dolce Vita.

'Good evening, sir.' The waiter holds the door open for me. The restaurant is small and decorated in charcoal grey and matte bronze, with padded grey chairs and glass bell-shaped lights that hang at differing heights from the ceiling.

'I am here to have dinner with Skye.'

It seems awkward and pretentious not to use her surname or, for that matter, even know what it is. The waiter doesn't seem fazed. Perhaps everyone really does know who Skye is.

'Of course, sir. May I take your coat?' He speaks with a heavy Italian accent. After hanging up my coat, he picks up two leather-bound menus, and I follow him to a table in the middle of the small restaurant. I am surprised to see that Skye is already here.

'I thought I was early!' I say jokingly, remembering not to look surprised when she greets me with a kiss on both cheeks.

'I am always early, and I can't abide people who are late. I think it implies that they consider themselves more important than you, that their time is of higher value. Anyway, it's lovely to see you again, Nathan. Please, sit down.'

'Can I get sir an aperitif?' the waiter asks as he hands me two menus.

'Just a sparkling water, please.'

'I'm afraid I'm already onto the cocktails.' Skye holds up a wide-brimmed glass with a cherry floating on the surface. She is looking glamorous in a low-cut black velvet dress with a simple silver cross on a chain that hangs into her cleavage. I try to keep my eyes on her face, which is more heavily made up than on the two previous occasions we have met, with red lips and long black eyelashes. Most of her hair is affixed to the top of her head although blonde tendrils have escaped and frame her face. During our previous two meetings, I didn't think she was exceptionally attractive. Tonight, she is undeniably beautiful.

Two couples arrive and sit down at the adjacent table. The women stare at Skye and unsubtly whisper and point at her. Skye doesn't seem to notice, but I suppose she is used to the intrusive effects of fame.

'I've already chosen,' she says. 'I always eat the same thing here. The asparagus to start with, followed by the Dover sole. You can choose the wine.'

'Actually, I'll only have half a glass. I'm driving.'

I think I see a flash of annoyance on her face, but it quickly morphs into a smile.

'In which case, we had better order by the glass. Where do you live?' she asks.

'Near Horsham, in West Sussex. And you?'

'No way!' she exclaims, clapping her hands. 'I'm just north of Horsham. I can't believe we've both come from the same place. I would have chosen somewhere closer to home if I'd realised.'

I'm surprised that she isn't aware of the location of Sacha's Sanctuary. Our offices are in Horsham, and Tiana knew where we are located. Perhaps Skye isn't involved in the business side of things, and the set-up between her and Sacha's Sanctuary has been initiated by Tiana, even though Tiana is giving Skye the credit.

I glance at the menu and, noticing the eye-water-ingly expensive price of the Dover sole, select a chicken dish.

After the waiter has taken our orders, along with

two glasses of Sauvignon, I lean back into my chair. Skye leans forwards.

'So, Nathan, tell me about you. Are you married? Do you have children?'

I try not to show my surprise. I thought we were here to discuss business.

'I'm engaged, and I have two girls, aged fifteen and twelve.'

'How lovely. Is your wife-to-be the girls' mother?'

'Um, no.'

'Divorce is a difficult thing. I hope your girls weren't too badly affected.'

'My first wife passed away,' I say quietly.

Her eyes widen. 'I'm sorry to hear that.' She looks shocked, as so many people do when they learn about the death of someone who dies too young.

'And you?' I ask, keen to remove the spotlight from my life.

'Holden and I have been together for a couple of years, not that it's public knowledge. In my job, I have to be very careful not to share too much of my personal life. He's a professional sailor, which is hard for both of us, because he is travelling for most of the year. But we're committed to each other, and I'm hopeful that it will work in the long term.'

'What does a professional sailor do?'

'He races yachts all around the world and captains super yachts for the rich and famous. It's good, because he understands my world. Have you ever been touched by fame, Nathan?'

I hesitate. It's a strange question, and the answer is definitely no. She places her hands on the table and slides them towards me, her head also edging towards the centre of the table. I catch that strong apple-blossom scent again.

She lowers her voice to a whisper. 'There are currently seven people in this room staring at me.'

I turn to look around.

'Don't,' she says. 'Keep your eyes fixed on mine.' I do as I'm told. 'The two women behind you are trying to take a covert photograph of me, and the man to our left has already rung his wife to say that I'm in the same restaurant as him and wants to know if he should ask me for a photo.'

I draw my chin back in surprise.

'You get used to this nonsense in a position such as mine.' She sighs, slowly unfurling herself backwards into her chair. Her voice returns to its normal volume. 'Which is why I want to work with your charity. To do some real good in this world of artifice.'

Our starters arrive, the asparagus concoction for Skye and a red pepper soup for me. I thank the waiter, but notice Skye doesn't even glance at him.

'You see, shared values are the most important thing to me. Far more important than looks or money. Honesty, compassion, thinking of the greater good, integrity. That's what struck me about you and your charity, and why I see our relationship as having so much potential.'

I take a spoonful of soup. It's as if she's reciting back to me words she's lifted from our website. I must try not to be cynical.

'Excuse me, but you're Skye, aren't you?' The girl standing next to us must be about the same age as Isla.

'Yes,' Skye says, throwing her a dazzling smile.

'Can I have a selfie with you?'

'Of course.'

The girl bends down next to Skye, holds her phone out in front of her, and pouts as she takes a couple of photos of them both.

'Thank you!' She scurries back to a table behind us.

'Don't you mind being interrupted?'

'It's part of the job. At least she was polite. You have to remember that your audience is your currency. If you don't give them what they want, they'll abandon you in a nanosecond.'

'But how do you balance your business life, which is all about being in the public eye, and your private life, which, by its very definition, is meant to be private?'

'That's the perpetual dilemma,' Skye says, staring wistfully at her plate.

I can't imagine how dreadful it must be, having every aspect of your life scrutinised all the time. I think of Marie and how I haven't even told the team at Sacha's Sanctuary that we're engaged. Ash is the only person who knows we're in a relationship. I was worried how it might seem; me hitching up with the au pair just eighteen months after my wife's death. Perhaps I shouldn't worry. I doubt anyone in my professional network would be the slightest bit interested.

'Tell me more about Sacha's Sanctuary and what your ambitions are,' Skye says.

And so, in between eating our main courses, I do. I tell her why I set up the charity, what we do on a day-to-day basis, and what our ambitious plans are to eliminate homelessness in the south-east. By the time I have finished, she is leaning so far forwards across the table, I can feel her breath on my face, and it's hard not to look at her cleavage. I lean back into my chair, but my foot catches hers.

'I'm sorry,' I mumble.

She runs her tongue over her bottom lip and strokes her neck with her right hand. She is wearing a large aquamarine ring that catches the low light.

'You know, it's such a relief to be spending time with

someone with your values, a true kindred spirit. Since I lost my best friend some years ago, other than Holden, I've never found anyone else with whom I have such shared values. Thank you for coming into my life, Nathan.'

I smile tightly. Embarrassed.

She evidently doesn't sense my unease and, to my relief, leans back in her chair. 'The people around me tend to be so sycophantic. Everyone wants to bask in my fame rather than appreciating how hard I've worked for this, how much I have had to sacrifice.'

She leans forwards suddenly, placing her right hand on mine. 'Let's talk about what I can do for you. I'd like to tell my audiences on all the platforms about Sacha's Sanctuary. Perhaps we could run some stories and interview homeless people you have helped. I will ask some of the brands I work with to donate funds to your charity, and we can run some joint sponsorship events. Tiana mentioned that Sacha's Sanctuary currently has a revenue of just under one million pounds, is that right?'

I nod. Considering we have only been in operation for three years, I'm immensely proud of our success. About a third of our income comes from a couple of government-awarded grants and contracts, but the vast majority of the revenue comes from donations from charitable foundations, legacies and fundraising initiatives. We have worked tirelessly, and with our healthy revenue, we are beginning to make a real difference.

The waiter interrupts us to ask if we would like the dessert menu. Skye shakes her head, and I follow suit.

'Any tea or coffee?' he asks.

'A black coffee,' Skye says.

'And one for me too, please.'

Skye leans forwards again. 'I have every confidence

that I can help you triple that income over the next eighteen months.'

I gawp at her. She speaks with credibility and has clearly achieved great success, but that is a wild claim.

'You look like you think I'm trumpeting hot air.' She winds a tendril of hair around a finger in a surprisingly girlish gesture.

'It's a rather ambitious goal.'

'Ambition is my middle name, Nathan. You don't get to having as many followers as me without hard work and single-minded focus. Obviously, I can't tell you the value of my influencer contracts, but between you and me, it's over seven figures.'

I can't stop my eyes from widening and feeling impressed. We talk about the ways she intends to fundraise for us, name-dropping brands and famous people, many of whom I suppose I should be familiar with, but I'm not. And then she clicks her fingers at a passing waiter. 'The bill.'

'Let me,' I say. It grates with me that she never says please. She is warm, attentive and polite to me, yet to the waiter she is offhand, verging on rude.

'Out of the question. I invited you,' she insists.

When the waiter places the little silver platter with the folded-up bill on it, Skye grabs it and places a black credit card on top, without even glancing at the bill. He returns with a card reader, and she pays the bill. I wonder if she's added any extra for tips.

As we get up from our table, I feel all the other diners' eyes on us; the noise level falls, and it's as if the star of the show is about to exit the stage with the audience holding their breaths in anticipation of a speech. Instead, Skye and I walk to the doorway and collect our coats. I thank her for such an enjoyable evening and realise that despite my initial misgivings, the hours have sped past.

'Can I give you a lift back to Sussex?' I ask.

'It's kind of you to offer, but I'm staying overnight at the Mandarin Oriental hotel and meeting a brand sponsor for breakfast.'

'Can I walk you there?'

She laughs. 'You're such a gentleman. I'll be just fine, but thank you for asking.'

She stands on tiptoes and places a kiss quickly, but firmly, on my lips. Stunned, I take a step backwards, but Skye is already striding away, raising her hand to wave goodbye, her black cashmere coat swinging.

As I drive home, I can't stop thinking about her, how she is clearly very astute and able, but at the same time, her social boundaries blur. She told me how she has a steady boyfriend, yet to her, it is perfectly acceptable to kiss a business colleague on the lips. She is extremely polite, if a little overfriendly towards me, yet dismissive of the waiter.

I shake my head and switch on Radio 2. I have no doubt I am overthinking things. So long as Skye really does raise the profile of the charity and increase our revenue, my personal feelings towards her are immaterial.

THE NEXT MORNING, Marie is making breakfast in the kitchen when I come downstairs. She was asleep when I arrived home, and I was careful not to wake her.

'Coffee for you,' she says as she hugs me tightly. 'How was dinner?'

'Interesting,' I say. 'Skye is a curious–'

We are interrupted by Chloe, who comes hurtling into the kitchen. 'Oh my god! Dad, you're all over social media! Look!' She holds her phone outstretched in front of her. 'Look, Dad!'

Isla is just behind Chloe. 'It's hilarious, Dad. They're saying you're Skye's new mystery partner, and everyone is wanting to know your identity. I can't believe you're famous. Did you get a selfie with her?'

'Of course I didn't.' I take Chloe's phone. The photo shows the two of us in profile, looking intently at each other, deep in discussion. I hand Chloe's phone back.

'Okay, calm down, both of you. This is all nonsense. I had a business dinner with Skye, and we discussed strategy for Sacha's Sanctuary.'

'It's so cool!' Chloe says.

Marie stands with her back to the stove, her arms crossed, her big eyes narrowed. 'Can you both go and get ready for school? Otherwise you'll be late.'

The girls sigh.

'Do as Marie says,' I say.

They slouch back upstairs. I walk over to my fiancée and take her in my arms.

'I'm sorry, darling. I guess that's what happens when you meet with a social influencer. People were taking photos left, right and centre. It can't be easy being that famous.'

Marie is tense, and I rub her shoulders, kissing her gently on her soft lips, so very different to Skye's. Thank goodness that moment wasn't caught on camera.

'It's alright,' she says. 'If the woman helps you grow the charity, that's all that matters.'

But the tense muscles in Marie's back tell a different story.

Then my mobile phone rings.

'It's her,' I say, unsure if I should answer it.

'Go ahead,' Marie says, waving her hand at me.

I answer my phone just before it goes to voicemail.

'Nathan, firstly thank you for a wonderful evening. I'm just on my way to the breakfast event and have seen all that speculation about us on social media. I'm terribly sorry.' She sounds breathless, and I can hear the clip-clopping of heels. 'I'm sure it's the last thing you want, to have your photo splashed everywhere. And all that speculation. Anyway, I just wanted to let you know that I'm going to put the situation straight. Don't worry. I must go, so *ciao* for now.'

She hangs up.

8

Tiffany doesn't require much persuading to bunk off college. There's only one problem: her distinctive car. I suggest that we go into a multi-storey car park in the centre of town, and she drives it up to the very top floor, which is totally empty. We sit there for a moment.

'What will we do all day?' she asks.

I think it's funny that she's at a loss. 'Go shopping, have lunch. You've got money, haven't you?' I ask. It'll be a bit of a bummer if we have to slum it.

'Yes,' she says.

'Maybe we could go to the seaside. I'd like to do that sometime,' I suggest.

Tiffany wrinkles her nose. I decide not to tell her that I've never actually stood on a beach. And despite dreaming of swimming in the sea, I've never done it.

We mooch around town all day and, on one occasion, dart into the changing rooms at Next because Tiffany thinks she spotted one of her mum's friends.

'How did you get money when you were on the streets?' she asks.

'I begged. Had one of those sad bits of cardboard with "I'm hungry, please help" written on it. I got three pounds and seventy-four pence. Do you want to give it a go? See how much dosh we can get?'

'Think I'll pass,' she says.

Of course she'll bloody pass. When you've got thousands of pounds in your bank account, why do you need to worry about small change?

At the end of the day, when I'm getting bored and am about to suggest we go home, Tiffany stiffens and plasters a strange smile on her face. There are three girls walking towards us, arm in arm, their long hair all bouncy, thick lines of kohl around their eyes, large bags slung over their shoulders, each wearing skinny jeans with holes in them.

'Hello,' Tiffany says awkwardly as they approach us.

'What are you doing, Tiff?' the tallest one in the middle asks.

'Um, nothing.' Tiffany glances at me, and I think I see fear in her eyes. I raise my eyebrows and link my arm through hers. That seems to embolden her. 'Do you want to go for a coffee?' Tiffany asks them.

'With you?' The dark-haired one curls her upper lip and laughs.

'Oi, no need to be uppity with my friend,' I say. Tiffany may be a spoiled princess, but I'm not going to let them be bitches towards her.

'Who are you, then?' the tall one asks, nudging her head towards me.

'I'm Skye, and you are?'

'Melinda.'

'Skye has come down from London. She's homeless and is staying with me,' Tiffany says.

'For real?' Melinda narrows her eyes at me. 'You don't look homeless.'

'And what is homeless meant to look like?' I scowl at her and put my hand on my hip.

'Sorry, it's just, well, none of us know any homeless people.'

'Fortunately, my friend Tiffany here is both cool and kind. We look after each other, don't we, Tiff?'

'Yeah,' she says, pulling her shoulders back and standing up straighter.

'You can join us for a coffee if you'd like,' Melinda says.

'I think we'll pass, won't we, Tiff? Got more important things to do.'

I start striding away, pulling Tiffany with me. When I turn around to look at the three bitches, they're standing there gawping at us. It isn't until we've turned onto the next street that Tiffany unlinks her arm. 'Thanks for doing that,' she says. 'That was really good of you.'

'You need to stand up to them. Grow some balls, Tiffany.'

She nods.

'But you don't need friends like them. Find yourself some real ones.'

'They don't like me because they think I'm too posh, because I went to boarding school.'

'What, because you speak funny?'

'No, I don't!' She stops walking and juts her chin out.

'Yes, you do.' I laugh. 'You speak in a drawl, and the tone of your voice goes up at the end of every sentence. But it's no biggie. I speak souff London, but I can speak like you if I want to.' I clearly enunciate all the consonants and drawl out the vowels. I'm good at copying people's voices, and Tiffany bursts out laughing. We're ambling now, back along the main shopping street. 'What was boarding school like?' I ask.

'Horrid. It was a girls' school stuck on a hill in the

middle of nowhere, with views to the sea. But at least I had some friends there.'

'I thought boarding school was all midnight feasts and music lessons and walking around with books on top of your head?'

Tiffany chuckles. 'No. My first year, I had to share in a dorm of six, and after that in rooms of two.'

'Sounds like in the children's home.'

'We had a horrible house mistress, and the house assistants used to patrol the corridors at night to make sure we were in bed. We played lots of games, and fortunately I was good at that. If you were rubbish at games, you didn't stand a chance.'

'What sort of games? Board games or on the computer?'

'Not those sorts of games! Sports like lacrosse or tennis. We had matches most Saturday mornings, and afterwards we were allowed into town, but not until we were sixteen.'

'Why did your parents send you to boarding school? Did they want to get rid of you?' We are back in the car park now, and Tiffany places both her palms on the top of her car.

'No! My parents love me. They wanted what was best for me, and as Dad is rich, they chose the best education they could afford.'

It sounds like she's parroting the nonsense that her parents have fed her. Looks like I'll have to teach her how to stand up to them. 'Your dad paid money for you to be in a prison?'

'It wasn't like that. Most of the time we had fun.' Tiffany opens the car doors.

I simply can't imagine why anyone would think boarding school was fun. It sounds like I had more freedom in care, and even though Tiffany has all that money, I'm not sure that I would have wanted her childhood.

WHEN WE PULL up in Tiffany's parents' garage, I have to kick myself that this is home, for now at least. I could get used to this. I need to ask Tiffany if I can borrow a swimming costume and use the pool. We trot along the corridor and into the black kitchen.

'Hello, girls, did you have a good day at school?' Adina is turning out a home-baked cake that smells delicious.

'Ordinary day, wasn't it, Skye?' Tiffany says. 'I've got some homework to do, so I'll be in my room until supper.'

I'm impressed. Tiffany is a good liar; or perhaps it's just that I'm a good teacher.

SUPPER IS the most delicious fish pie I've ever tasted. I eat it so quickly; I just can't help it. Adina seems thrilled when I come back for a third helping. Jeffrey scowls. I don't know why he's narky about it, because I see what Adina does with the leftovers. She shoves them down the sink and jams on a noisy incinerator-type thing. Such a waste of good food.

'What do you want to do in the future, Skye?' Adina asks as I shovel the last mouthful in.

I pause. I realise that Adina is the only person who has ever asked me about my future, except at that stupid Pathway Plan meeting that I had with Sandra, where we talked about what I could do because that's what the council demands. I just told her what she wanted to hear, because it was all a pipe dream. Becoming an actress. Getting a part on a soap. I knew it wouldn't come true. I've survived from day to day, being shunted from one place to another, knowing that if I had any hopes for the future, they would be dashed. So rather than thinking about the what-ifs, and praying that things will get better, I've stopped myself from dreaming. What do I want to do? It's a bloody good question. The acting thing is a stupid idea.

They're all looking at me, waiting for an answer.

'I don't know. There are so many exciting possibilities, aren't there?' I reply, my head tilted to one side, my eyes raised upwards, as if I'm deeply considering my future.

'Most kids your age don't know what they want to do,' Adina says. 'The world is your oyster.'

What she doesn't realise is that most kids don't have any choice. When you've got money and your parents know the right people, the world may well be your oyster. But for people like me, it's about survival. I wonder what Adina and Jeffrey would think if they knew the truth. And that's why I need to concentrate on the here and now and take from these people as much as I possibly can before this little fairy tale of scrumptious food and feather-filled beds comes to an abrupt end. Because it will; good things never last.

'I don't want to!' Tiffany slams her palm on the table, and the cutlery rattles on our plates. What's going on? I have zoned out of the conversation and missed whatever it was Jeffrey was saying to her. His monotonous voice is such a bore.

'It's your legacy, Tiffany. You should be bloody grateful!'

But Tiffany flees the room, slamming the door behind her.

Now what? Am I meant to run after my supposed

new best friend, or sit here politely with her dreadful parents?

'I'm ashamed at my daughter's behaviour,' Jeffrey says, his triple chin wobbling. 'She should be grateful that her future is secured, that she knows what she will be studying and where she will be working.'

'I think I'll just go upstairs and check she's okay,' I say.

'She's lucky to have you as such a kind friend.' Adina smiles at me and pats my hand. It's like I'm one of those stupid therapy animals. 'Pop back down when she's calmed down. I've got chocolate fudge cake and fruit salad for you both.'

I almost sit back down now. It sounds delicious. But no, I need to act the part.

UPSTAIRS, Tiffany is lying on her bed, sobbing her eyes out.

'What's all this about?' I ask, plonking myself down next to her.

'My life isn't my own. Everything I do has to meet their expectations. They didn't even let me choose which A levels I wanted to do. I'm the one who is studying them. It's not fair.'

'And if you go against their wishes, what happens?'

'They stop my pocket money. They'll take my car away, and then I'll be stuck here in the middle of nowhere. I don't want to work in a bloody salad factory! But Dad says it's my destiny, that everything they do is to secure my future. They've even named me after the stupid business.'

'Is Tiffany the name of a plant?'

'No.' She sniffs. 'It's Lettice. My middle name is Lettice. Spelled with an *i*, not a *u*.'

'Your parents called you lettuce?' I snigger. I can't help it.

Tiffany lets out a sob. ''My dad is known as the King of Salads, and he called me after a fucking lettuce!'

It sounds odd when she swears; it's as if the word somehow jars on her tongue. 'Your parents are weird. But at least you have parents, Tiffany Lettice Larkin.'

'Don't call me that!'

We're both quiet for a while. Tiffany may think she's suffering, but she has no idea of the meaning of the word. She's bathing in self-pity and acting like a spoiled princess. She sickens me, but I'll have to play along, for now, anyway.

'So what do you want to do?' I ask eventually.

'Be a YouTube make-up blogger like Jilpa Tang or Candy Phelan.'

'Never heard of them,' I say. But as the only make-up I own is a kohl eyeliner pencil and a lipstick I stole from Superdrug, I suppose it's no surprise.

'It's going to be the next big thing, vlogging and being a social media star. Look, I'll show you what I tried to do.'

Tiffany jumps off her bed and opens her wardrobe. It feels like my eyes are going to pop out on stalks when I realise her wardrobe includes a desk that slides forwards, with a fancy-looking computer and a video recorder standing next to it. She types into the keyboard and brings up a page on YouTube.

'This is me.'

The page is titled Tiff's Tips. Then up comes a video of Tiffany pouting at the camera. I watch it for maybe half a minute and turn away. It is cringe-making. Tiffany is peering into the camera, applying make-up, talking in a silly high-pitched voice and pretending to be funny.

'What do you think?' she asks.

'Doesn't matter what I think. What do the comments say?'

'They're not great.'

She tries to shut the page down, but I'm too quick, and I grab the mouse. The comments are vile.

F-off, you fat, ugly cow.

Tiff the toff. Why would anyone want to watch you?

Did you now that her middle name is Lettuce? Ha ha. Can't even spell the word know properly.

Another rich bitch telling us how fab dab AMAZING her life is. Get real, bitch.

Gorgeous Tiffany. Luv u xxx

I turn to Tiffany. 'Except the last comment, these are horrible. Why don't you switch off the comments?'

'Because then I can't engage with my followers, and it's all about engagement.' But she doesn't speak with conviction.

'How many followers have you got?'

'Thirty-seven,' she says quietly. 'Most of them are from school or my old friends.'

'So it's not exactly a roaring success, is it?'

Tiffany sniffs and turns the computer off.

'I'm going to buy followers. You can do that, apparently. It'll up the numbers, and then I'm going to write to companies and ask if I can be a brand influencer. I'll get free make-up and stuff.'

I bite my tongue to stop myself from saying, *You can afford to buy your own.*

'I follow all the stars on YouTube. I don't see why I can't be like them.'

'It's no good being the same as other people,' I say. 'You need to be different. It's just like opening up a shop that sells the identical things to Top Shop, right next door to an existing Top Shop. What can you tell people that's new?'

She shrugs her shoulders and picks at the threads on her jeans.

'The thing is, you're just a little rich girl in her fancy bedroom, trying on stuff that ordinary people like me could never afford. Why are people going to respect you when you've done nothing to earn their respect?'

Tiffany recoils as she opens and shuts her mouth. 'I thought you were my friend!'

'I am your friend, because I'm telling you as it is. Your supposed friends either kiss your arse because they're impressed with all of your stuff, or they're bitches who say mean things. I couldn't give a toss whether you're successful on YouTube or not, so I'm just telling you the truth.'

Tiffany jumps onto her bed and buries her face in her pillow. Her voice is muffled. 'Leave me alone now.'

And so I do. I go back downstairs and eat chocolate cake; so much of it, I think I might be sick.

9

By the time I have arrived in the office, my team have worked themselves up into a frenzy about my dinner with Skye.

'Was she amazing?' Sophie asks. She's our newest and youngest recruit and probably the member of staff I should listen to the most regarding anything social media.

'Amazing isn't necessarily the word I'd use to describe Skye. We had a good dinner, and she's got an array of initiatives she wants to embark on to help us raise funds.' I hang my coat up on a hook on the wall behind my desk.

'Have you seen what she's written about you?'

'No.'

I'm not sure I want to see it, but Sophie thrusts her mobile phone towards me. There is a photo of her and me sitting at the table. She is leaning forwards, her hand is placed over mine, and we are staring at each other intently. Shit. Taken out of context, I can see why gossip mongers might think we were on a date. And then my eyes slide to the text.

Had a wonderful dinner last night with Nathan Edwards, the brains behind Sasha's Sanctuary, one of the UK's most important charities for the homeless, a cause close to my heart.

'She's spelled Sacha wrongly,' I say.

'It doesn't matter,' Sophie says. I'm not sure I agree, but I carry on reading.

Nathan is an amazing man, he does great work, but I can reassure you all that our dinner was purely business, and he and I are not an item. Nathan is a family man, so please respect his privacy. I'll be posting soon how you can support Nathan's amazing charity. Hugs to you all and speak later. Skye x – If I can reach for the sky, you can too. Be true to you. Xx

'It's great for us,' Sophie says excitedly. 'She only posted that twenty minutes ago, and it's already had 13,459 likes.'

'What!' I exclaim.

'She's really popular, Nathan. Anything she says about the charity will be good for us.'

'Even if she spells Sacha incorrectly,' I say between gritted teeth as I pull my chair out to sit down.

Ash leans back on his chair, balancing on two legs. He's very adept at it, but as he is such a large man, my stomach lurches a little every time he does it.

'An email arrived from Tiana saying that they're finishing off their proposal and we should have it early next week. I'll work on the PR we can do from our side, how we can shout about our new figurehead.'

Ash and I spend the rest of the morning in our meeting room, going through our numbers in preparation for the next meeting with our trustees. It's close to lunchtime when Sophie pops her head around the door.

'You're not going to believe this! Skye has announced that she's going to be donating ten percent of every purchase of her new Reaching For The Skye lifestyle app to Sacha's Sanctuary!' Sophie hops from foot to foot with a wide grin on her face.

'And what is that, exactly?'

'It's super hush-hush, so we don't know. But it'll probably be something along the lines of Gwyneth Paltrow's Goop.'

Ash and I look at each other blankly.

Sophie giggles. 'Never mind. It'll be great. Would either of you like a sandwich? I'm nipping down to the shops.'

When I get home, I can tell Marie is in a bad mood. She answers my questions in monosyllables and swears in French under her breath. When the girls are out of the room, I grab her.

'Hey, what is it?' I wrap my arms around her and whisper into her hair.

'I don't like all these pictures of you with this Skye. You wouldn't like it if it was the other way around, would you?'

'No, you're right. I wouldn't.' I kiss her gently. 'And I hate that my photo is on social media.'

'You're a private man, Nathan,' Marie says. 'And I love that about you. Don't change.'

It never crossed my mind that Marie might feel insecure or threatened by Skye. I have to reassure her that it's a ridiculous notion. 'And I love you too, with all my heart. I would never do anything to upset you.'

'You have this life I know nothing about, and this Skye, suddenly, she seems to be everywhere. What's she like really?'

'You're right,' I say. 'You should meet her. Why don't we invite Skye and her boyfriend for Sunday lunch? She's announced she's going to be donating the proceeds of a new app to our charity. What do you think? I'd like you to meet her.'

'Meet who?' Chloe says as she pads into the kitchen with bare feet and grabs a bag of crisps from the larder.

'Skye,' I say. 'I'm going to invite her to our house for Sunday lunch.'

'OMG!' Chloe says, throwing the bag of crisps into the air. Marie is too quick for her and catches it, hiding it behind her back.

'We're about to have supper!' Marie laughs, a glint in her eye.

But Chloe doesn't care about the crisps. 'Skye is coming to our house!' She screeches and then runs out of the room and shouts up the stairs, 'Isla, Skye is coming for lunch!'

Another high-pitched scream comes from upstairs. Marie and I grin at each other.

'Let's just hope she accepts the invitation,' I say.

I'M NOT sure how we get through the next few days, because the girls' excitement is close to a manic frenzy. Apparently they are the most popular kids in their classes, and I have to have a stern word with them, explaining that this is a private visit and under no circumstances can we have a group of teenage girls hanging around our house, begging for selfies, and that they are strictly prohibited from posting anything about Skye on social media. I get them to promise that they will both act coolly. I'm not hopeful.

And now it is Sunday, and the doorbell rings on the dot of 12.30. The girls are in the kitchen with Marie, because I have forbidden them from sitting by the window, waiting for Skye's arrival.

I open the front door, and Skye is standing there,

dressed in a caramel-coloured belted coat and a wide smile on her face. 'It's so kind of you to invite me over,' Skye says, handing me a bottle of red wine and a very large bouquet of pale pink and cream roses wrapped in brown paper; they must have cost a fortune.

I glance outside and see a gleaming navy BMW parked behind my car.

'Is your partner here?' I ask.

'No, sorry. Holden couldn't make it. Unfortunately, he's stuck out at sea. Weather conditions were such that they couldn't sail. I asked my assistant to contact you. I'm dreadfully sorry if she didn't. I'll have to have words.'

'It's no problem. Welcome anyway,' I say, standing back so that she can pass me.

I'm relieved that she doesn't attempt to give me a kiss today. I place the bottle of wine and flowers on the hall console table and take her coat, hanging it on the coat stand. Skye is wearing a white fitted sweater, probably made from mohair, because there is the faintest fuzz on its surface, and tightly fitting brown suede trousers with high-heeled brown leather boots that come up to her knees. Long silver earrings make a little tinkling sound as she moves.

I lead her along the hallway and into the living room. We have a fire going in the hearth, and the room looks cosy with two cream sofas facing each other, throws over the back of each and stacks of cushions on the sofas and chairs. There are recessed bookshelves either side of the fireplace and an upright piano pushed up against the back wall. Taupe curtains are tied back with giant tassels. Table lamps on two small side tables throw a warm glow.

'My girls are dying to meet you,' I say.

'And I can't wait to meet your daughters.' She smiles as she sits down in one of the armchairs.

'What can I get you to drink?'

'Anything non-alcoholic. A sparkling water or orange juice would be great.'

'Coming right up. Please help yourself to nibbles.' I point at the small platter of nuts and crisps that Marie has left out on the glass coffee table.

I leave the room and walk straight into the girls, who are bright-eyed and quivering in the corridor. 'Go and introduce yourselves,' I whisper to them. I stride into the kitchen to get Skye's drink.

'Lunch will be ready in ten minutes,' Marie says. She is standing in front of the hob, stirring something that smells delicious. She is wearing a dark burgundy dress that I haven't seen before. I place a kiss on the back of her neck.

'I'm afraid we're one down. The boyfriend hasn't turned up.'

'More food for the rest of us,' Marie says.

I'm grateful to her.

I pour some sparkling water into a glass and carry it back into the living room. The girls are sitting opposite Skye, their eyes wide, hanging on her every word. I have never seen them in awe of anyone before, and I have to stifle a grin. We make small talk for a couple of minutes, and then Marie comes in.

Skye stands up, and the women shake hands. Marie's smile is tight, and I want to tell her that she has nothing to worry about.

A few minutes later we are seated at the table, in the dining room, a room that gets little use. As a family, we always eat in the kitchen, and in the years since Sacha died, I can count on one hand the number of times we've used this room. At Christmas, mainly. The room has beams running across the ceiling, and the walls are covered in a wallpaper that has a faint silvery fleur-de-lis pattern. A series of prints of Venice hang on the walls. I sit in my normal place at one end of the table, and Marie sits at the other end, opposite me, nearest to the door. Skye sits in the middle of the side facing the window, and the girls are opposite her. Marie has laid the table with a flower arrangement in the middle, our best crockery and white linen napkins.

'I've made a smoked salmon and fish mousse starter, followed by roast chicken. I hope that's okay,' Marie says.

Skye's hand rushes to cover her face. 'I'm terribly sorry, but I'm a pescatarian. I'll happily have the starter, but afraid I won't eat the meat. Didn't you get the message?'

Marie glances at me, and I shrug, mouthing *sorry* to her.

Conversation flows easily enough, although it's mainly Chloe and Isla asking Skye questions, grilling her on all the celebrities she's met, which clothing brands she wears and how very glamorous her life is.

'I make it sound like I'm a movie star, but I'm really not.' Skye laughs. 'I wouldn't have anything if I hadn't worked incredibly hard. But I am lucky. My life is so fulfilling, and doing things for charity is so rewarding. I guess you must feel like that every day, Nathan?'

I notice how she loves her superlatives. 'On the whole, yes. Although running a charity is a constant bureaucratic uphill battle.'

'And what do you do, Marie? Other than being an amazing cook and next in line to be Mrs Edwards.'

Marie tenses, her fork hovering in mid-air. 'I look after the children,' she says, her voice tight.

'I realise that. What I meant is, what do you do for a

job? It's funny how the vagaries of language sometimes get lost in translation.'

'Marie's English is fluent,' I say.

'Yes, I'm very impressed by your grasp of the language, Marie. I can't speak a word of a foreign language. Hats off to you. So work-wise, what keeps you busy?'

'The girls and the house are my work,' she says, quickly putting another forkful of salmon mousse in her mouth.

'A house fiancée, then! I gather you are engaged. How very cute. So when is the big day?'

'In eight weeks' time,' I say. 'And I can't wait.' I try to catch Marie's eye, but her gaze is firmly on her plate.

'Are you looking forward to having a new mother?' Skye leans towards the girls.

I need to stop this conversation now. The room is bristling with tension, and I'm surprised Skye can't sense it. 'Marie has been part of our family for nearly four years, and we're looking forward to formalising things, aren't we, darling?'

Marie nods, but her jaw is set forwards and her lips tightly pursed.

'This is delicious, by the way,' Skye says to Marie. She turns to Isla and Chloe. 'Do you cook, girls?'

'Isla cooks a little, don't you, love? The problem is, Marie is such an amazing chef, she puts the rest of us to shame. Isla is doing a GCSE in food technology, though.'

'Goodness, I didn't know such a thing existed.'

'Do you like cooking?' Isla asks Skye.

'No, I rarely have time. And because I grew up in care, I didn't have a role model in the kitchen. I do intend to have basic recipes in my new lifestyle app, meal ideas that are easy and cheap to make, but still very nutritious and tasty. Perhaps I could call on you for recipes, Marie?'

'Perhaps,' Marie mutters. I wish I could put my arms around her and tell her to relax.

'Do you help out in Nathan's soup kitchens and homeless shelters?' Skye asks.

Marie doesn't answer, but stands up, scraping her chair backwards. 'Please excuse me. I need to check on the cooking.'

I search for something to say, and am relieved when Skye breaks the silence.

'I've been meaning to ask you, Nathan. Would you be willing to accompany me on the Piranha Sailing Regatta?'

I try to keep my face impassive. I would rather jump out of an airplane than bounce up and down on waves in the English Channel.

'What's the Piranha Sailing Regatta?' Chloe asks.

'The UK's biggest charity yacht race,' Skye explains. 'Last year, we raised over a million pounds for various charities.'

'You know, Chloe,' Isla says. 'It's when Skye sailed with Purple Dollarz.'

'Oh my god! Will Dad be going with you and Purple Dollarz?' Chloe's eyes glisten with excitement.

'And who is Purple Dollarz?' I ask.

My girls groan, and Skye laughs. 'He's a world-famous DJ,' she explains. 'He accompanied me last year, and we came second. And no, your dad would be attending instead of Purple Dollarz. It's a two-crew sailing race.'

Marie walks into the dining room, holding a large platter piled high with vegetables, and places it on the chrome plate-warming trolley in the corner of the room.

'Skye has invited Dad to do a sailing race with him!' Chloe exclaims.

'Nathan doesn't know how to sail,' Marie says, carefully placing the platter on the table.

'That's no problem,' Skye says, smiling. 'I'm an experienced sailor, and I will look after him. So long as you're able and willing to follow instructions, Nathan, it will be fine.'

'I'm curious how someone with a background such as yours becomes an experienced sailor?' Marie says.

'My boyfriend is a professional sailor, and my best friend from years ago had a boat. I'm lucky enough to have had lots of experience.'

'You'll be famous, Dad,' Chloe says. She stands up to help Marie clear the dishes, and Isla follows suit. It's one of the few times neither of us have had to ask the girls to help clear up.

'Isla, stay sitting. No need for both of you to help,' Marie says.

The last thing I want to do is go on a yacht or court fame. I had a cousin who tragically drowned in a swimming pool aged three, so my parents were reluctant to allow my brother and me to have swimming lessons. Consequently, I've always been a pathetically weak swimmer, coupled with feeling seasick on the few times I've been on a boat. I change the subject.

'If it's not confidential, please tell us about your new app,' I say to Skye. 'I gather you're intending to give Sacha's Sanctuary a percentage of your profits.'

'Yes, I'd love to,' Skye says, licking her lips and holding my eyes. 'I have a ten-step programme that helps people achieve their dreams. I was doing individual and group coaching, but my coaching prices are increasingly beyond most people's reach. And frankly, with all the brand endorsement stuff I'm currently doing, I don't have much time for supporting people through the programme. My team thought an app would be the best way to bring my programme to the masses. What I'm hoping is that we can give it free to people who really need it. People who are coming to the end of their drug rehabilitation programmes, for instance. We'll raise funds by getting brands to advertise on the app.'

Marie has returned with the roast chicken.

'That sounds fascinating,' I say. I stand up to go and help carve the chicken.

'Skye, would you like some more smoked salmon, or just vegetables?' Marie interrupts us.

'The vegetables look delicious,' Skye says. 'I'm sorry I won't eat the chicken, but I'm very principled about it.'

'It's fine,' Marie says, turning her back to the table.

'In fact, why don't you join me sometime, Marie?' Skye suggests.

'Join you doing what?' Marie asks as she ladles vegetables onto a plate.

'You could come to the drug rehabilitation centre and help me when I'm giving some of the ladies a makeover.'

Marie pauses for a moment and then turns and walks towards Skye. She puts a plate laden with vegetables in front of her. As she's walking towards me, she mutters under her breath, '*Peut-être, mais probablement pas.*' *Perhaps, but probably not.* Let's hope Skye really doesn't talk French.

I am carving the chicken, and Marie is standing next to me, holding out a couple of empty plates. 'How do you make money as a social media influencer?' Marie asks.

I look up, surprised. Marie is astute, and although

she professes to have no interest in business, she invari-
ably asks the critical questions.

'I get paid by brands. They pay me for talking about
their products or featuring them in a post or video, but
it's much more than that. My followers trust me. They
know that when I vouch for something, it will bring
them real benefit. It's all about engagement and trust.
You should try it sometime. I can tell that trust is difficult for you, Marie. Believe me, if you trust in yourself
and those around you, it will make you so much
happier.'

I can feel the waves of hostility bouncing off Marie,
and I wish I could envelop her in a hug and tell her not
to listen to Skye. The two women are chalk and cheese. I
love Marie, and I will never compare her to Skye. Isla
throws me a quizzical glance, which I have to ignore. By
the time Marie and I are seated again, Chloe, our little
saviour, asks Skye some questions about a clothing
brand she represents, and conversation once again
flows.

Dessert is a treacle tart with a bowl of fruit salad.
Skye nibbles at some fruit but doesn't touch the treacle
tart. I suppose that's how she stays so thin. After we've
finished eating, I suggest that the girls accompany Skye
to the living room while I prepare coffee.

Marie is loading the dishwasher when I walk into
the kitchen, and I embrace her from behind.

'She's dreadful. Holier than thou and so pleased
with herself,' Marie says.

'I suppose so, but it is admirable what she's
achieved.'

Marie pushes away from me and turns around.

'Oh, come on, Nathan. You're not buying into all the
bullshit, are you?'

I don't argue. I can't argue. I am wedged into a

corner and wish I had never brought my work back home.

I get the sense that Skye is a storm. When you're in the storm's eye, all is idyllic, but if you catch its outer edges, then the waters are so turbulent, you might fall in.

10

SKYE – THEN

Yesterday I found the swimming pool, and I'm in heaven. Tiffany loaned me a scarlet swimsuit that is too big for me and gapes in places it shouldn't, including showing my scars, but who cares. I swam yesterday evening, and now I'm here again. It's just gone 7 a.m., and I'm alone in the pool. It's much smaller than public pools, but the water is gloriously warm, and it doesn't smell of that heavy chlorine that makes me want to puke. There are even underwater lights. I haven't swum in three years, but it all comes back to me, and before long I am in a rhythm, swimming crawl up and down the pool, luxuriating in the water and loving the way my body feels so strong.

It isn't until my limbs start to ache that I lift my head up and tread water whilst I catch my breath and wipe my eyes, blinking hard so that I can see. I let out a little yelp.

Jeffrey is standing at the far end of the pool, watching me, bare legs and feet poking out under a navy towelling robe.

I tug at the swimming costume, worried that I'm exposing bits that I shouldn't. He stares, expressionless.

'Enjoying it?' he asks.

'Yes.'

He nods and then undoes his robe, letting it drop onto a lounger at the side of the pool. I can't look at his gross, flabby, old body. I turn and swim quickly to the steps in the shallow end, as far away as I can get from the diving board, where he is standing. I adjust the costume once again and quickly climb out of the pool, making a dash for my towel. Then I hear a massive splash and turn to see him in the water.

Just as I'm about to walk away, he appears, right by my feet.

'How long are you going to stay with us?'

'Um.' I'm startled. 'Just until the weekend, if that's okay with you,' I say, adding as an afterthought, 'but thank you for having me to stay.'

He doesn't give me an answer, but turns in the water, splashing like a hippopotamus. I hurry out of the pool and rush up the stairs to my bedroom. The question worries me. There is absolutely no way that I want to be leaving this palace anytime soon. I'm happy being Tiffany's pseudo sister and eating Adina's delicious food. But it's not difficult to sense Jeffrey's dislike for me, a feeling that's mutual. As I get dressed, I realise I need to come up with a story to persuade them to let me stay.

It's the third morning that I've stayed with the family, and once again, we're in Tiffany's car, supposedly heading towards college. I am just about to suggest we go to the seaside when Tiffany speaks.

'I'm going to go into some classes this morning.'

'Why?'

'Can't risk them reporting my skiving to my parents,' she says. 'I'll meet up with you at lunchtime. I haven't got any classes this afternoon, so it's legit for me to be off.'

I'm not going to argue with her. If she wants to toe the line, that's her choice. 'Okay. Drop me in the centre of town. And can I have some money?'

Tiffany sighs. 'My wallet's in my bag,' she says.

I reach over to the back seat and grab her wallet. It's stuffed full of notes.

'Take fifty quid.'

We're at the traffic lights, and Tiffany glances over at me. I remove one hundred and wait for her to say something, but she doesn't. It's as if she couldn't care less. As if money is on tap and she never needs to think about the possibility of it running out.

The lights turn to green, and she drives forwards. 'Oh, I forgot,' she says. 'I put my old phone in my bag. I thought you might like to have it.'

I grin at her. My Nokia is knackered: The screen is broken, and the phone is about to die.

'Thanks,' I say as I fish out what looks like a brand-new iPhone. I can't believe that Tiffany has discarded such an expensive phone that is barely a year old.

I spend the morning in a coffee shop, drinking fancy coffees and playing with the phone. It's awesome. I count the money I've accumulated since meeting Tiffany. Just under five hundred pounds. Bloody hell. She's given me some of it, but the rest I've just taken from her wallet, and I found a lonesome fifty quid in one of her coat pockets. If she's noticed that I've taken her cash, she hasn't said anything. I really don't think she cares. Money is like toilet paper to her. Use it, dispose of it; they'll always be another roll.

A little part of me feels bad for taking it and squirrelling it away, but I have to grasp every opportunity that comes my way. It could be months or years until I get easy money like this again, and I need to do everything I can to save up enough so I don't have to sleep rough if the Larkins chuck me out.

By 1 p.m., Tiffany and I are back at her house for lunch, which is a quiche and salad. As normal, it's delicious.

'Would you like some more, Skye?' Adina asks. 'You're such a little scrawny thing.'

Scrawny? That's a bit harsh. 'Yes, please.' I push my plate towards her.

'Can I have some more, too?' Tiffany asks.

Adina scowls. 'No. Skye needs feeding up; you most definitely don't.'

Tiffany bristles, and I don't blame her. It's not like she's fat; she's just well-padded, with boobs to die for. I reckon she's a size twelve, possibly a fourteen, whereas I'm a six or an eight.

'Girls, as you've got the afternoon off, I thought I'd take you for a treat.' Adina leans over and picks up a strand of my hair. 'If you don't mind me saying, Skye, your hair looks like it could do with a good chop and perhaps a few highlights. I thought we'd go to the salon. While we get your hair done, Tiffany and I will have a massage. Then we can all have a manicure. What do you think?'

'That's lovely,' I say as demurely as possible. 'But I can't possibly afford to get an expensive haircut.'

Adina laughs. She has a throaty chuckle that seems at odds with her blonde, movie-star looks. 'It's my treat, dear. My treat.'

I glance at Tiffany. Her eyes are narrowed and her

lips pursed, a fury bouncing off her that I don't understand. Surely she should be happy that her mum is treating her to a massage? Or is she peeved that Adina is being particularly nice towards me whilst being critical towards her? There's nothing much I can do about that. Tiffany will have to suck it up.

I've never been to a proper hairdresser. People like me don't sit for hours with foils in their hair, reading celebrity magazines. I admit that I flinch when the hairdresser approaches me with a pair of sharp scissors, but generally it is wonderful, and so relaxing. When she has finished and I look in the mirror, I don't recognise myself. My hair is no longer mousey; it's ash blonde with lighter highlights, and it's cut into a bob that's longer at the front than the back. I turn my head from side to side, wondering where the old Skye has gone.

'You look amazing!' Adina gushes as she appears at my side. She's right. I do. It makes me look older and sophisticated and, dare I say it, even a bit pretty. Tiffany doesn't say anything; in fact, she barely glances at me.

The three of us are led to the other end of the salon and sit side by side at a nail bar station, waiting for our manicurists to arrive. I flick through the colours and think I might go for a navy blue.

'Jeffrey mentioned you're leaving us at the weekend,' Adina says.

Shit. Tiffany looks at me, her eyes wide. She throws me a strange glance, and I can't tell if it's relief or disappointment. Sometimes she's really hard to read. I turn to Adina slowly, giving myself a moment to allow the tears to well up in my eyes. It's good that I'm accomplished at turning on the taps.

'I'm devastated,' I say, pretending to swallow a sob. 'I'm going to have to move to Glasgow to live with a horrid aunt. They're selling Grandma's home, and I've got nowhere to go. It means I've got to change colleges midway through the term, and I don't even know if they do the same subjects or exams in Scotland. I've been trying not to think about it.' I wipe my eyes with the back of my hand and sniff loudly. 'Aunt Dorothy used to hit me when I went to stay with her as a child. She's an alcoholic, too. But I've got no choice. There is nowhere else for me to go.' I bury my face in my hands and shake my shoulders.

'Oh my goodness. That's terrible!' Adina says, jumping up from her chair and putting an arm around me. She smells of sweet exotic spices, a medley of divine scents. 'We can't possibly let you go to Glasgow. I'll have a word with Jeffrey tonight. For now, you must stay with us and carry on going to college with Tiffany. We'll see what we can work out.'

'Seriously?' I ask, blinking rapidly, then wiping my eyes with the back of my hand. I throw my arms around Adina's neck and inhale that glorious perfume. I look over her shoulder at Tiffany and throw her a wink. I get a scowl in return.

LATER THAT EVENING, Tiffany and I are in her bedroom.

'Would you rather I leave?' I ask. I really need to butter her up, because Tiffany could scupper all my plans.

'No, it's okay. I know it's hard to believe, but my parents are nicer to me when you're around.'

'Really?' I ask, but she ignores me. She's watching some stupid make-up blogger on YouTube.

'Do you think I should try to get on *X Factor*?'

'Doing what?' I ask, lying on my stomach on top of the pink bedspread of her sumptuous bed.

'Dunno. That's the problem.'

'Do you really want to be famous?' I ask.

'Yes. Don't you?'

'I suppose so, but I've never really thought about it.'

That's true. It is so beyond the realm of anything I could imagine. I sort of wanted to be an actress, but could never see myself doing it for real. I suppose I assumed that the only thing I might be famous for is getting involved in some heinous crime and being hauled up in front of a judge and being featured on the front page of the newspapers. The problem with that is I'll be locked away in prison for years afterwards, and that's the last place I want to go. No. Fame isn't high up on my agenda. Not right now, but who knows what the future might bring.

'I wish I could sing or juggle or something,' Tiffany muses.

'Most of the people on X *Factor* or *Britain's Got Talent* have got some sort of talent or skill, but the people you're watching on YouTube don't have any talent at all, do they?'

'Suppose not,' she says.

'So what do they have?'

She screws her face up at me.

'They've got to have something; otherwise no one would watch them.'

'Jeez, you're right!' Tiffany jumps up from her chair, as if struck by some divine inspiration. 'They don't have a special talent, but they do have backstories.'

'What do you mean?'

'Something tragic has happened to them in the past. They've overcome adversity. It makes them feel more real.'

'Exactly. And that's what you need,' I say. 'A backstory. Not living the life of Riley with all your fancy stuff.'

'You're right.' Tiffany starts pacing around the room. 'I need to be like you. Or I heard a story about a woman who had cancer in her late teens, and she wrote a recipe book off the back of it. She's got her own YouTube channel and writes for women's magazines.'

'You could do that,' I say.

Tiffany moans. 'I can't pretend I've had cancer! I'd look terrible without any hair. You need to have a cute round face, more like yours, to be able to pull off the hairless or pixie look. But you're right. I need an authentic backstory, and I don't have one. I've got horrid parents, but I live in a lovely house, and I've got my own car, and I'm learning to fly my dad's airplane–'

'You're what?' I exclaim.

'Dad's got a small plane in the hangar in the field next door.'

'Holy shit!' I say. 'You've even got a plane.'

'And a yacht.'

I can't believe this. I really have landed on my feet with this family. 'You're learning to fly?'

'Yup. I'm quite good at it, actually. My teacher says I'm a natural. I wouldn't mind being a pilot, but Dad says pilots are staff, souped-up chauffeurs. And he's right, I'd hate to have to be polite all the time and stick to timetables and all that crap that comes when you're a pilot. And you only get famous as a pilot if you save your plane from crashing or survive a hijacking. No. I want to be a vlogger and be famous that way.'

I don't tell Tiffany that I've never been in an airplane or in a boat. That I have no idea what it's like to be a pilot, or whether her ambition of being a vlogger is realistic or not. But one thing is for sure. I need to do everything I can to stay a part of this family and get as much dosh out of them to set myself up for the future. I think Adina will be an easy touch, but I need to keep out of

Jeffrey's way. He's creepy, and it's as if he sees right through me.

But actually it's Tiffany who is likely to be the trickiest. She's happy to have me around at the moment, because I deflect the heat from her parents. And I make her look edgy, cool even, as if she's got a friend, even if she's had to buy my friendship. But I know how people tick. She'll get bored of me sooner or later, and then she'll want to go back to being the princess of the household. I need to make her dependent upon me, to help her get everything she wants – recognition and fame, ideally. If I don't do that, then my time in this household might be over a lot sooner than I want. And there is no way that I am leaving this place empty-handed.

I roll onto my back. 'I was thinking,' I say languidly, 'I could do a guest spot on your YouTube channel. You saw how those bitches from college reacted towards me. They thought I was cool, and that made you cool too, by association. If people know that we're besties, and they find out that you took me in, a poor homeless girl off the street, it might give your story a bit of authenticity. What do you reckon?'

She hesitates for a moment. 'That could work.'

I bet she's thinking I'll be crap at it. Without her fancy education, what do I know about standing in front of a camera? The only potential problem is if Adina or Jeffrey see the footage. But what are the chances of that? They don't seem like the sort of people who watch social media. Jeffrey has his nose in *Horticulture Week* or *The Commercial Greenhouse Grower* magazine while Adina flicks through the *Daily Mail* or *Hello* magazine. And if they do come across it, we can always tell them that we were lying about my background; we were taking part in some kind of social experiment or project for college. I look at Tiffany expectantly.

'Yeah, okay. Why not? But you'll have to wear old clothes, not all the gear we've just bought you. And your hair is looking a bit smart with this new haircut.'

'It's fine. I'll wear a beanie. I'll put on my old, ripped jeans and make myself look as if I've slept rough.'

Tiffany throws me a sideways glance, and I can tell exactly what she's thinking. That I'll be absolute crap at talking on camera. She might be right – but then again, she might be totally wrong.

11

'Oh my god!' The screech comes from one of the girls upstairs. It's early evening. Skye left a few hours ago, and Marie and I are in the living room. I drop the newspaper on the floor and look up with alarm. I know that ninety-nine times out of one hundred, my daughters' screeches are an overreaction to something minor, but since Sacha died, I've felt so over-whelmingly responsible for them, I jump at the slightest thing.

'Would you mind going up to find out what all the noise is about?' Marie asks. 'I've got a headache.' It is only since we got engaged that she has eased out of her role as au pair and into the role of stand-in mother and my future wife. She looks pale and is lying on the sofa, reading a novel in French. I lean over her and place a gentle kiss on her forehead.

As I walk up the stairs, it sounds as if there is a roomful of teenage girls having a party – impossible, unless they've managed to sneak into the house without us knowing. I knock on Isla's door and poke my head around it. No. There is no party, just my two daughters screeching. And then I hear more voices and realise they are both talking to multiple friends on their phones.

'What's with the racket?' I ask.

'Be quiet for a moment, everyone. Dad's walked in!' Isla says. 'We're putting you on mute!'

'Look at these photos, Dad! Aren't they the best?' Chloe shoves her phone in front of my face. 'Skye is awesome!'

And there are my two daughters standing beside Skye, who has her arms around both of their shoulders. Chloe swipes the screen and shows me more photos. One of Skye kissing Chloe on the cheek and another of her doing the same with Isla. The message underneath says, *My new little besties – Isla and Chloe! Aren't they just the cutest?*

'When were these taken?' I ask, utterly horrified.

'This afternoon, when you and Marie were in the kitchen, making coffee. I can't believe it! We're famous! Look, Dad! It's already got over thirty thousand likes. People from all over the world. And look at the comments!'

'Oh my god, Purple Dollarz has commented! He's said we're babes!' Isla screeches.

'Did Skye ask your permission before posting these photographs?' I ask.

'Of course, dah!' Isla says. 'We wanted her to do it, obvs.' She pulls a face at me.

'You don't need to be rude,' I say. I turn my back to my daughters. What the hell can I do now? The girls switch the volume back on their phones, and the gaggle of young female voices returns. I walk out of the room, shutting the door behind me.

I walk slowly back downstairs. I feel as if I've failed as a father. As if I've failed Sacha. I promised her that I would also protect the girls, but now their faces are on view to millions of people all over the world. How can I protect them in the face of social media? I slump back into my armchair and put my head in my hands.

'What's up?' Marie asks.

'Skye has posted photos of the girls.'

'What!' I'm relieved that Marie's reaction is the same as mine. 'You need to ask her to take the photos down.'

I sigh. If I do that, I'll face a mutiny, not only from Isla and Chloe, but most likely from the team at the charity, as well as Skye and her hangers-on. 'I can't,' I say dejectedly.

'Did she actually ask permission?'

'Of the girls, yes. Of me, no.'

'But they're children!' Marie exclaims. 'She needs your permission, not theirs.' Unfortunately, Isla most definitely does not view herself as a child. 'You need to say something. Do something,' Marie urges.

'I will,' I say quietly. 'Tomorrow.'

THE OPPORTUNITY ARISES when Skye telephones me at work.

'Thank you so much for lunch. It was wonderful to be welcomed into your lovely family. And please commend Marie on her delicious cooking.'

'It was great to get to know you better. I was a bit upset about you posting photos of the girls, though.'

There is a long silence, and I wonder if she's hung up on me.

'Hello?' I say.

'Sorry, I'm still here. Did you say you're upset about it?'

'Yes.'

'But it's what your daughters wanted. They specifi-cally asked me to post photos of the three of us, and as it wouldn't do any harm to my brand, I agreed. I thought they'd be happy.'

'They are happy. It's just I don't think it's appropriate to be posting photographs of underage girls without their parents' permission.'

'Oh my goodness, Nathan. I am dreadfully sorry.' I can hear her footsteps, and it sounds like she's pacing around a room, heels clip-clopping on a hard floor. 'Honestly, it never crossed my mind that you might have a problem with it. The very last thing I would want to do is upset you or your lovely family. Would you like me to put out a statement or something?'

'No, no, that won't be necessary.' I certainly don't want to bring more attention to the girls.

'I could take the post down, but I fear that may upset the algorithms and garner more public interest. I've never removed a post, so it's bound to raise questions.'

'It's fine. Just leave things as they are. I don't want to sound like an old stick in the mud; it's just I need to protect the girls.'

'Of course you do, and I think you're an amazing father. I wish I'd had a daddy like you.'

There is another awkward silence, and for some reason, a shiver runs through me.

'Once again, thank you so much for lunch. My team will be in touch about all the new initiatives.'

We say our goodbyes and end the call.

THAT EVENING, I arrive home, and Marie grabs me. 'We need to talk,' she says, pulling me into the living room and shutting the door behind us.

'What is it?'

'Skye has sent the girls the most outrageous gifts.'

'What do you mean?'

'They were hand-delivered by a courier about an hour ago. She has given each of them a luxury make-up set from Charlotte Tilbury, worth about three hundred pounds apiece.'

I frown. 'The girls are too young to wear make-up,' I say. 'Particularly Chloe.'

'It's not only that, but to give them such valuable gifts is outrageous. Either she has no understanding of the value of money, or she's trying to buy the girls' friendship.'

'That's ridiculous, Marie. I accept that the gifts might seem excessive, but it's probably a result of my chat with her earlier. I told her that I wasn't happy about the photos of the girls on social media.'

'You have to tell the girls they need to send the make-up back,' Marie says.

I swear under my breath and rub my hands over my face. 'I can't do that, Marie. Skye would see that as a snub, and we've already seen an increase in donations to the charity, just in the last twenty-four hours.'

'I don't like her, Nathan, and I don't like the way she's inveigling her way into the children's lives.'

'Come on, love. That's a bit of an overreaction.'

'I know she's pretty and successful, and you're hoping to ride on her coattails, but you need to be careful, Nathan.'

I stare at Marie. I have never had reason to think that she's the jealous type. In fact, she's played our relationship very cool for a long time, being reluctant for anyone to find out we were dating, in case it didn't work out and the girls might be hurt. Something has changed. Is it just Skye who has provoked this reaction, or is there something else going on too?

• • •

TWO DAYS LATER, we receive a detailed proposal from Skye and her team. The document is professionally put together and outlines the many ways in which Skye proposes to support Sacha's Sanctuary. In return, she wants to be our key "ambassador" and figurehead. The contract itself is simple, and I don't see anything in it that is onerous on us. It's Skye who is committing to do things.

'It's awesome,' Ash says, leaning over my desk and running his fingers through his too-long red hair. 'Have you seen the spreadsheet at the back, how she intends to raise funds for us, and how she's quantified the reach her campaigns will have?'

'Yes, it's impressive, if it all happens,' I say. 'I still don't understand how she thinks she can raise this amount of money.'

'Her income stream is predominantly from promoting brands. I'll show you.' He grabs his chair and wheels it around to my desk. He brings up Instagram on my computer and hops on to Skye's profile. He then clicks on a post where Skye is holding a frying pan with what looks like a pancake inside it.

'Right, look at this post. She'll have earned top bucks for this. She's promoting the non-stick clean-living frying pan, the gluten- and dairy-free pancake mixture, and Dotty & Potty, the designer of the apron. She could be making upwards of twenty-five thousand pounds for just one post.'

'How do you know it's a sponsored post?'

'She has to say it is. All the social media platforms are demanding transparency these days. Also, check out the hashtags to see if any of them say "sponsor" or "ad". Look here in the text. Skye says she's the official partner of Free Up To Fry pans and Gourmet Graphics.'

'I suppose companies wouldn't pay her so much if it wasn't worth their while,' I muse.

'Exactly. This is a much stronger form of advertising than your typical adverts on TV or in magazines, which are scattergun in their approach. Skye's followers all love her. If she says jump, most of them will. It's like trusting your best friend when he suggests that you'll love a particular beer from a local microbrewery, or that you should take a test drive in the car he's just bought. You're more likely to believe him and to take action on that advice than you are to follow up from an advert.'

'All those millions of people trust the likes of Skye?'

'Yup. And then she's got a host of other potential income streams such as talking at events, affiliate marketing, getting free products, not to mention the book and app deals she's already got, and the ones coming on board. And then there's the considerable banner advertising that she'll get from ads on YouTube and her website – and so it goes, on and on. Anything that she can be sponsored for, she will be. She'll be earning six figures from all of this, too.'

'Seven figures,' I say under my breath. It's impossible not to be impressed. 'But the thing that makes me suspicious is that ostensibly she's wanting nothing in return from us. I suppose it's all about being seen to be doing good.'

Ash laughs. 'Exactly. For someone like her, everything is about image. She needs to be seen to be affiliated with good causes. It'll make people believe in her even more. She obviously thinks we're an up-and-coming charity, and she wants to piggyback.'

'Which is true, of course.' I chuckle.

'From our side, we'll need to invite her to events, and as the face of the charity, you'll have to attend events with her.'

'Like the charity yacht race she mentioned.'

'You could do a lot worse than having Skye on your arm.' Ash winks at me. 'So, are you happy to give the go-ahead for all the initiatives she's listing?'

'You seem very eager for me to commit.'

'I am. It's not every day that an influencer of Skye's magnitude offers to help a small charity. I think we should grab the opportunity of a lifetime, in the lifetime of the opportunity.'

I know Ash is right; it's just I can't banish the look of dismay on Marie's face. The way that she has immediately taken a dislike to Skye.

'What's stopping you?' Ash asks, frowning.

'Nothing,' I say. I pick up my pen and sign the contract. I then write an email to Tiana thanking her for the proposal and saying that we're happy to go along with all the initiatives she and Skye are suggesting. I just pray I've done the right thing.

'All done,' I say to the team. 'We have ourselves a new figurehead and brand ambassador.'

They let out a cheer and raise their mugs of tea into the air.

WITHIN THE HOUR, I receive an effusive email back from Tiana saying that Skye is thrilled I've agreed to their proposal and signed the contract, and she's inviting me to be Skye's plus one at the Social Media Awards of the Year dinner, to be held this coming Friday night in a sumptuous five-star hotel near Brighton. I wonder why she's inviting me so close to the event. Surely she would already have a partner lined up. I telephone Tiana.

'Nathan,' she gushes, 'I do hope you'll say yes. Skye is very eager for you to attend with her.'

'Can you be honest with me?' I ask.

There's a beat of silence before Tiana replies, 'Of course.'

'Am I a substitute?'

She laughs. 'Skye would kill me for telling the truth, but yes, you are. Holden was meant to be attending with her, but he's stuck on a yacht somewhere in Southern Spain and won't make it back in time. I hope you don't mind being the fill-in.'

'I don't.'

'That's a relief, because Skye wants to take the occasion to formally announce her endorsement of Sacha's Sanctuary. All the media will be there, and it will be the perfect opportunity to officially launch your partnership.'

'Yes, I see that.'

'So I hope the answer is yes, that you will be attending.'

'Thank you. It will be a privilege.'

12

SKYE – THEN

Tiffany is uptight. Apparently, there's a teacher-parent evening coming up this week at college, and she's worried that her absences will be mentioned. I don't know what she's stressing about. She's missed less than a week's worth of school. Hardly a big deal. Anyway, it means that for the next couple of days, I'm alone to wander around and do my own thing.

I decide to go up to London, and I've slipped Tiffany's video camera and my iPhone into my rucksack. I was going to go to my old turf, but at the last minute, I decide to go into the West End. I can't take the risk of running into Sandra, my social worker, or getting the video camera nicked, which might well happen if I'm hanging around the rough streets where I grew up.

I get lots of strange looks as I saunter jauntily along Oxford Street, holding the camera out in front of myself, talking about the best places to lay my head for the night, rifling through bins to show what sort of food is safe to eat and which are the best types of cardboard to sleep on. It's not like I've got real experience of this, but

I know plenty of folk who do. People stare at me. Particularly Japanese tourists who film me filming myself. It's quite a laugh. I go into a restaurant and tell them that I'm filming a piece on homelessness, and could I have some of their leftover food? They offer to give me lunch in return for mentioning them on the film. I have a steak and chips followed by the biggest ice-cream sundae I've ever seen, let alone eaten.

In the afternoon, I'm back in Horsham in time to meet Tiffany come out of school. I don't tell her where I've been, because I want the video to be a surprise.

'I've got to get home on time because I've got a flying lesson.'

'Really? Can I come, too?'

'No, but I'll show you the plane.'

I suppose that will have to do. After parking her car in the garage, next to Adina's Porsche, Tiffany leads me to the massive shed that sits behind the house, with its corrugated iron roof and wide sliding door.

We walk in through a side door, and Tiffany switches on the lights. Inside is a small airplane, white with red curvy lines across its nose. It's rather strange-looking, with wings that seem to come out from the roof. As it's the first time that I've seen a small plane close up – or any plane, for that matter – for all I know, it could be perfectly normal.

'I can't believe that you can actually fly this thing. Aren't you scared when you're up there?'

'Nope. I sit in the left seat, and my instructor or Dad sits in the right. It's all really logical; I just have to follow a clear set of instructions in a certain order. Honestly, if you can learn to drive a car, you can learn to fly one of these.'

She opens the door and climbs into a seat. I perch on

the step and lean in. 'I thought it was super complicated.' I stare at all the buttons and levers in awe.

'It's the same with anything. Practice makes perfect. And I love flying. That deep throaty sound gives me goosebumps, and flying high above the countryside, you feel so powerful.'

She glances over her shoulder before continuing in a quieter voice. 'Dave, my instructor, is so gorge. Last week, he was telling me what to look for when buying a new plane, like checking for wrinkling in the firewall and doing a compression test. OMG, I was getting seriously hot. I'll be getting my private pilot license next month, fingers crossed.'

'Where's the runway?' I ask, confused now, as I thought planes had to be flown from airports.

'We've got our own strip in the field round the back.'

'So you could literally wake up one morning and decide to fly off to New York.'

'No, silly. This is a small airplane. It can't fly that far. It can do about nine hundred miles, so Dad has flown us to France a few times, and to Jersey, of course.'

'I don't know why you don't just hop in the plane and fly far away, and tell your parents where to stick it.'

She rolls her eyes at me. 'You think you're all tough and worldly-wise, but you're so naive sometimes.'

'Bitch,' I mutter softly under my breath, but Tiffany's attention has turned to the man who is standing behind me. She may think that she's superior to me because she has all this stuff and she knows how to fly a plane, but she's not. She's weak and spoiled, whereas I'm like a stray cat, wily, manipulative and alert. A survivor.

'Good afternoon, ladies. All set for the lesson, Tiffany?'

She smiles at him coyly, flicking her hair over her

shoulder. I don't know what she sees in him. He's too old and not in the slightest bit good looking.

'See you,' I say as I leave them to it. I've got something better to do.

While Tiffany is having her flying lesson, it's the perfect opportunity for me to get onto her computer and upload the video to her YouTube channel. I sit there and watch myself, and considering I've never done anything like that before, I'm rather proud of my film. I'm a bloody sight better at it than Tiffany.

It's the day of the parent-teacher meeting, and I tell Adina that I've got massive period pains and I'm not up to going into college. I can't risk her wanting to go with me to chat to my non-existent teachers, or chatting to someone in authority and discovering they've no idea who I am. She gives me a packet of paracetamol and tells me to stay in bed. She's out all day doing something or other, and I reassure her I'll be staying in bed and not to worry about me.

With the house to myself, I start by having a good snoop in the rooms I don't normally have the chance to look inside. Their bedroom is enormous, with luscious thick white carpet that leaves footprints when you walk through it. I open Adina's wardrobe doors and run my fingers along all the silken fabrics. I find a pouch full of jewellery stuffed at the back of her knickers drawer and have a rifle through it. Most of it is vulgar and not to my taste. Chunky pieces in gold and gaudy coloured stones. But when I open Jeffrey's wardrobe, I see a safe. I guess the jewellery in the pouch is artificial, and the good stuff will be locked away. Their bath has a jacuzzi tub, and I'm almost tempted to get in and have a soak. I'm sure Adina wouldn't mind, but instead I go downstairs and swim in the pool. It's heavenly, knowing I'm all alone and free to do whatever I want.

Adina returns home in the afternoon. As soon as I hear her car, I rush upstairs and lie on my bed. She pops her head around the door and tells me she's leaving me supper in the fridge, which I can heat up myself. They're taking Tiffany out for a meal before the parents' evening. Goodness knows why. I spend the rest of the day watching films and gorging myself on chocolates.

The three of them return home about 8 p.m. I hear Tiffany running up the stairs, sobbing loudly. Poor little rich girl obviously hasn't been getting good grades.

'Come back down here now, Tiffany!' Jeffrey roars.

I poke my head around the side of my bedroom door. 'Is everything alright?' I ask, an expression of concern furrowing my brow.

'Did you know that Tiffany has been bunking off college? That she's failed tests in all three of her subjects? Is this anything to do with you?' He jabs his finger in my direction.

'I'm sorry,' I say, with big eyes. 'I had no idea. Tiffany and I do different subjects, so I don't know what she gets up to.' I slink back inside my room. Oh dear. Poor little Tiff is in trouble.

Heavy footsteps come up the stairs, and there are raised voices. I stand with my ear to the door.

'I'm stopping your pocket money and confiscating your car for a month. You clearly can't be trusted!' Jeffrey yells.

'I'm sorry. I've said I'm sorry,' Tiffany sobs.

'You can have your flying lesson, but nothing else.'

Blimey. What weird values this family has.

I hear Adina's placating voice, but Jeffrey roars, 'This is my decision, Adina. Enough is enough!'

Shit. If Tiffany hasn't got any money, it means my income source will also be drying up. That's bad news.

The voices disappear downstairs. I wait for a bit and then go downstairs myself. I tiptoe past the living room.

'Tiffany has never skived before. It's got to be Skye's bad influence,' Jeffrey says.

'Sixth-form college is very different to boarding school,' Adina says. 'Perhaps she's just got in with a different crowd.'

'No. I'm telling you, it's that Skye's bad influence on our Tiffany. I want the girl out of our house.'

'She's going to have to go to Glasgow to a horrible, abusive aunt if we chuck her out.'

'She's not our problem, Adina. We need to concentrate on our own daughter.'

'But Tiffany said that Skye is helping her with her homework, and Tiffany seems so much happier with Skye around.'

'You've told me they're not even doing the same courses, so I can't see how she's helping her. Fat lot of good it's done, too, if Tiffany has failed all those tests. Our daughter needs to get her head down and concentrate on getting into a good university. I haven't sweated blood and tears for all these years to have our daughter dropping out. I want Skye out of this house by the end of tomorrow, and that's the end of the discussion.'

I tiptoe back upstairs. Shit and double shit. I can't leave! I've got nowhere to go, and I need to have more than five hundred quid in my pocket to set myself up for the future. I pace the bedroom. I wonder whether I should steal some silver or Adina's jewellery pouch; even if the jewellery is fake, it still looks expensive. I could go through her handbags and his jacket pockets when they're out tomorrow.

But no, I'm not a thief. Not a proper one. And if stuff

goes missing, they'll know it's me. I'm already a missing person, so the last thing I need is for the police to be looking for me and nailing me for being a thief. This is a disaster.

After racking my brain for a while, I reckon I've got only one option, and that is to tell Adina the truth. The woman obviously has a soft spot for the underdog, and I will have to play on her emotions and just hope that she persuades miserable Jeffrey to let me stay.

I WAIT until the next morning and tell Adina that I'm still not feeling well. Tiffany leaves with Jeffrey, who is dropping her off at college on his way to work. Neither of them says goodbye to me.

Adina is in the kitchen, flicking through the *Daily Mail*. She glances up at me, a worried expression on her face.

'I've got something I need to say to you.' I look Adina in the eyes and bite my bottom lip, folding and unfolding my hands. She can't hold my gaze.

'And I'm afraid I've got something to say to you, too,' she says. I can tell she's nervous.

'Can I go first?' I ask.

She nods. I sit down opposite her at the kitchen table and make my legs bounce up and down.

'I've lied to you,' I say, placing my hands on the table, my palms facing upwards. 'I am sorry from the bottom of my heart. I don't go to college, and my grandmother hasn't died recently… and I don't have a horrid aunt in Glasgow.'

'What?' Her big blue eyes almost pop out of her head.

'I'm homeless. I don't have any parents. I was brought up in children's homes and foster care. Tiffany found me on the street in Horsham, and she took me under her wing. Your daughter has a heart of gold. She's a truly wonderful girl. I'm so very, very sorry that I lied. That she lied, too. She knew you'd never let me stay if she had told you the truth.'

Adina opens and closes her mouth, but no words come out.

'I have never been anywhere as lovely as your home. I've never stayed with such wonderful, generous, honest people, and now I've seen that people like you exist, I don't want to go back to how it was before. Please, Adina. Please don't chuck me out.'

I wring my hands and let tears flow down my cheeks. It's easy to pump up the emotion, because I'm telling the truth. 'I have nowhere to go. I don't want any money, I just need a roof over my head, and I'll look for work. I want to work, to earn my own money, and then I can leave here and get a place of my own. And I'll pay you back every penny you've spent on me.'

I almost feel sorry for Adina. She looks totally blindsided.

She stands up and then sits down again. 'How long were you in care?'

'Since I was five years old. My mother is a drug addict, and I was taken away by social services. I lived in foster care and children's homes in London.'

'You say that you befriended Tiffany?'

'She gave me money. We got chatting. Tiffany is lonely; she doesn't have many friends. Anyway, we just hit it off.' I don't tell Adina that she likely befriended me as a finger up to her parents, and because she was desperate to have a friend.

'You haven't got her into drugs or anything bad, have you?'

That pisses me off. 'Just because I had a rough start

in life doesn't mean that I'm into drugs or prostitution. I saw what it did to my mother, and I'm never doing that. It's the reason I ran away from where I was living. They wanted to get me into selling drugs.'

'Oh, Skye,' Adina says, shaking her head. 'I really don't know what to say.'

'Please let me stay here, just for a little bit longer.'

'I'm sure we could give you money to help you out.'

I burst into tears. What the hell? I never cry in front of anyone, not real tears, anyway. Furiously, I rub my eyes with the sleeves of my jumper and take deep breaths to control the sobs. I should be happy. She's just offered me money, but I've shocked myself. Yes, money would be nice, but what I really want is a family. People who look out for me, who ask my opinion, who care, even just a little bit. And money won't buy that.

'I don't want money.' My voice sounds croaky. 'Well, I do, obviously. But really, I want to be here with you. You are the first person in the whole of my life to ask me what I want to do in the future and actually be interested in my answer. No one has ever cared.'

She throws her cashmere-clad arms around me then, and I snuffle into her shoulder. Tiffany doesn't know how lucky she is, having a mother like Adina.

'What was it you wanted to tell me?' I ask Adina when we eventually pull apart.

'Nothing, dear. It's not important.'

THE DAY CRAWLS PAST. I know the decision will be made this evening when Jeffrey comes home from work. In the meantime, I do everything I can to butter up Adina. I make her cups of tea; I offer to cook supper; I tell her that I'm writing my CV, that tomorrow I'll go to the job centre. But she looks at me differently now. I hate that expression of pity. I never want to be pitied.

In the afternoon, I go through everything in Tiffany's room, ferreting out coins and forgotten notes stuffed in coat pockets and handbags. I find an expensive-looking watch that she doesn't wear, and another couple of pieces of jewellery. If they chuck me out, I'll keep them. If they don't, I'll put them back. The money, I shove into my backpack.

Just before 4 p.m., Adina shouts that she's driving to college to collect Tiffany. I have twenty minutes to search the house for any other things I can steal; my security blanket if things go wrong. I don't want to do this, because I'm not a thief, but I have to have a backup plan. If they agree for me to stay, I'll put the items back.

My hasty trawl includes a small silver plate, a little clock in a cabinet in the living room that looks expensive, a pair of gold earrings that belong to Adina, and a diamond ring that I remove from a drawer in her bedside table. I feel bad about nicking the ring, but I need to look out for my future.

Half an hour later, Tiffany walks into my room without knocking. 'I can't believe you told Mum the truth!' she says.

'Are they going to chuck me out?'

Tiffany shrugs.

'Can you do something to persuade them to let me stay?'

'Why should I?' she asks.

'Don't you want me around anymore?'

'You might have noticed that I'm not the one who calls the shots around here. Dearest father and mother decide everything. And no doubt I'll be blamed for bringing riff-raff into the home.'

'Are you calling me riff-raff?' I stride towards Tiffany so that my face is just centimetres from hers.

'Well, you are, aren't you? You're from the gutter.'

I am shocked that Tiffany is holding her ground. I'd have thought that this little princess would crumble at the slightest hint of a fight.

'You bitch!' I say. I'm going to make her pay for this.

And then she grabs a lock of my hair. But at that very moment, Adina shouts, 'Girls, can you come down for a family meeting, right away.'

Tiffany lets go, and I straighten my clothes and walk out of the room with a rigid back, listening to Tiffany's footsteps behind me.

'Tiffany, your father has come home early. We want to talk to both of you,' Adina says as she stands at the bottom of the stairs.

JEFFREY IS in the living room, pacing backwards and forwards. His multiple chins are wobbling, and he has undone the top button of his beige shirt, exposing tufts of chest hair.

'Sit down,' he says, without looking at us.

Tiffany sits at one end of the enormous white leather sofa, and I sit at the other end. Adina sinks into an armchair.

'I'm very unhappy that you both lied to us about Skye's circumstances.' He turns around and glares at us, his hands on his hips.

'I'm sorry, too,' I murmur. I glance at Tiffany. She is staring at the ground. I notice a bead of blood on the side of a fingernail. She sucks at it.

Jeffrey carries on talking. 'But I came from nothing. Not as difficult a situation as yours, Skye, but my family were paupers. It was chance that I got an opportunity to get into horticulture. If that door hadn't been opened and I hadn't stepped through it, who knows what would have happened. I certainly wouldn't be living in a house like this with a beautiful wife.'

Tiffany glances up for a second, but as her father continues talking, her shoulders sag again. I suppose she was hoping for a compliment from her father.

'My wife is a soft touch, and she has persuaded me not to throw you back out onto the streets.'

Relief courses through my body. 'Thank you,' I murmur.

'I've grown surprisingly fond of you,' Adina says, with a coy smile.

Tiffany throws me daggers.

'You may stay living in our home, but I can't abide idleness. You will work in my salad business.'

Tiffany lets out a little sarcastic laugh. 'Good luck with that!'

Jeffrey ignores her. 'Tomorrow morning, you will come with me to work, and our head of human resources will find you a position.' He stares at me.

'Thank you,' I say again, fluttering my eyelids, then holding his stare. 'I am so very grateful.'

13

NATHAN – NOW

Marie doesn't say a word when I tell her about the awards dinner. She doesn't have to. The expression on her face says it all. The girls, on the other hand, are effervescing with excitement. It's blatantly obvious that for the first time in their lives, they think their dad is cool.

For my part, I'm ambivalent. I don't like being the centre of attention. I don't like big fancy events where everyone is showing off, and the very last thing I want is to be a media star. It's ironic really, considering I used to organise such dinners in our previous business. But in those days, I was firmly behind the scenes, and I rather wish that were still the case. In addition, I don't drink much. Call me boring perhaps, but I loathe that out-of-control feeling you get when you're drunk.

That night in bed, Marie turns to me.

'Sorry I've been grumpy about you going to the dinner with Skye. I know you have to go for work, and I want the charity to be a success. It's not me who has to like her.'

I pull Marie closer to me. 'I don't like her particularly either, but for every pound she raises for us, the easier it will be to help our clients.'

'I know that,' Marie says as she kisses me. 'And that's what I love about you.'

On Friday morning, despite her obvious misgivings about me attending the dinner, it's Marie who suggests I take a taxi rather than driving.

'It will be difficult to park, and you'll need to have at least one glass of wine,' she says as she digs my dinner jacket out from the back of the wardrobe.

And so here I am, in a taxi en route to Brighton.

'Collecting you at 11 p.m., is that right?' the driver asks as he deposits me at the front door to the hotel.

'Yes, please. I'll let you know if that changes.'

'Enjoy your evening.'

There are enormous flame torch lights either side of the entrance. A woman dressed in skintight Lycra in the pattern of leopard skin, her eyes and nose covered with a leopard print mask, stands by the door, holding a clipboard.

'Good evening, sir. May I have your name, please?'

I find it hard not to smirk at her bizarre outfit. She checks me off her list, and I'm permitted to go in. The entrance hall is identical to any corporate-type hotel anywhere in the world. Anodyne. I glance at other people milling around, dressed in evening wear, voices raised as if they're trying just a little too hard to be effusive or endearing or interesting.

'Nathan, darling! I'm so glad you're on time!' Skye flings her bare arms around me and plants a kiss on my cheek.

'Whoops,' she says as she stands back. 'Red lip mark on your cheek.' She licks her finger and wipes my cheek. I try not to flinch or appear embarrassed.

Skye is dressed like a fairy princess from the children's books the girls used to read, in a low-cut strapless silver dress that shows off her cleavage and then hugs her curves, fanning out widely over her hips, with the skirts grazing the floor. A diamond choker around her neck and large diamond earrings sparkle in the low light. She slips her right arm into mine, but it isn't until we're walking and I glance downwards that I realise her dress is split up the right-hand side the whole way to her waist, meaning that she can't be wearing anything… I can't think about that.

'Now let's get you a drink!' Skye says. She stops next to a woman clad in tiger print and takes two glasses of champagne, thrusting one into my hand before I have the chance to say I'd prefer an orange juice. 'I have so many people I want to introduce you to!' she gushes.

We walk into a large room, a conference room by day that has been transformed into a ballroom for the night. It has been decorated with enormous white-and-green flower arrangements and silver paper lanterns hanging from the ceiling. There is a podium-like stage at the back of the room, but on the main floor are numerous circular tables laid with white linen tablecloths, silver cutlery and sparkling glasses. In the centre of each table there is a large white-and-green flower arrangement bedecked with silver baubles and silver tinsel. I can't decide if they're gaudy or tasteful. Marie would be able to tell me. How I wish that she were here with me.

In front of the area sectioned off with tables, there is floor space crammed with people: women in evening gowns and men in black tie, with the occasional man breaking the mould by wearing a kilt or velvet jacket with a stand-up collar. There must be a few hundred people here, but it seems as if Skye is the strongest magnet, with people flocking to her, showering her with compliments, asking what she's up to. A famous newsreader, whose name escapes me, grabs her hands and kisses her on both cheeks.

'Meet Nathan Edwards,' Skye says to him. 'He's my new partner.'

'Business partner,' I say awkwardly. The man winks at me.

As soon as I finish drinking my glass of champagne, Skye thrusts another one into my hand.

'I mustn't drink too much,' I say.

She throws me a scornful look. 'It's the only way to get through these events.'

'I assumed you enjoy this sort of thing.'

'Ha,' she mutters scornfully. 'It's my job.'

SOMETIME LATER, the master of ceremonies announces that dinner is to be served. I follow Skye through to the far side of the room. Our table for ten is near the front, just steps from the raised podium. We have name places, and I am seated between Skye and a woman called Natalia Brinkman. About my age, she looks thoroughly out of place, in a tartan taffeta gown, the type that might have been popular in the 1980s. She has greying hair and minimal make-up.

'How do you do,' she says. 'I'm Skye's accountant.'

We shake hands. Tiana is sitting on the other side of the table, at too great a distance to be able to converse with. All the other guests are men. Starter is a beetroot salad with goat's cheese. It looks pretty but is tasteless, or perhaps my senses are numbing due to the amount of alcohol I'm consuming. I am drinking in moderation, but my glass seems to be perpetually full, which makes it difficult to know exactly how much I've drunk.

'So, everyone, I want to introduce Nathan.'

All of the guests around our table lean forwards, straining to hear what Skye is saying over the loud din of chattering guests and clattering cutlery.

'He's my new partner, and between us, we have enough passion to fire a furnace. We're going to use that hot fire to extinguish homelessness in the south-east.' Skye places her hand on top of mine and gently strokes the top of my hand with her first finger. I desperately want to pull my hand away, but I can't without appearing rude. I smile, but it feels awkward.

I try to converse with Natalia, who is sitting next to me, eyes firmly on her food and quite evidently being left out of the discussions. But every time I turn towards her, Skye puts a hand on mine or says my name, pulling me back into conversation.

After a main course of perfectly cooked sirloin and some whitefish for Skye, there is a shift in the atmosphere. It's time for the big announcements. The *compere*, a Scottish comedian, walks onto the stage and silences the room. He has a relaxed manner, but even so, I sense Skye becoming increasingly tense. She sits very still, her fingers clasped together on her lap, her jaw clenched. I lose track of all the awards, there are so many different categories – and then, finally, it's time for the Social Media Influencer Award of the year to be announced. I glance at Skye, who looks as if every muscle in her body is tensed, her eyes unblinking, the vein at her temple throbbing.

'And the winner is…' There is a drum roll that goes

on and on. I always think it's ridiculous to leave a long pause, and this one is even lengthier than normal. The *compere* swivels towards our table, pointing both index fingers at us.

'The winner is… Skye!'

The cheer is deafening. Everyone at our table leaps to their feet, with me following suit a couple of beats too late. I wobble slightly, the effects of too much alcohol. And then Skye flings her arms around me and places her lips directly over mine. The cheers are deafening. Flashes of light catch the sides of my eyes, and I pull away, and then Skye is weaving her way between the tables and lifting her dress to navigate her steps up to the stage, her bronzed, toned body on show.

She shakes hands with the comedian and holds the glass trophy high up in the air. Cameras click and flash again. And then she steps in front of the microphone. She waits until the clapping dies down, repeatedly mouthing *thank you* and tilting her head downwards whilst coyly looking upwards.

Eventually, she holds one hand up. 'Ladies and gentlemen. Thank you. Please stop clapping; I'm embarrassed. This honour is not really for me, it's for my amazing team. The crew at So She & All, Tiana Johnson and everyone who has worked tirelessly to make sure I'm on-brand. To all the wonderful sponsors and brands who have supported me. And of course, most of all, my millions of followers. I love you all!'

There is a loud cheer, but Skye puts her hand up yet again to stop the noise.

'And there's someone else who has recently come into my life, who shares my values. Together, we will be making a real difference. As many of you know, my childhood was difficult, and I experienced the inexplicable hardships of sleeping on the streets, of having no home, no one to care for me, no future and no hope. Together, Nathan Edwards and I intend to work tirelessly to banish homelessness in the south-east of England. I will raise funds for his charity, Sacha's Sanctuary, donating proceeds from my new app and encouraging the big brands I work with to donate, too. He is a wonderful man, inside and out, and I'd like you to join me in raising a glass to Nathan Edwards!'

I feel hundreds of eyes upon me, and all I want is for the ground to open up and for me to sink into a hole. I know the gushing is fake, but Skye barely knows me. How can she possibly say something like that? All I can think of is thank goodness Marie isn't here, and I pray to the lord that Skye's speech isn't broadcast on social media or, worse still, the news.

How the hell am I going to get through the rest of the night?

'HELLO, GORGEOUS.'

I try to wake up. My head is pounding. I can see light through my closed eyelids, but it is so difficult to open them. How much did I drink last night? Surely not that much. I turn over in bed and shiver as Marie's fingers trace a line down from my chest. I throw a leg over hers, but something doesn't feel right. I force my eyes open, and the brutal light makes me blink and then–

What the hell!

I shift away. I am in bed with Skye, her long blonde hair splayed on the silken pillow, the duvet pushed down so that her naked body is on show. I glance down at myself. I am naked, too. Surely not. Surely I didn't sleep with her! I try to recall what happened, but my brain doesn't work. There is blackness from shortly after

Skye received her award. I'm not good with drink, but I've never passed out. Never.

'How are you feeling?' Skye turns over to face me, her fingers reaching over to play with my chest hair. I try to shift towards the edge of the bed, but get a stab in the centre of my forehead. I can't stop the groan.

'That was a special night, wasn't it? Have you got a hangover?' Her voice is husky. She runs her tongue over her bottom lip.

'What happened?'

She smiles at me, a knowing expression playing at the edges of her lips. 'You're a beautiful and charming man, Nathan Edwards.'

I swing my legs out of the bed, my back towards her. I glance at the alarm clock. It's gone 8.30 a.m. Marie will be beside herself with worry. I put my head in my hands.

'I'm engaged to be married,' I murmur.

'Hey,' she says, wriggling so that she is on my side of the bed. She strokes my back with long firm fingers and then uses her fingernails to lightly run up the back of my neck, ruffling the hair on the back of my head.

'I'm also in a relationship,' she says. 'But these things happen.' She lets her hand fall away. 'There's obviously chemistry between us, but we're both grown-ups, Nathan, and we can approach this in an adult way. I want to work with you, and you want to work with me. We have our own lives. I'm not going to rock the boat, and I assume you won't either.'

I shake my head, which does nothing for the pounding headache behind my eyes. I don't do things like this. I vowed to myself I would be a good person and never succumb to temptation for the rest of my life. I know it's not a rational thought, but I've often wondered whether it was my behaviour that brought on

Sacha's cancer. I tell myself that Sacha and I were each other's true love, and I do genuinely believe that. But I'm not the honourable person I pretend to be.

I cheated on Sacha. It was the year before her diagnosis. I had a one-night stand with a client of our catering company. It was spontaneous, but it was wrong, and afterwards, I was deeply ashamed. I think Sacha might have found out, but I will never know for sure. She didn't say anything to me directly, except shortly before she died, she held my hand and said, *I forgive you.* I've had to live with that, the hurt I caused the person I loved more than anyone else in the world. And that is why I will never cheat again. It's unconscionable; even if I was paralytically drunk, I wouldn't do that. It's not as if I even like Skye.

I glance around the room and see our clothes scattered over chairs and on the floor. It certainly looks as if we were discarding clothing in the heat of passion.

'I'm going to use the bathroom, and then I'm going home,' I say, more to myself than her.

'Of course,' Skye says softly.

I pull on my boxer shorts and stand up carefully, but still see sparks in front of my eyes. I turn to look at her. She is lying on the bed, her arms above her head, her large breasts on full display, but her eyes are closed, and tears are slipping down her cheeks. At least she feels as bad about this as I do. I pick up my clothes and slink off to the bathroom and stand for some long minutes underneath the burning hot shower, hoping that it might banish my hangover and my shame. When I'm dressed, I come out of the bathroom, and Skye is sitting up in bed, wearing a fluffy white dressing gown.

'Can I have one last goodbye kiss, because I assume we'll never be doing this again,' she asks, running her fingers down her neck.

'Skye, I can't. I'm sorry.'

She throws me a sad glance. 'It's alright,' she says. 'I had a truly wonderful evening.'

'Thank you, me too.' Although I am only being polite, as I have no recollection of most of the night.

'Don't go out the front door,' Skye says as I put my hand on the doorknob. 'The press will be there. You'll need to check no one is in the corridor and then go out the back of the hotel. You're not meant to be here, remember.'

I nod, grateful for the advice. I edge the door open and glance into the corridor. There is no one in sight. I walk briskly towards the lifts and take the staircase instead. My fingers curl around my bow tie, which is wedged in my pocket along with my phone. I take it out and stare at it for a moment, wondering why I don't have lots of missed calls. And then I realise the phone is switched off. My brain really isn't working this morning. I turn the phone on and immediately it beeps at me. Seven missed calls from home, two from the taxi company and four text messages from Marie. My heart sinks. Did I switch off my mobile, or did someone else?

I am in desperate need of several black coffees and paracetamol, but first I'm going to have to go home and face the music. My first call is to the taxi company. Luckily, they can get a car here in twenty minutes. I am about to call home, when I stop myself. What the hell am I going to say to Marie? I need some more time to work out an answer. Instead, I send her a text message. 'I'm so sorry I haven't called before. I'll be home in forty-five minutes. Will explain all.'

I find a door that leads to the gardens at the back of the hotel. I slip through it and, keeping close to the bushes, I walk around the edge of the property to the front. When the taxi arrives, I run towards it and jump inside. Leaning my head back against the seat, I focus on my breathing, just hoping that I can stop myself from throwing up on the journey home.

I OPEN the front door cautiously. It's a Saturday morning, so at least the girls will still be asleep. My head feels as if it's going to split open. I walk into the kitchen and see Marie seated at the table, her iPad in front of her. She looks up at me and immediately glances away.

'I'm so sorry!' I say, rushing towards her and throwing my arms around her neck.

She tenses and wriggles away from me. The tendons in her jaw are tight, but she says nothing.

'I should have rung you. I'm so sorry.'

'I waited all night,' Marie says, still refusing to look at me. I pull out a chair and sit down next to her.

'My phone was out of battery. I know it's unforgivable not to have rung you.' I hate having to lie, but what would she think if I said my phone had been switched off?

'Where were you? What did you do?' She speaks quietly, with the hint of a tremble. I have never seen Marie lose her temper, but she doesn't need to shout for me to know that I have hurt her terribly.

'Nothing. I did nothing and remember nothing. I might have been drugged.'

'Really?' Marie's voice is laden with contempt.

I know it sounds unlikely, but drugging seems to be the only possible explanation for having a complete memory blank. I know that alcohol doesn't agree with me, and I did drink a lot, but surely it wouldn't result in a total blackout? It's never happened to me before.

'Look at the headlines.' She swipes the iPad, which

skates across the kitchen table towards me. I catch it just in time.

I glance at the screen, and it feels as if my stomach is going to implode.

'No,' I whisper. 'It wasn't like that.'

But I know I'm lying. It was worse than that. Much worse than that.

The photograph shows Skye and me in an embrace, our bodies locked together, her face tilted backwards and eyes staring up to mine, a look of such tenderness, it makes me want to scream. My bowtie is undone, and I look a rumpled mess.

'Swipe through,' Marie says in a whisper.

I don't want to see any more, but I know I have to. The next picture is worse. It has been taken from behind us, and it looks as if I am kissing Skye, my head lowered over hers, her hands clutched around my back.

'Nothing happened, Marie. You've got to believe me! The stories paint a lie.'

'You didn't come home last night. You didn't call me or text me. In fact, you totally forgot I existed. And look at you now, all hungover in a dreadful state. Those photos show you with your tongue down Skye's throat. I told you she was after you, and you didn't believe me. I hoped that you would live up to your morals, and even if she flung herself at you, you would restrain yourself. But no, you're weak and dishonest.'

'You can't believe those photos,' I say, standing up and wringing my hands. 'Marie, they're not true. I love you. I would never cheat on you. You can't believe what you see on social media.'

'Do you think I'm a total idiot, Nathan? Just be honest with me. I need the truth. Tell me what happened.'

I groan and pace around the kitchen. The honest truth is, I have no idea what happened. I can remember absolutely nothing between Skye winning the award and waking up this morning. I know I wouldn't willingly cheat on Marie and that I would never switch my phone off.

But do I really know that? Could I have been seduced by Skye? It just doesn't seem possible, yet we awoke, naked, in the same bed. The most likely thing is that I was drugged, most probably by her or, at a stretch, by someone else. But if I tell Marie about my suspicions, then I will have to tell her that I slept with Skye. There is no easy answer. 'I don't know what happened,' I say softly. 'I don't remember.'

'Where were you all night?'

'I don't know,' I say, yet again.

She stands up and rushes towards me, grabbing my upper arms, shaking me hard. 'Where did you wake up this morning?'

I turn my face away from her. 'In Skye's room.'

Marie releases her grip and staggers backwards.

'On her sofa,' I say, desperate to stop Marie's pain.

'So it's true.' Tears flow down her cheeks.

'It's not true,' I say as I rush over to her, trying to hold her pretty face between my hands, but she shoves me away, knocking over her cup of coffee, which spills onto the table and drips onto the floor. Neither of us touch it.

'You're treating me like an idiot, Nathan.'

'I would never do anything to hurt you. You have to believe me.'

'But you just did. You have broken all the trust between us, Nathan. You spent a night with that woman. I can't do this, I just can't.'

'Do what?'

Marie turns away from me. 'I need some time alone.'
She walks out of the room.

'Where are you going?'

'Away. To think. Back to Switzerland.'

'Please, no, Marie.' But she doesn't listen to me. She walks up the stairs, her back rigid, her shoulders trembling.

14

The next morning, Tiffany comes barging into my room as I'm getting dressed. Any annoyance that her parents have welcomed me into their home seems to have been forgotten. Her face is lit up, and she thrusts her phone at me.

'You didn't tell me you were doing that guest post on my channel! I can't believe it! Look at all the likes and the comments. Rhiannon says it's such a cool video she thinks it's going to go viral!'

I haven't got a clue who Rhiannon is, but Tiffany is right. My post has been reshared scores of times, and comments are coming in as I watch. This is bloody awesome. I hand the phone back to her.

'What should I do now? I need to build on what you've done,' Tiffany says.

I shrug my shoulders and tug on a sweatshirt, ready for a day at work.

AN HOUR LATER, I am sitting on the cream leather passenger seat of Jeffrey's Rolls-Royce as he navigates the road, listening to some repetitive country and western music that he sings along to, out of tune. I've taken a visceral dislike to the man, and I'm glad this is such a big car so I don't have to sit too close to him. I can't work out exactly what it is about Jeffrey that gives me the creeps. He's no oil painting, and he's horrible to Tiffany, but those aren't reasons enough to give me goosebumps. I wonder if it's because he stares at me as if he knows my secrets. Or perhaps he has secrets that he's worried I'm going to uncover.

The journey is interesting, with roads cutting through countryside that I have never seen before, and at one point, when we are at the top of a hill, I think I see the sea glinting pale silver on the horizon. After forty minutes, the landscape flattens, and Jeffrey turns this monster of a car to the left, passing a huge sign that says "King Salads". We drive past vast greenhouses that spread as far as the eye can see, then skirt a massive tarmac area where three lorries are parked up, their backs towards the opening of a greenhouse. There is a small single-storey office block to the right, with a car parking area in front. Jeffrey guides his car into a space with a sign that reads J. Larkin Esq, Managing Director.

'Out you get, then,' he says, the only words he has spoken to me during the entire journey. He reaches into the back to pick up his soft leather briefcase and heaves himself out of the car with a wheeze. He locks the car and then walks into the office block, with me trotting behind him like a bloody stupid lapdog. Just beyond the entrance lobby, on the left, there is a sprawling open-plan office with lots of people sitting at tables, typing away or on the phone, but Jeffrey turns to the right. We pass three offices, each with their doors open and men seated at their desks busy with something or other.

'Suki!' Jeffrey shouts before opening a door that has another little plaque with his name and job title on it.

'Good morning, Mr Larkin. How are you this morning?' A woman, perhaps mid-thirties, comes bustling up behind us, glasses perched on her head, clutching a notepad, pen and phone. She's wearing a tightly fitted brown straight skirt and a shiny burned-orange blouse with a bow.

'Suki, find Timothy whatever-his-name is, the new chap who's running HR, and get him to give this girl a job. I want her properly employed. On the books.'

'Is this a temporary or permanent position, Mr Larkin?' she asks. Her voice is high-pitched, little-girl-like.

'Temp full-time for now. Might lead to permanent. No concessions.'

'Of course.' She turns around and starts walking in the direction we've just come from. I stand in the corridor.

'Follow her, then!' Jeffrey says, batting his hand towards me.

Suki makes me wait in the entrance lobby, sitting on a hard plastic chair. I can see the big office through a large internal window and watch the office workers on their phones, typing away at keyboards. Not one of them smiles, so I deduce this must be a miserable place to work. I look at the photographs on the walls. Most of them feature Jeffrey shaking hands with people I don't recognise.

'Gather you're waiting for me.'

'Maybe,' I say, without getting up.

He's a tall man with long, dark brown sideburns that meet a neatly trimmed beard. He has green, hawklike eyes and I decide immediately that I don't like him. He stares at me, expressionless.

'I'm Timothy Tranter. Come along, then,' he says. He doesn't extend his hand. Reluctantly, I follow him into the open-plan office and then into a little room hidden around the corner. He shuts the door.

'Sit down.'

He takes a seat behind his desk while I remain standing.

'Name?'

'Skye Walker,' I say.

He snorts. 'Your parents fans of *Star Wars*?'

I throw him a filthy look, as I always do when someone comments on my name.

'Age?'

'Seventeen?'

'Work experience?'

'None.'

'Qualifications?'

'Two GSCEs in English and drama.'

He sighs. 'To summarise, no skills and no experience. Address?'

'Um, I'm not sure.'

He looks up at me and frowns.

'I'm staying with the Larkins at the moment, so whatever their address is.'

He sighs again. 'In summary, as a favour to Mr Larkin, you need a job. You're qualified for nothing. You've missed the weekly training sessions for picking, so you'll have to work in the packing shed. You'll be making up cardboard boxes and placing cartons on Danish trolleys.'

I haven't got a clue what he's talking about, so I just nod.

'You'll be working shifts. Twelve hours, from 7 a.m.

to 7 p.m., seven shifts in every fourteen days, which means week one you'll work for five days, including Saturday and Sunday. Week two you'll work two days, then the following two weeks you'll work nights in the same pattern.'

'But I'm not even eighteen yet!' I exclaim, wishing I knew what my rights were. 'How much will I earn?'

'£3.57 an hour.'

'That's nothing,' I say.

'It's all regulated under the Agricultural Wages Board. Don't like it, the door's over there.'

'How am I meant to get here to work those hours? Jeffrey doesn't work those hours, does he?'

He tuts and shakes his head. 'First of all, so long as you're working here, it's Mr Larkin to you. And secondly, Mr Larkin is our managing director, the owner of this business, and he works the hours he chooses. All I've been told is that I need to find you a job. I am following instructions. How you get to our premises is your problem.'

'Shall I tell Mr Larkin how helpful you're being?' I cross my arms. There is no way that I'm going to be intimidated by this jerk.

He gets up, his face expressionless. 'Come.'

I follow him out of the office block and into a vast warehouse. It's noisy with beeping forklift trucks and the sounds of machinery. But most of all, it's freezing cold. I shiver.

'Jim!' Timothy shouts to make himself heard. An older man with a kindly face hobbles towards us.

'This is Skye. She'll be working here. I thought she could help make up cardboard boxes.'

'That'll be good. We could do with all the extra hands we can get.' He looks me up and down. 'Got some gloves with you?'

I shake my head. Timothy strides away.

'Right. Yeh know how to assemble a box?' he asks.

'Never done it.'

He rolls his eyes but in a kindly sort of way, not sarcastic and mean like Jeffrey or Timothy. I walk along-side him towards piles of flat cardboard boxes towering up as high as a house. Jim grabs one from an easy-to-reach pile, places it on a metal bench and in a matter of seconds has turned it into a box. It was like he was performing a magic trick, he did it so quickly.

'Can you do it again, a bit slower?' I ask.

'Once more. But haven't got all day. We've got a lot to get done here.'

He does it slightly slower the second time.

'Each made-up box goes onto this conveyor belt, ready for the packing machine.'

'Don't you have equipment for making up the boxes?' I ask.

'Too expensive,' he mutters before shuffling away.

TWO HOURS LATER, I've had enough. It's a horrible job, not least because the sharp cardboard is ripping my hands to shreds, and I'm bloody freezing cold. There's no one to talk to, and it's boring as hell. I'm going to have to ask Jeffrey to get me a better job. Sitting in that office perhaps, where I'll be warm. My arms and back are aching, so I sit down on the floor and blow into my hands to warm them up.

'Oi! What the hell are you doing down there?' a male voice shouts at me. I can't see anyone. It isn't until I look upwards that I realise there's a person leaning out of a giant forklift truck. 'You get paid to work, not to sit on your ass.'

I stand up. 'I need to use the toilet.'

'Shift break at noon. You can go then.'

This is worse than a bloody prison. I feel like walking out, but if I do that, I'll be leaving behind my luxury living with the Larkins, and as we're stuck out here in the middle of the sticks, I doubt there's even a passing bus. Besides, I've got to go back to their house, as the money I've accumulated is safely hidden under the mattress of my bed. I stand up and scowl, returning to the bench, and slowly make up yet more cardboard boxes.

'SKYE, can you follow me? Mr Larkin wants to go home.' Suki hovers by the entrance, looking awkward and out of place. I glance at the big clock on the wall. It's 4.15 p.m., and I have never been so relieved to be called away from something. Today has been one of the longest of my life. How anyone can do twelve-hour shifts of this soul-destroying, hand-ripping work is beyond me.

'Have you checked out?' Suki asks.

'What?'

'You need to punch your card when you leave,' she says. 'I'll show you.'

I follow her to a strange-looking machine attached to the wall. She searches through little cards that are listed in alphabetical order, finds mine and slots it into the machine. 'You have to do this when you arrive in the morning and when you leave.'

'Timothy said something about working twelve-hour shifts. Will I get into trouble for leaving early?'

I cross my fingers behind my back. I hope he'll fire me, and then Jeffrey will have to find me another job.

'You will need to discuss that matter with Mr Larkin.'

. . .

JEFFREY DOESN'T EVEN GLANCE at me as we get into the car, but he seems stressed. He's tapping his fingers on the steering wheel, and he has this weird involuntary twitch above his left cheek that makes him look as if he's doing a half wink. We drive in silence for ten minutes or so; then all of a sudden he speaks. It makes me jump.

'Bugger it. I need to get away. We'll take the plane to Jersey for the weekend. Ever been in a private plane, Skye?'

'Um, no.' I don't tell him that I have never been in any kind of plane, that I've never been abroad.

'I'll fly. Tiffany's lessons are going well, so she can co-pilot. It'll do her good. Did she tell you that we've got a place over in Jersey?'

I shake my head.

'And a place in southern Spain and a chalet in the Alps, not that I like it there. Too bloody cold, and nowhere nearby to land the plane. We'll leave first thing Saturday morning.'

Is he trying to impress me, or is he such a bastard that he enjoys gloating about his four mansions to a homeless person? I choose to ignore him. I'll find a way to rub his ugly face in his gloating soon enough.

'I need to ask you about my job,' I say, keeping my tone of voice meek.

'What about it?'

'I'm meant to work twelve-hour shifts and nights every fortnight, but I don't drive, and I've got no way of getting here if I'm not getting a lift with you.'

He sighs. 'I'll discuss it with that Timothy.'

'When do I get paid?'

'When you've earned it.' He turns on the radio.

. . .

THE NEXT MORNING, my fingers ache, my back aches, and every time I wash my hands, the cuts sting.

'I need to borrow some gloves,' I say to Tiffany as I watch her pack her bag with books for college.

'Do you have to?' she asks, in a moaning tone.

'Ergh, yes. Look at my hands!'

I thrust them in front of her, but she barely glances at them. She walks over to her wardrobe and takes out a pair of pale pink woollen gloves shot through with silver thread. She throws them to me. I reckon they'll be torn to shreds in no time and won't give my hands much protection, but Tiffany seems as if she's in a sulk, so I don't say anything. The euphoria about the good reactions to my blog post seems to have gone. I wonder if she's posted something and it hasn't gone so well. I haven't had the chance to look.

'Skye, can you hurry up! I've got a meeting to get to,' Jeffrey shouts up the stairs.

Tiffany has her back to me, and while she's not looking, I swipe her headphones. I can't get through another day of boredom without at least listening to some music.

'Bye,' I say as I stuff the headphones into my jacket pocket. She doesn't respond, so I hurry downstairs.

WEARING the gloves and listening to music makes the tedious work semi-bearable. It's 11.30 a.m. when Jim hurries over to me.

'Take those things out of your ears now!'

I frown, removing the earphones.

'Mr Larkin is doing a walk-around with some bigwigs from one of the supermarkets. You need to keep your head down and work hard. Got it?'

I nod. Suddenly, the ambient sound notches up

several gears. The machines seem to be working faster, people walk briskly rather than ambling, and it feels degrees warmer, as if a jet engine is pumping hot air into the warehouse.

And then I spot them. I count seven men and one woman. They're all wearing dark suits; they look middle-aged, dull and deeply serious, as if they're discussing matters of life and death rather than whether to buy a few thousand extra boxes of lettuces. A couple of them are carrying clipboards and write furiously on them as they walk around. The deeply etched frown on Jeffrey's forehead looks like crevices, and he is sweating profusely, wiping his face repeatedly with a white hand-kerchief. Goodness knows why, because despite the increase in heat, it's still freezing cold in here.

Jeffrey spots me, and they walk towards me. I stop gawking and return to my thankless task of making up cardboard boxes. An edge of a box cuts through the wool on my right index finger and slices into my flesh.

'Shit,' I say, and immediately suck my finger, spitting out little fibres of wool.

'This is our rough diamond. Our charity case,' Jeffrey says, beaming widely, his frown smoothing out. He steps towards me and puts an arm around my shoulders. Yuk.

What the…

They stare at me as if I'm a specimen in a jar. A few of Jim's team stop working and step a bit closer, obviously listening to Jeffrey speak.

'Young Skye here was wandering the streets and picked up by my daughter, and we've taken her into our home despite all the obvious risks, et cetera. If it works out, we'll start a training programme for the down-and-outs. Corporate social responsibility and all that.'

Everyone is staring at me.

Down and out. Risks. How dare he!

'Skye has no qualifications and would otherwise end up on benefits. If she proves herself, this could be an interesting new venture for us. Prevent us from having to import foreign labour.' Jeffrey gives my shoulder a further squeeze and steps away. I am shaking with fury and want to speak, but no words come out.

'Get along now, Skye,' Jeffrey says, waving his hand at me and throwing the people in suits a fake grin.

I want to spit at the man. Tell him what a jerk he is. An ignorant bigot. But the humiliation is too much. Those pitying eyes gnaw at my insides, so I turn away from them and take pleasure in the masochistic pain of tearing my fingers to shreds on the corrugated boards.

My anger makes me more productive. I listen to heavy metal music, which cuts out the voices in my head, and before I know it, Jim is in front of me, telling me it's time for a break. I glance at the big clock on the wall. It's 5 p.m. How did that happen? And for that matter, why hasn't Jeffrey called for me to go home?

The staffroom is a cavernous space with lino floors and lots of plastic tables and chairs. There's a canteen at one end where they serve lunches for free, ordinary dishes like macaroni cheese and spaghetti bolognese. Suits me fine. There are big urns where we can help ourselves to tea or coffee and bowls of biscuits and fruit. It's a good perk, and like everyone else, I tuck in heartily. I'm surprised they don't provide more salads, though, considering this is a lettuce factory. I don't speak to any of the other staff, and they don't speak to me. I think they assume I'm a spy for Jeffrey, or else they overheard Jeffrey's little speech and think I'm some charity-case tramp. That's a joke.

I grab two chocolate biscuits and a cup of milky tea

and settle into a chair. It's weird that he's still here so late. Normally Jeffrey is home shortly after 5 p.m. And that's when I get nervous. I leave my half drunken cup of tea and make my way towards the offices. Suki walks out of a room, her coat on, a large red handbag over her shoulder, and says goodnight to someone inside.

'Suki!' I shout.

She turns around.

'Where's Jeff – Mr Larkin?'

She blinks rapidly. 'Mr Larkin left about an hour ago. He didn't say where he was going. Home, I assume.'

'So he's fucking well left me here, has he?'

She flinches. 'We don't use that language at work, my dear.'

Dear. She's calling me dear! It's obviously gotten around to everyone that I'm the Larkins' charity case.

'How am I meant to get home?'

Suki fidgets with her handbag. 'Bus? Taxi?'

I turn around and stomp back to the staffroom. I jab Tiffany's number into my phone and let out an audible breath of relief when she answers after two rings.

'You need to come and get me. Your darling father has forgotten me.'

Tiffany starts laughing.

'It's not bloody funny!'

'Actually, it is.' She snorts. 'Anyway, I'm definitely not driving all the way to Chichester and back. Mum, Dad and I are going out for supper tonight with my cousins.'

'How am I meant to get home?' I ask.

'Taxi.'

'Will you pay?'

'For god's sake, Skye. Why can't you do anything for yourself? You're earning money now. You should be able to sort yourself out.'

'They haven't paid me yet, and why should I have to pick up on your father's mistake?'

'Just sort yourself out, okay. You should be grateful you've got a job. Hitch a lift.'

She hangs up on me. The bitch hangs up on me.

I call her straight back, but she has switched her phone off. I leave a string of expletives as a message. Although Tiffany deleted all of her contacts from her old mobile phone, she left her home telephone number in the address book. I ring the Larkins' landline, and to my relief, Adina answers.

'Tiffany darling, why are you calling me? Aren't you in your bedroom?'

'It's not Tiffany. It's Skye.'

'Oh, Skye.' Adina's voice flattens.

'Is Jeffrey at home?'

'Yes, he's in the bathroom. We're going out for dinner.'

'He forgot to bring me home.'

She pauses and then gasps, and then, just to rub salt into the wound, she also laughs. 'Oh, goodness, we totally forgot about you. Poor Jeffrey has so much on his mind at the moment. Where are you?'

'At the salad factory.'

'I'm afraid we won't be able to collect you. We're going out for dinner. Let me have a quick word with my husband.'

She puts the phone down with a clatter. I hear raised voices in the background, including what sounds like Tiffany yelling, but despite straining my ears, I can't make out what they're saying. Eventually, Adina picks up the phone again.

'I will arrange for a taxi to collect you and bring you home. We won't be here, but I'll leave the alarm off and the key under the mat by the back door. Help yourself to food in the fridge. Oh, and you might want to pack a few things in preparation for our trip to Jersey for the weekend. I'm not sure if Jeffrey will want you to come, but if he does, best be ready.'

I want to hurl the phone across the room. I thought Adina was better than Jeffrey, but perhaps she's not. She's got no backbone, no ability to stand up to her foul husband. Jeffrey is using me, treating me like a skivvy and an idiot. And Tiffany, she's not much better. I'm just a plaything for her, someone to make her feel better about herself. To hell with them. I'm going to make them pay.

15

SUNDAY, 9 NOVEMBER 2008

KING OF SALADS FEARED DEAD

A rescue operation has been called off following a plane crash into the English Channel. The single-engine plane is reported to have hit water twenty miles off the island of Jersey. A search operation involving helicopters was launched. Some wreckage is believed to have been found, but no bodies have yet been recovered.

It is believed that the Cessna 182 registered in the UK is owned by Jeffrey Larkin, known in the world of horticulture as the King of Salads. The plane took off from his private airstrip in West Sussex on Friday at 6 p.m. It is believed that his wife, Adina, a former Czech model, was travelling with him. Neighbours say that the family own a house in Jersey and regularly visit for the weekend. They are survived by their seventeen-year-old daughter, Tiffany Larkin, who is being comforted by friends.

A States of Jersey Police spokeswoman said: 'Following a comprehensive search and rescue mission by the RNLI, fire *and rescue service, Channel Island Air Search and assisted by private boats, we now believe there were no survivors of yesterday's light aircraft crash.*

'The States of Jersey Police will now be working alongside the Air Accidents Investigation Branch (AAIB) to establish what happened.' No time has been given as to when the aircraft lost radio contact.

Colleagues at King Salads, one of the UK's leading producers of lettuces and salad crops, expressed their dismay and condolences for the loss of their majority shareholder. Timothy Tranter, Director of Human Resources, issued a statement on behalf of the 120 staff. 'We are all unified in our grief for the Larkin family.'

I follow Marie upstairs and watch with dismay as she packs a large suitcase.

'Can we talk about this?' I ask.

'There's nothing more to say.' She opens her underwear drawer and sweeps everything into the case.

I pace the room, feeling futile. 'How long are you going for?'

Marie doesn't answer.

'I love you, Marie.' I attempt to touch her, but she shakes me off and carries on packing.

'You'll have to arrange for the girls to be collected from school, or they can walk home. Maybe enrol them into after-school clubs.'

My chest is constricting; it's as painful as my throbbing head. I can't lose my second love. There was nothing I could do to stop Sacha from dying, but Marie's not in peril. This situation is of my own making. Or if not mine, Skye's.

Then there's my daughters. Marie's departure is going to have such a negative impact on them.

'What should I tell the girls?'

'Tell them the truth. That you cheated on me, and I am not prepared to be a pushover.' Her voice is acerbic. 'Not that you'll need to tell them. It's all over the media, so it won't come as any surprise.'

I sit down on the side of the bed and put my head in my hands. It feels like I am caught in a nightmarish maze with no route out. Whatever I say or do will be wrong. I could go to the police, but if I tell them that I think I was drugged by Skye – not just any woman, but a famous woman – will they really believe me? If I heard a man make such a claim, I doubt I would believe him. But if I don't get tested for drugs, then I have no way to clear my name. And then there's the association with the charity. If I make any claim against Skye, I don't see her adoring public turning against her. The inevitable backlash will be towards the charity; everything we've worked for over the last three years and most impor- tantly to the detriment of the people I help.

As heartless as it sounds, I would do that if it would persuade Marie to stay. I beg her, I make promises I don't know I can keep, but she is resolute. 'I'm not an idiot,' she says scornfully.

When Marie has packed her case, we both walk downstairs, in silence. The girls are in the kitchen. They look up in surprise, seeing Marie dressed in her brown leather jacket, her handbag slung across her body.

'I'm going back to Switzerland.'

'Why?' Chloe asks, with her mouth full.

'I need to have some time to think.'

'Are you coming back?' Chloe's face is a picture of dismay. Isla, who has clearly worked out what has been going on, doesn't seem the slightest bit concerned. She's never hidden her disdain for Marie.

'I don't know.'

'What about the wedding?' Chloe asks.

'We'll temporarily put the plans on hold,' I say.

I follow Marie out into the hall.

'Please, Marie. Believe me. Nothing happened. I don't even like the woman, and I love you. Truly love you.' I step towards her and try to pull her into my arms, but she pushes me away yet again.

'Will you call me?' I ask, watching with dismay as she picks up her suitcase.

'I'll check up on the girls.'

'Is there anything I can do to stop you?'

'No. I need to go.' She edges past me.

'Can I at least drive you to the airport?'

'No. An uber is arriving in five minutes.'

'I'm sorry, Marie,' I say. 'I'm sorry that you feel the need to go, but please know that I love you with all my heart and would never knowingly do anything to hurt you.'

She turns her back on me, opens the door and walks outside.

I want to sob, pummel the walls, scream that she is mistaken, that Skye drugged me. But who the hell will believe that? If Marie, the person I thought loved me most in the world, doesn't believe me, I don't suppose anyone else will.

I DON'T KNOW how I get through the rest of the day. It takes me back to those dark times after Sacha died. But once again, it is Chloe and Isla who keep me sane. My beautiful Isla is particularly sensitive, surprisingly so, as if she can feel my pain. She brings me cups of tea and makes supper for the three of us and tells me that Marie wasn't so bad after all.

I send Marie three text messages, but she doesn't respond. It isn't until 9 p.m. that she sends a short message saying that she is at her parents' house and that I shouldn't contact her.

THAT NIGHT, I take a sleeping pill, something I haven't done in years. Although I feel physically better when I awaken, that gnawing pain of loss has only increased. Mid-morning, I receive a call on my mobile from a with-held number. I answer it, hoping it's Marie.

'Nathan,' Skye says huskily. My heart sinks.

'I'm so sorry about all the publicity. How are you?' She lowers the volume of her voice. 'How are you *really*?'

Previously, she has called me through the office switchboard, and I don't recall giving her my mobile number.

'Unhappy,' I say.

'Me too. Holden has dumped me. Via text message. Can you imagine the brutality of that?' She lets out a little whimper. 'I thought he was the one, and now it's all over.'

'Marie has left me,' I say. 'Those photographs weren't real. Can't you put out a statement to say it was all staged, and that we're not in a relationship?'

There is such a long pause, I wonder if she's still on the line.

'I don't know, Nathan. I will have to ask my publicity team as to the implications,' she says. 'I am so dreadfully sorry about Marie. That is utterly devastat-ing. Would you like me to have a word with her? To explain that it was a mistake? I'm more than happy to do that. Surely she would understand that it was a one-off and will never happen again. I can drive around to your house right now.'

'No, that's fine,' I say hurriedly. I can't believe I'm

relieved that Marie is already in Switzerland, but I am. The thought of Skye rocking up to our house and telling Marie that we slept together, woke up naked in the same bed, but *don't worry, it didn't mean anything* is too horrific to contemplate.

'I can't bear the thought of being responsible for the breakdown of your engagement,' she gushes.

'Hopefully, it's only temporary. I intend to win her back.'

'Of course you do,' she says.

Should I ask her if she put anything in my drink? No, I can't. It's a criminal offence, and she's hardly likely to admit to it. 'I'm worried about the effect that this publicity about us will have on the charity. I have always stayed out of the limelight.'

'Oh, you don't need to worry about that. All publicity that links the two of us will be brilliant for your fundraising campaigns, especially as I won the Influencer of the Year Award. The phone hasn't stopped ringing with proposals for collaborations, and it's still the weekend. Tiana is giddy. One of my passion projects is a self-help book that I'm compiling. We've been in discussions with a couple of publishers, and yesterday, they emailed Tiana and me with an offer I can't refuse. I intend to donate all the proceeds to Sacha's Sanctuary.'

'Thank you, that's very kind of you.'

'Try not to worry too much, Nathan. I promise you that our association will be very fruitful for us both.' The line goes dead for a moment, and then she's back. 'I must go now; Tiana's on the other line.'

MY TEAM LOOK at me with expectant faces when I walk into the office, but I have no intention of answering their questions about Skye. I know I'm wimping out, but I lock myself away in one of the side offices and bury myself in work.

I decide to leave early and collect the girls from school. I have allowed them to walk home together on the odd occasion during the past couple of months, much to Isla's delight. But I'm not comfortable with it, even though it's only a twelve-minute walk, along reasonably well-lit pavements, necessitating just one crossing of the road. I knew I had to give in, because Isla was becoming increasingly petulant about not being given any independence, especially as all of her friends are allowed to walk home alone. In the end, it was Marie who persuaded me.

'You need to show that you trust Isla. She must text either you or me to let us know when they're leaving school, and I'll be at home waiting for them.'

The system worked. The problem now is that unless I leave work very early, they'll be returning to an empty house. I'm not sure what I'm going to do about that.

It's been a long time since I've stood at the school gates, so I hang back slightly and send Isla a text message to say I've arrived. I expect her to be grumpy and am surprised that she comes out of school in the centre of a gaggle of girls, none of whom I recognise. She gives me a little wave, and then the other girls stare at me, open-mouthed, and start whispering between themselves.

Chloe appears at my side. 'I'm hungry.'

'Isla!' I beckon to her and, reluctantly, she saunters to my side.

'Let's go home. It's good to see that you've got so many friends,' I say.

'Most of them aren't my friends. They're just sucking up to me because they think you're dating Skye. Are you?'

'Absolutely not.' I am walking too quickly for the girls to keep up with me. 'Marie and I are engaged, and Skye has a boyfriend.'

We reach the car, and I unlock the doors. Isla gets into the front passenger seat.

'She dumped the sailor,' Chloe says as she climbs into the back seat.

'No, he dumped her,' I say.

'That's not what she said on social media,' Isla interjects.

'Don't believe what you read.' I start the car engine and pull out of the parking space.

'Are you going to marry Skye?' Chloe asks.

'Don't be ridiculous, Chloe,' Isla says. 'Skye isn't the marrying type. She's much too cool and independent.'

'I'm going to marry Marie,' I say quietly.

'Doesn't look like that one's going too well,' Isla says. Her words choke me.

'I hope Marie comes back,' Chloe says. 'She's a brilliant cook. And she makes Dad happy.'

'Thanks, Chloe,' I say, gritting my teeth to stop the emotion in its tracks.

17

I t's been one hell of a day, and I want to celebrate. Winning the Social Media Influencer of the Year award has fired a jet stream underneath all of those mediocre middle managers in charge of recruiting influencers to promote their bands. Success attracts success, and everyone wants a little piece of me. The phone has rung off the hook, and Tiana's inbox is being inundated with contracts that need checking by the legal team. I instructed her to play hard to get. I have no desire to be stretched in too many different directions. Any associations must be on-brand and must be extremely lucrative.

I am standing in my living room and slowly swivel around, having a good look, trying to view it through the eyes of an estate agent. Yes, it's classy with the soft furnishings in muted grey and cream hues. Yes, it's brushed with my unique style, but I know I can do better. Winning this award has pushed me up to the next level, and soon my life will look very different. I need a new house, with lots of bedrooms, much bigger and glossier. Ideally a new build, perhaps down on the coast with views across the English Channel. A couple of properties have caught my eye – sumptuous modern houses constructed from endless panes of glass. Or maybe a small country estate would be better, a house set at the end of a long private drive. I will put this house on the market, and with the Skye effect, I have little doubt that it will achieve at least double its market price.

I hang my coat in the cupboard in the hallway and walk barefoot into the kitchen. It's not a bad size, but the time has come for an upgrade. I want one of those kitchens where everything is hidden. I open the fridge door and look at the contents. Half a dozen eggs, three bottles of Laurent-Perrier, four lemons, a carton of almond milk and some kefir yoghurt. The interior is spotless, mainly because I never cook. Despite being the face of many healthy-living brands, I simply don't have the time to cook. If I did, I'm sure I would be loyal to those brands. Well, not totally sure, but I'd give it a go.

I take out a bottle of champagne and am about to pop open the cork when my mobile phone pings. I put the bottle on the white marble countertop and pick up the phone.

Shit.

It's a Facebook message from that bloody woman again. I wonder if I should block her. Instead, I delete the message without reading it. Stupid cow. I wish she'd go to hell and leave me alone. Just another sad hanger-on. That's the downside of fame. All the losers crawl out of the woodwork, desperate to leech me for whatever they can get.

I turn to the bottle of champagne, but the thought of drinking it alone has lost its allure. That's the other problem with fame. It may look like I've got lots of friends, but in reality, I don't. The relationships are all transactional, and occasionally, very occasionally, I wonder if it's all worth it. Perhaps if I didn't have all this, I'd have a bevy of girlfriends, people who genuinely cared and would rally around when I felt low. I can't go there. I shove the champagne back in the fridge. I've got a better idea.

I hurry to the bathroom and take a quick shower, my hair carefully protected under a shower cap, and smother myself in a delicate apple-blossom body cream. It's a scent that was made especially for me, and I have it as a cream and a perfume. With my towel wrapped around my torso, I pad into my dressing room. I want to look casual, but not too casual. I take out a short brown leather skirt and a soft mohair sweater. From my under-wear drawer, I select a cream-coloured silk bra and matching knickers.

Fifteen minutes later, I've done my make-up, put on some understated jewellery and tugged on a pair of tightly fitted dark brown suede boots.

I call Italia Deliziosa and ask to speak to Vince.

'Bella Skye, how are we this evening?' he asks, with his fake, sing-song Italian accent. I overheard him once swearing in the kitchen, and his natural accent is defi-nitely Brigh'on and not Italiano. He does a good job of pretending, though, and I have no intention of exposing him.

'Good, thanks. Can you make me four pizzas to take away? At least one of them should be vegetarian. I want them to be as upmarket and delicious as possible.'

'For you, anything, *mia cara.*'

'I'll be with you in fifteen minutes.'

'They'll be ready and waiting for you. *Ciao, ciao.*'

I eat at Italia Deliziosa at least three times a week, normally collecting takeaways, occasionally eating in the restaurant. I never go to the front of the restaurant, as it wouldn't do to be seen in an Italian when I'm promoting a gluten- and dairy-free lifestyle, so I park up at the back of the restaurant, where the tradespeople go, telephone when I'm there, and Vince pops out with my order. I'm too good a customer for him to expose my true eating habits.

I take one of the bottles of champagne out of the fridge and select a bottle of red wine from the cupboard. When I move to a new house, I will get a dedicated wine cellar with a specialist wine cooling system, perhaps installed in a basement accessed via a spiral staircase. For that matter, I also need an integral garage. It's humiliating having to step outside, worrying whether someone will snap a photo of me balancing an umbrella in one hand to keep my hair dry, my keys in the other and my bags over my shoulder. But that is what I have to do right now as I make a dash for my handsome navy BMW.

A quarter of an hour later, I am at the back of Italia Deliziosa and Vince is handing me a large plastic bag holding four boxes of pizza. Less than ten minutes after that, I am parked outside Nathan's house. With a quick glance in the mirror to check I have no lipstick on my teeth, I hop out of the car, grab the pizza bag and bottles, lock the car and walk up to the front door. I take a deep breath, plaster a smile on my face and ring the doorbell.

A few seconds later, the door is swung open by one of the girls.

'Skye!' she exclaims. 'Have you come to see us?'

'Ergh, yes.' *Stupid question.* 'And your father. Is he home?'

'He's making supper, but he's a crap cook. Are you any good?'

'So-so, but I've brought pizza, so perhaps I can save you from a rubbish home-cooked meal.'

'That's awesome!' She claps her hands and then turns around and shouts up the stairs, 'Isla, Isla, come down! Skye is here!'

There is a loud clatter from upstairs, a door slamming and the sound of running feet.

'Can I come in?' I ask.

'Oh yeh. Sorry.' She stands back and lets me through. 'Dad's in the kitchen.'

'Hello, Skye.' Isla comes hammering down the stairs.

'It's so lovely to see both of you young ladies again,' I say, oozing an eagerness I don't feel. I follow Chloe along the corridor and into the kitchen.

'Dad, look who's here!' Chloe says, flinging her arms open wide and bouncing like an overexcited puppy.

Nathan is standing at the stove, an apron around his waist, his hair mussed up, looking utterly delectable. He swivels around. When he sees me, his face falls. It's only for a split second, but I see it.

I take a step backwards and collide with Isla.

'Sorry, sorry,' I say, unsure whom I'm directing my apologies to. 'I hope you don't mind me just turning up unannounced, but I was going to get myself a pizza and thought that as you're alone, you probably would be left with the cooking. So I picked up a selection for you and the girls.' I know I'm overexplaining, but that momentary look of dismay has wrong-footed me.

'That's cool,' Chloe says, pulling out a chair and sitting on it.

'Yes, very kind of you, and no doubt a relief to the girls, who despair of my cooking,' Nathan says, wiping his hands on his cream-and-black apron.

'I assumed you would be a good cook, considering you owned a catering business.'

'I like food, but I'm a lousy cook. I've been lucky enough to leave that to others.'

I take the pizza boxes out of the bag and place them on the table. Chloe leans forwards and lifts the lids. I thought the child would have some manners.

'And here are a couple of bottles,' I say, holding the champagne and wine out to Nathan.

'Goodness, thank you.'

This is certainly not the excited, grateful reaction I was hoping for. I do a quick calculation and decide to change my plans.

'Well, I must be off now. Enjoy the pizza.' I smile tightly.

'What? You can't go!' Chloe exclaims. 'You only just got here.'

'Chloe, I'm sure Skye has somewhere else she needs to be.'

'Actually, I don't,' I say. 'Just another evening with the television to keep me company.'

'In which case, you must stay.' Nathan steps towards the table and pulls out a chair. 'Please have a seat. We should eat all of this together.'

'Only if you're sure,' I say.

'Absolutely.'

I try to read Nathan, but his face is closed. 'What would you like to drink, Skye?' he asks.

'Just a glass of red, but don't open anything especially for me.'

He takes a corkscrew out of a drawer and opens the bottle of red that I brought. We all sit down. I notice that he is sticking to water, but I don't say anything.

'This is scrumptious,' Chloe says, taking a big bite of pizza. The cheese creates long, gooey bands.

'Thanks, Skye. It's really kind of you,' Nathan says, smiling at me awkwardly.

'So,' Isla says, turning towards me. 'Are you and Dad an item?'

'Isla!' Nathan exclaims.

Isla ignores him and stares at me, her head tilted to one side.

'Goodness, no. Your father and I are just colleagues who happen to live near each other.'

'All those photos of the two of you on social media, and the massive argument that Dad had with Marie, has that got nothing to do with you?'

I don't like this girl's sarcastic tone of voice. I had assumed she approved of me, based on her gushing admiration last time we met. Perhaps her apparent anger is directed more at her father. It can't be easy seeing your father work his way through a harem of women.

'Enough!' Nathan grits his teeth and glowers at Isla.

'It's fine,' I say, leaning towards Isla. 'The thing with being in the public eye is that people want certain stories to be true. I'm sure my followers would love for me to find happiness, so they simply put two and two together and made five.' I turn towards Nathan. 'Didn't they?'

He nods. I can't help but notice the nerve pinging in his jaw. I carry on speaking. 'It happens all the time,' I say. 'And that's why you should never believe every-thing you see or read in social media. Your father and I have developed a good working relationship very quickly, and that is all there is to it. Why Marie left is none of my business.'

'I'd rather Dad was with you than with Marie,' Isla says.

Interesting. My assumption was right; her feelings are directed towards her father.

Chloe stares at me with big eyes.

'Please, Isla, let's change the subject,' Nathan says. 'Those pictures were not what they seemed, and next time – if there ever is a next time – I will be very careful to ensure that I keep my distance. I've never had experience with the media, and I guess it shows. As Skye says, don't believe everything you read or see.'

'So, girls,' I say as brightly as possible, 'I was wondering if I could pick your brains. I want to do an awareness campaign about drugs, and I need to target it towards teenagers. Obviously, I'm much too old to have many teenage followers, but I thought I might link up with a couple of other high-profile celebrities, pop stars or actors perhaps, who have the ear of teenagers. Who would you suggest?'

And then the conversation flies. The girls banter between themselves as to who they admire the most. I interject every so often and throw Nathan knowing glances. His smiles are cautious. We finish the pizzas – or rather, I should say, Isla and Chloe finish off the pizzas, and Nathan offers up some ice cream from the freezer, which the girls devour, though I abstain.

'What time do you girls go to bed?' I ask as casually as I can muster.

'Chloe's bedtime is 9 p.m., and Isla's is 10 p.m.,' Nathan says.

Isla rolls her eyes at me. Nathan collects the plates, and I discreetly glance at my watch. I can't risk anything until both the girls are well out of the way.

'I'll clean up,' I say.

'Absolutely not,' Nathan insists.

'But I was the one who arrived uninvited. How about you wash and I'll dry?'

He laughs uneasily and then hands me a clean tea towel featuring a National Trust property.

'We could add a tea towel to our range. I'll put my thinking cap on,' I suggest.

We wash and dry up in a companionable silence.

When we've finished, Nathan says, 'Would you like a tea or coffee?'

'Actually, I was thinking about that bottle of champers.' I nudge him gently.

'Um, I don't drink during the week. My tolerance for alcohol seems to be rapidly diminishing.'

'I rather like the alcohol-intolerant Nathan.' I step very close to him. Frustratingly, he steps backwards. I change tack.

'Would you like me to help get the girls to bed?'

Nathan frowns. 'They're teenagers. They don't need help getting ready for bed. These days, all I get is a shout from upstairs saying goodnight, and that's if I'm lucky.'

I laugh uneasily. 'Shows how little I know about children. That's what happens when you grow up in the environment I did. Anyway, shall we talk about our plans for the charity?'

He hesitates and then says, 'Sure.'

Annoyingly, he doesn't offer me another drink, but he does lead me into the living room. I push the door so it almost closes behind us.

'It's a bit chilly in here. I'll light the fire,' he says.

'Mmm. I love a log fire.' Not that I love this one. The fireplace is too small, faced with an ugly stone surround. If it were mine, I would rip it out and install a glass-fronted stove, ideally one of those that open and close with a remote control. I'll have a couple like that in the new house.

I wander around the room as Nathan makes the fire. There are photos on the top of an upright piano.

'Do you play?' I ask, running my fingers over the smooth lacquered keys.

'No. It was my late wife's. Chloe is musical and has piano and violin lessons.'

I pick up a photograph on top of the piano. It's of a younger Nathan and his beautiful, carefree bride, who looks radiant in a loose flowing white wedding dress, strawberry blonde ringlets cascading over her shoulders, her head thrown back, laughing as she leans into Nathan's arms. The adoration on both of their faces makes my stomach curdle.

'Was this your wife?'

Nathan turns and nods. 'Yes, Sacha and me on our wedding day.'

Nathan bends over and takes a couple of logs out of a wicker basket.

As he does so, I walk up behind him. He turns, and we are nose to nose, so close, I can inhale his masculine scent. I stand on tiptoes as I lean in to let my lips press against his.

'No,' he says, stepping sideways away from me. He drops a box of matches. They scatter all over the carpet, but he ignores them and runs his fingers through his hair.

'I'm sorry, Skye, but I think you've got the wrong end of the stick. I really appreciate your assistance with Sacha's Sanctuary, but whatever happened the other night should never have happened.'

'I can't stop thinking about you,' I say huskily. I think of all the messages I've received on social media saying how gorgeous Nathan is, how right we look together, how happy people are for me. 'You seemed to enjoy me the other night.'

He stares at the matches, but still makes no move to pick them up.

'I don't remember a thing,' he says. 'I think I might have been drugged.' His voice is low. He raises his eyes to look at me.

I step towards him and lay the palm of my hand on

the side of his cheek and run a fingernail along his jawline. He shivers and tries to step backwards, but the sofa is behind him, so there's nowhere for him to go. The sexual tension between us is like a thin shard of ice, ready to be melted.

Nathan takes hold of my wrist and removes my hand from his face, his fingers gripping tightly. So he likes to play rough. That's fine with me. I lean forwards, but he releases his grasp and steps to the side, so I stumble and have to grab the sofa for support.

'You need to leave, Skye. I'm sorry if you got the wrong impression, but I don't want an affair. I don't do affairs.'

'Goodness, nor do I! Marie has gone. This is a new beginning. For you and for me.'

'I love Marie!' he says gruffly. 'She is the woman I'm going to marry. I am not interested in having a relationship with you, Skye. Please leave my house.'

I stand there and stare at him. This beautiful man who is the ying to my yang, or whatever the saying is. He cannot reject me. No one rejects me. How is it possible that I can see how perfect we are for each other, how much my followers want us to be a couple, yet he is denying it? I have never been so brutally rejected. That's why I have such a love-hate relationship with fame. Your life looks so glossy and perfect on the outside, but inside all you crave is real human connection. Love. Nathan is going to give that to me. Come hell or high water, he will.

'You've led me on,' I hiss, feeling anger bubbling up inside me. 'You might have denied your feelings in public, but privately, your actions have spoken louder than words. I don't believe you can't remember how passionately you made love to me. Lovemaking like that is impossible under the influence of drugs. It was real, Nathan, even if in your own mind you try to deny it.'

He flinches.

'Is that how you make love to Marie? No, of course it isn't. You told me that yourself, but I suppose you've conveniently forgotten that, too. One thing you might like to remember is that I can make or break your little charity.' The fury is now boiling through my veins.

'What are you trying to say?' he asks, eyes narrowing.

'I've lost my boyfriend over you. Was it all for nothing?' I feel tears smarting my eyes, and I can't work out if they're real or not.

'That's not true, Skye. You said on social media–'

'Don't you bloody believe everything I write, too! My life is a mess. I can't help it if I've fallen for you, if everyone else thinks we're perfect for each other. All I'm trying to do is be kind to you, but if that's the way you treat me, then you can go to hell. As can your little charity.'

I storm out of the room, grab my handbag and coat and stomp straight out of the front door.

As soon as I'm by myself in the car, I am riddled with regret. What the hell was I doing, losing my cool like that? I am tempted to go back inside and apologise. I slam my fist against the dashboard before starting the car. I drive away, my tyres screeching over the tarmac. Why can't Nathan feel the same way as me? Most men throw themselves at my feet.

I pull up in front of a set of red traffic lights, and then I have a moment of deep insight. Maybe that is why I have fallen for Nathan. Maybe it's because he isn't like all the others. He is indifferent.

I remind myself that I always get what I want in the end, but sometimes it takes patience. Time is on my side. It's not as if I want children, and Nathan already has a family. I need to take stock, be cool as I normally am. Make Nathan realise that I am indispensable in every aspect of his life, from his girls to his charity to his bedroom. Calm settles over me as the lights turn green, but rather than jamming my foot hard onto the accelerator as I normally do, I pull away slowly. I realise that must be a metaphor for my life now. Calm, patience, result.

18

I can't sleep. I toss and turn, thinking about Skye, wondering how she can be so delusional. How could she really think I would lose Marie one day and jump into bed with her the next? And her behaviour makes me increasingly suspicious that it was she who put some drug in my drink so that I loosened my inhibitions and slept with her. If she wasn't in the public eye, I would be down at the police station immediately, but I know I'm going to have to take this one on the chin.

And now, I need to extricate myself from the tentacles she has wrapped around Sacha's Sanctuary. All I want to do is hold Marie, but my bed is cold and empty. I have sent Marie several text messages, and I can see that she has read them, but she hasn't replied.

I'm up early. I take some lasagne out of the deep freeze, ready for supper, and prepare some sad-looking sandwiches for the girls' packed lunches.

'How do you feel about returning home to an empty house?' I ask Isla, in the car on the way to school.

'Cool,' she says nonchalantly.

'I will try to be back earlier than normal, but if I'm not home, will you grab a bite to eat for both of you and get on with your homework? Can you promise me that you won't misbehave?'

'All of my friends are left alone in their houses without their parents breathing down their necks. We're hardly going to have a party in the hour between getting home and you coming back.'

'Text me when you leave school and again when you're at home. And leave your phones on so I can contact both of you.'

I get the normal rolling of eyes and my-dad-is-so-embarrassing looks when I drop them off outside school; then I make my way to the office, arriving five minutes late for our weekly catch-up meeting.

'Sorry,' I say as I sink into my chair at the head of the table.

'You okay?' Ash asks. 'You look rubbish.'

'Just a bit under the weather, but nothing to worry about.'

'We've had another amazing, record-breaking week.' Ash beams at everyone. 'Skye's involvement with Sacha's Sanctuary has resulted in the most dramatic increase in donations, so much so that we've received more donations last week than we did in the whole of the three previous months. On top of that, the value of PR she's generated for us is off the scale.'

I consider telling them that Skye is likely to dump us, that the easy revenue days were successful but short-lived, but something makes me hold back. Ash hands out a couple of sheets of paper to each of us. The numbers are impressive, that's for sure. And I would be even more impressed if I didn't think that Skye wanted something from me personally. There is absolutely no one I can tell; it would make me look delusional, assuming that someone as glittery as Skye would want a relationship with an ordinary man like me. All I can do is keep her at arm's length and hope that she continues to support the charity despite my rejection of her advances. What worries me the most is not the halting of the publicity and the associated increased donations, but how misinformation about Sacha's Sanctuary could destroy us as quickly as she's boosted us. That is what I can't allow to happen.

Rosie, the youngest of our team, pokes her head around the door.

'Skye is on line one for you, Nathan.' She grins widely.

'Speak of the devil.' Ash laughs.

I do not smile. 'I'll take the call in room one.' This is not a conversation I want my team overhearing.

'NATHAN,' she says, her voice honey-smooth, 'I want to apologise unreservedly for my behaviour last night. I was totally out of order, and I just want to reassure you that my personal feelings will have absolutely no impact upon my business decisions.'

I let out a puff of air in relief.

'Please understand that one of my many failings is that I can't switch off my feelings easily. I'm not going to pretend. I do have very deep feelings for you, but I totally understand that it's too soon to embark on a new relationship. Both of our lives have been tumultuous of late, and we need to take things slowly.'

'But I don't–'

She interrupts me. 'Please hear me out, Nathan. I am a patient person and I will wait. However long it takes. You need to think about your girls, too, and I under-stand that. So for now, let's concentrate on the Sanctuary. I've got so many fundraising ideas and can't wait to share them with you. In a perverse kind of way, rejection spurs my creativity. I suppose that is the story of my life. Rejection by my mother, rejection by foster parents – all of that has made me fight harder. So your rejection was a trigger for me. I hope you understand and will forgive me.'

I simply don't know what to say. Her words suggest that she thinks we will have a romantic relationship at some point in the future, whereas I think she's totally psycho. Even if she didn't drug me, throwing herself at me like that is repellent.

'It's fine, Nathan. You don't need to say anything. I'll get Tiana to set up a meeting between us so we can discuss next steps for fundraising. In the meantime, I just want to apologise once again. I want to settle things before we meet up for the sailing race. Have a great rest of the day.'

And she hangs up on me.

I stare at the phone. How has such a screwed-up woman managed to be so successful? Her exterior image bears no resemblance to the person she really is. And now I'm caught right in the middle of this mess. I sit for a couple of minutes in the small meeting room and then wearily get up and walk back to the larger meeting room.

My team look at me with expectant faces. I'll discuss the bizarre situation with Ash later, but for now I just smile.

'All good. She's got some more fundraising ideas and will be setting up another meeting for So She & All. When we next meet Skye's team, I'd like Ash and Sophie to accompany me.'

Ash rolls his eyes, but I'm not letting him get out of

this one, while Sophie looks like all her dreams have come true.

'It's staggering how one influencer can make such a big difference to a charity,' Ash muses. I smile through gritted teeth. I know how long it takes to build up a business, and I also know how quickly it can be destroyed. I just pray that Skye will keep her word.

SOMEHOW, I get through the meeting, contributing very little. Afterwards, I hurry back to my computer and do some online searches on Skye. It looks like things really kicked off for her about six years ago. She was posting regularly, mainly on YouTube; she then upped her game on Instagram. Even I, with my limited artistic appreciation, can tell that her feed looks beautiful. The pastel tones carry through everything, and although I find her words too touchy-feely and overly demonstrative, I can see how less secure people might be inspired by her. The rags-to-riches story is a strong undercurrent, but it's not in your face. She really paves the way with concrete action steps as to how someone might overcome their personal tragedies.

FOR THE BEST part of an hour, I get lost in Skye's social media. There are YouTube and TikTok videos, Facebook posts and blog posts on her own website. It's impressive, and I can see how she has increased her following, like a snowball growing exponentially over the past few years. But it's the real Skye I want to learn more about, not her public veneer, and that is proving much harder to unearth.

I go onto Companies House website and see that she registered Skye Official Ltd as a company five years ago.

The accounts filed last year show that she has net current assets in excess of £2 million. Impressive. Her registered office is an address in Crawley, which I discover belongs to a firm of accountants; nothing suspicious about that. Her filed company accounts also give me her real name: Skye Walker, and her month and year of birth: March 1990. I try searching for her under births, marriages and deaths, but find nothing. Despite trawling through pages and pages of Google searches, I can find no online presence for Skye Walker prior to six years ago.

I sigh. I suppose it's not that unlikely. If she was in care during her youth and then lived on the streets, why would there be any digital footprints? What I want to do is find out who the real Skye is. Who are her friends? What about past boyfriends? I consider reaching out to Holden, Skye's ex-boyfriend, but quickly discount that. It would be odd.

At 4.10 p.m., Isla texts to say she and Chloe are leaving school to walk home. By 4.30 p.m., I haven't received a text to say they've arrived. I call our landline, but it goes to answer machine. The girls never use the landline, so I'm not unduly worried. Nevertheless, I decide to go home. With my thoughts preoccupied by Skye, it's not like I'm doing anything productive in the office. I pack up my bag, wave at the team and call Isla's mobile. It's busy. I leave a message and tell her I'm on my way home.

Fifteen minutes later, my stomach clenches as I turn the car into our driveway. The house is in darkness. The girls should be home, lights on in every room, as is normally the case. I open the front door, switch the light on in the hallway and shout upstairs. Unsurprisingly, there's no answer. I try both of the girls' mobiles, and they go straight to voicemail. With trembling fingers, I jab on Find My Friend app, but their locations are unavailable. If their phones are off, that would be why. I grab the phone list pinned to the fridge, which lists the details of their closest friends and classmates. I call every single number, but the conversation is the same each time.

'No, I'm sorry. They're not here.'

'Yes, I saw them leave school. They were together, walking the normal way.'

It's Ellie Crawfoot, the mother of Bronwyn, Isla's best friend, who suggests I call the school. I decide to do one thing better. Go there. I scribble a note, which I leave on the kitchen table, asking the girls to call me the second they see the note.

I then rush out of the house, get into the car and drive very slowly along the route that the girls walk home, scouring the pavements in case they're walking back. A silver estate car behind me hoots and then over-takes, the driver giving me a middle finger as he speeds past. I couldn't care. My girls are nowhere to be seen.

I park directly outside the school and then rush up to the gates. I ring on the intercom and get the school care-taker. After checking their logs, he confirms that both the girls left at 4.08 p.m., which coincides with when Isla texted me. I return to the car, a spasm of panic causing me to double over. Sliding into the driver's seat, I try both their phones again, to no avail. I need to be rational. The chances that something terrible has happened to them on their short walk home is minimal. In all like-lihood, they are at a friend's house and have forgotten to call me. I will go home, wait twenty minutes, and if they still haven't shown up, I will call the police.

Back at home, I pace the kitchen and jump when the landline rings. I grab it with relief, only for the relief to be short-lived.

'Nathan, it's Ellie. Bronwyn says that your girls are
on Instagram live with some social media star called
Skye. Does that mean anything to you?'

'Shit,' I say, under my breath.

'Bronwyn is beside herself with excitement. It's a big
deal, apparently.'

'Do you know where this live session is happening?'

'Hold on a mo.' I hear Ellie shouting for Bronwyn,
but then I can't hear the rest of the conversation. A few
seconds later, she is back on the line. 'It's at a new
restaurant called Azure that's opening tonight on East
Street in the centre of town. It was written up in the
local paper. Apparently, they're sampling the food.
According to Bronwyn, if you go onto Skye's Instagram
right now, you'll see it.'

'Thank you, Ellie,' I say, relief dripping from every
pore. 'And thank Bronwyn, too.'

FIFTEEN MINUTES LATER, I find a parking space in the
multistorey car park in the centre of town and run full
pelt towards the restaurant. I pause to calm my breath,
standing on the opposite side of the street. It is obvious
why they've called the new restaurant Azure. The door
and window surrounds are painted in a strong, deep
turquoise. The window has a decal stretched across its
lower quarter that looks like a turquoise ocean, and
lights are ablaze from the inside. A man walks out of the
restaurant, a large camera swinging from his shoulder,
and the sound of a saxophone fills the quiet late afternoon air. I cross the road and open the door, ignoring
the closed sign.

'Good evening, sir. We're not open currently. We
have a private function taking place,' the baby-faced
waitress says.

'So I understand. Skye is here with my daughters.'

'I'm sorry, but we can't confirm or deny that.'

'I'm not asking, I'm telling you. I am here to collect my daughters, Isla and Chloe Edwards, who are here without parental permission.'

'Um, let me see if my manager is free to talk to you.'

I know it's rude, and I feel sorry for the flustered young waitress, but I haven't got time to be dealing with the gatekeepers. I push past her and stride through the restaurant.

'Sir!' she says, running after me.

The restaurant has been beautifully decorated, with blue velvet chairs and banquettes along the walls, and brass lights, reminiscent of ship pendant lights, pulled low over tables set with white cloths and blue linen napkins. I stride through the restaurant towards the back of the room where a group of people have gathered. The music starts up again, a saxophonist and a guitarist playing smooth jazz classics.

'Excuse me, but who are you?'

A man, at a guess in his late thirties, stands in front of me, a blue apron wrapped around his stomach, his arms crossed. He is wearing a name badge that says *Toby, Manager*.

'Skye has abducted my children, and I am here to collect them. Please let me through.'

His eyebrows shoot up to his forehead, and he glances over his shoulder. There are at least three photographers and a videographer. The last thing he will want is a scene played out on social media. I notice Skye seated at a small circular table, plates laden with food in front of her. Standing to one side, fortunately out of the camera shots, are Isla and Chloe. They haven't seen me yet.

'She's doing a Facebook live for the opening of our restaurant. I would be grateful if you didn't interrupt it.'

'If you get my girls for me, I won't.'

He hesitates, so I take one step towards him. I don't like being threatening, but I feel as if my blood is about to boil over. There is Skye, all dressed up in a low-cut dress, hair coiffured into golden wavy curls that cascade onto her shoulders, taking forkfuls of food and ooh-ing and ahh-ing, whilst my girls stand there, looking on adoringly. How dare she bring them here without telling me!

Toby steps to one side. I edge my way along the side of the room, out of view of the cameras, until I'm behind Isla and Chloe.

'We're going home. Now,' I whisper into Isla's ear. Both girls jump and turn to look at me.

'What are you doing here?' Isla hisses.

'That is the question I should be asking you. We are leaving now.'

'But, Dad, I don't want to–' Chloe sees the look on my face and halts mid-sentence.

'Move,' I say. It is rare that I am genuinely livid with them, but right now I have to clench my hands in order to contain my rage. I think they recognise the fury, because they walk in front of me without saying a word. When we're outside on the pavement, I speak. 'What are you doing here without my permission or knowledge?'

Isla juts her chin forwards and puts her hands into her coat pockets. Chloe answers, her eyes downcast, 'We were walking home, and Skye drove past. She saw us, stopped, and asked if we wanted to attend the restaurant opening.'

'And you didn't think you should let me know? You didn't think for one moment that I might be worried about you?'

Isla has turned her shoulders away from me and is bouncing her foot up and down.

'Isla, I'm talking to you! You are the one who is meant to be responsible. Why did you switch your phones off?'

'Skye said we had to, in case they got in the way of the filming. Besides, it's not like we got in a stranger's car, is it? You know Skye. You had a fling with her.'

'I did not have a fling with her. This is totally unacceptable behaviour.'

Exasperated, I start walking towards the car park, and the girls follow, shuffling slowly behind me. Somehow, I manage to restrain my temper. When we're at the car, I open the doors.

'Get in,' I say. 'Switch your phones on.'

I watch whilst they do so. 'Now you're to stay in the car until I get back. Understood?'

'Where are you going?' Chloe asks.

'To talk to Skye.'

'What are you going to say to her?' Isla swings her head towards me, a look of defiance on her face.

'To tell her never to contact you again behind my back.'

'But she was only trying to be nice!' Chloe wails.

'You're such an embarrassment,' Isla says. 'It's not surprising Marie has left you.'

I can't take any more. I inhale deeply and repeat, 'Stay here. I'll be back in ten minutes.'

I walk briskly back towards the restaurant, but as I'm approaching the street, I halt. I don't want to have this conversation in front of other people. Isla is right, but for the wrong reason. I turn around and go back to the car.

. . .

THE GIRLS' fury doesn't dissipate. Chloe thinks I've ruined their fun and is worried that Skye won't invite them to anything again in the future. Isla tells me I'm an embarrassment and I've torpedoed everything. I try to explain that I love them, that I worry about them, but I'm not sure the message gets through. I leave it an hour, and then I call Skye. I'm half hoping that she won't answer, but she does.

'Nathan, lovely to hear from you. I hope the girls enjoyed this afternoon.'

Her saccharine voice jangles my nerves. 'That's why I'm calling. I understand that you have little experience with children, but it is totally unacceptable to sweep them off the streets and take them somewhere without my permission.'

'Excuse me?' she says, her tone of voice rising into a question.

'I understand that you stopped your car, collected my girls, told them to switch off their phones so I couldn't track where they were, and didn't bother to let me know. Have you any understanding as to how I felt, how worried I was?'

'But Isla and Chloe were thrilled to see me! I was just trying to be nice. I saw them walking along the pavement, looking forlorn, and thought it would be a lovely treat for them to be at the opening and feature on social media.'

'Look, Skye. I appreciate what you're doing for the charity, but I have made it perfectly clear that I don't want a relationship with you, and that includes a relationship with my children. Any contact we have is to be through the office.'

I hear her inhaling through her teeth. 'So that's the way you want to play this.'

She hangs up.

I am enraged about Nathan's reaction. All I have done is be considerate towards him and his children. I couldn't care less if those bland girls were at the restaurant launch or not, but I thought it would give them pleasure. In fact, I know it did. What is the man trying to do? Hide the girls away and protect them? And from what?

By 7 p.m. I'm back at home, having been paid a small fortune for taking miniscule mouthfuls of the Azure restaurant's mediocre food while pretending it was delicious. Good luck to them. I pour myself a large glass of white wine and go upstairs to change. I pull on a pair of charcoal grey cashmere leggings and a matching hoodie and then return downstairs to slump in front of the television. I light an apple-blossom-scented candle, and I'm just flicking through Netflix when there is a rapping, I think on the front door.

I sit still. It comes again. A distinct three knocks on the door.

I'm nervous about people visiting. Not that I've had any problems to date, but being in the public eye, it's something that I have to consider. I have one of those web-based doorbell systems, which lets me view who is at the door. The problem is, it was installed after I moved in, so I had to select a battery-operated system. I log in to the system on my phone, and sure enough, it's out of battery. I've forgotten to recharge the damn thing yet again. It explains why the doorbell hasn't chimed.

I get up and walk cautiously to the front door, keeping away from the windows either side, and peer through the peephole. It's a woman. She's got short, thin grey hair that curls slightly around her forehead. She's wearing clear-plastic-framed glasses that do nothing to hide the heavy bags under her eyes, which she's tried to cover up with concealer. Her coat is a black-and-white dogtooth pattern, and it swamps her. I hope she's not a bloody journalist. I open the door a couple of inches.

'If you're selling something, I'm not interested,' I say, ready to shut the door in her face.

'Skye, it's me! Of course I'm not selling something.'

I frown. There seems to be an assumption that just because people know who I am, I am supposed to know who they are, too. It's ridiculous, because of course I don't. I remember the days when I just had a few hundred followers, and I might have recognised Sheila_Crazy65 or BigBoy1998, but those days are long gone.

'I'm Monica. Your mother.'

I place my palm on the door and try to slam it shut, but she has put her foot in the gap between the door and the frame.

'Please, darling, don't shut me out.'

'I'm not your darling, and kindly remove your foot.' I stare at the cheap white trainer that looks brand new.

'Please, Skye. Hear me out.'

'I don't want anything to do with you. Go away and leave me alone!'

'You have every right to be angry and upset, but I just want to be part of your life. Come on, Skye. It's been much too long.'

'I suppose you're after money,' I say. Why else would this scum of a woman appear out of the woodwork after all of these years?

'No, I'm not. I don't need anything from you. Just a relationship with my only daughter. I've been clean for a few years, and I want to reconnect. I get it that you may never forgive me, but can't you at least give me a chance?'

Shit. Shit. Shit.

No.

I cannot give this woman a chance. She could ruin everything.

Everything.

I lean my shoulder against the door. It must be hurting her foot by now, but perhaps she's done so much damage to her body over the years, she's killed off her nerve endings and doesn't feel pain.

'Skye! Stop this. I know I've hurt you, and I'm desperately sorry. I really am. I can't begin to tell you how proud I am of everything you've achieved. It's wonderful how you're in the public eye and all that good you're doing for charities.'

How has she found me? I've been so careful to ensure my address isn't in the public domain.

'Just go away!' I spit, pushing against the door even harder. 'I don't want anything to do with you.'

'You're hurting me!' she squeals. Of course I'm bloody hurting her! That's the point. I want her gone. Out of my life for ever.

'I got your details off that lovely journalist. What's

his name? Martin Rodriguez from the *Daily Mail*. He
was ever so interested when I told him that I was your
mother.'

All the strength evaporates from my body. I step
away from the door, and Monica stumbles as she falls
inside. I stand with my back against the wall, staring at
this woman who is now staggering to her feet. When
she's inside, facing me, I kick the front door shut. I don't
suppose there's anyone standing outside listening to
this horror show of a conversation, but I certainly can't
risk it.

She adjusts her coat and pats down her hair as she
stares at me. 'Martin thought you'd be thrilled to
meet me.'

'I'm not,' I say. I know Martin Rodriguez; well, I
don't *know* him exactly. I've met him once, and we've
spoken on the phone a couple of times. He writes for
various celebrity magazines and some of the tabloids.
It's quite the coup if he writes about you. He's won
various awards and is known for being one of the better
celebrity journalists. He does his job. Research, probing,
digging and squirreling until he uncovers all of the dirty
facts. I cannot have Martin Rodriguez anywhere near
me. I need to think. Fast.

'Are you going to offer me a drink?' she asks.

I glance at those wrinkled lips and shudder. The
woman disgusts me. I can see what the drugs have
done. Even if she has been clean for a few years, they've
left their mark. How old is she? Mid-fifties? She looks at
least seventy.

I turn and she follows me, her trainers squeaking on
the oak floor.

'Beautiful house you've got here,' she says. I don't
comment.

We walk into the kitchen, and I lean against a kitchen unit.

'What a fabulous kitchen. You have wonderful taste, love.' She sits down on one of my acrylic Ghost chairs.

'You know, my heart is bursting with pride, dear. If only I had been well... But it's no good having regrets, is it?'

'What do you want from me?' I say, my words sharp and harsh. I cross my arms in front of my chest.

She looks affronted. 'Nothing. I don't expect anything from you. I simply want to be part of your life, to be acknowledged by you. I know I can't make up for all of those lost years. All that time when my head was messed up and you were sent from foster home to foster home. I tried. I really did try, Skye. You must believe me. Anyway, that's the past. I've been clean for three years and eight months. I've even got a job. You'd be proud of me. I wash the dishes in an old people's home. They're all so lovely, and it's nice to be able to give something back after all this time.'

I shudder.

'Well, aren't you going to say anything? I know we haven't spoken in so long, and I'm sure you don't know me from Adam. Ha ha, Eve!' She laughs at her own pathetic joke. 'And of course you're nothing like the wee girl that I remember, but so long as we're both on God's earth, it's never too late, is it?'

Her verbal diarrhoea is making it impossible for me to think straight. I have worked so very hard to create brand Skye, and this woman could ruin it all.

'Please say something, dear. I was thinking I could make a public apology to you, perhaps on the telly or on your social media. Tell the world how desperately sorry I am for not being the mother you deserved. And that might inspire other people, mightn't it?'

'No,' I say.

'Why do you say no? It would mean the world to me, and Martin thought it was a great idea. It would make a lovely, up-beat story.'

Martin. Damned Martin.

'What if I refuse?' I ask, crossing my arms in front of my chest.

'Refuse?' She stares at me as if she doesn't understand the meaning of the word. 'Martin said he'll write a story on me whether you're involved or not and that I'll get good money for it. He said people want to know about Skye's mother. Amazing, isn't it? But I'm not in this for money. Believe me, I'm not. I just want a relationship with you. My chance to say sorry.'

I am totally sickened. Never for one moment did I think that Monica would crawl out of the woodwork. I need time to reflect, to work out how best to play this to my advantage.

'Does Martin know you're here?'

'Of course not. Some things have to stay in the family, don't they? But I promised to let him know how our reunion goes. It's the least I could do to thank him for giving me your address. You have no idea how difficult you are to find. I'm not very good with computers, so I went to the library. You're not listed anywhere, are you, Skye? The lady at the desk said it's normal for people who are famous to make sure their addresses and phone numbers can't be found. When I told her that I was your mother, her eyes nearly popped out of her head. She couldn't have been more helpful. We found the name of your agent, but I wanted to contact you directly. Those sorts of people always get in the way, don't they?'

'Enough!' I say. I want to put my fingers in my ears and stop all of this nonsensical chatter.

'Aren't you going to offer me a drink, dear?' she asks, tilting her head to one side.

I have an overwhelming urge to slap her.

'I'll give some thought as to what you want,' I say. I know that I must handle this extremely delicately. No rash reactions or decisions. I have to think it through, a bit like a game of chess, planning my moves, assessing all the possible eventualities. And that takes time. I will not be rushed. What was it I decided the other day? Calm, patience, result.

'Leave me your telephone number,' I say. I reach behind me to the little notepad and pen I keep next to the landline telephone. I hand her a piece of paper and the pen, careful to make sure that our fingers don't touch. She scribbles her number.

'Can I have yours, love?' she asks.

I want to scream no. The last thing I want is to have this haggard, pathetic creature anywhere near me, but if I refuse, she might share that with Martin. In the grander scheme of things, it will be better for her to call me on my mobile than turn up here unannounced or, worse still, at any of my events. I grab the pen and write it on another small note.

'Don't give my number to anyone. Do you understand? It's confidential.'

'Of course, love. I will never betray your trust. Believe me, now I've got you back, I will treat you like a precious jewel. I know this is a shock for you, Skye, but I hope in time you'll come to feel for me in the way I feel for you.'

She gets up from the chair, and I hope that she's about to walk to the door. But no. She's walking towards me, her arms outstretched. I step away from her at the last minute.

'Don't touch me,' I hiss.

Tears well up in her eyes. 'I think you should leave now,' I say. 'I will be in touch once I've worked out what to do. Once the shock has passed.'

She nods and lifts her scuffed beige handbag off the back of my chair, putting it over her shoulder.

I follow her to the front door. She opens it and turns to face me. 'I've always loved you, Skye.'

'Just go,' I say.

The second she's on the other side of the door, I slam it shut and bolt it, top and bottom. I stride to the utility room and find a packet of antibacterial wipes. I then wipe down every single surface that she might have touched.

20

I am missing Marie, not just because I miss her easy-going manner, the relaxed smile, the way we were so compatible in bed, but also from a practicality perspective. I suppose I have taken for granted how well-run our family life was with her around. She made our weekly routine possible.

It's Thursday, and every Thursday evening I attend one of our soup kitchens and homeless shelters that Sacha's Sanctuary established three years ago. I rather assumed that our smart town wouldn't have need of such services, but how wrong I've been proven. These shelters are at the very core of the services our charity provides. During the daytime, we offer counselling and skills support, such as learning how to budget and cook, or how to look for a job, write a CV or practice for interviews. We have a large clothes bank and even help people dress to impress. Needless to say, we work with other charities, social services and GPs to help people with addictions, but our most important work is offering homeless people a decent meal, for free. Whenever we can source suitable accommodation, we also set up hostels.

Back when I established Sacha's Sanctuary, I decided that I wasn't going to be some remote, hands-off chief executive, who just loaned their signature and mug shot. So I've made it part of my routine to meet the people who use our services, to understand their stories and to be one of the team every Thursday evening. Sometimes, I wander the streets, talking to homeless people, trying to understand what they need and ensuring they know about our services. Other times, I'm ladling out food or just listening to what one of the regulars has to say.

Without Marie, I'm reliant on friends and neighbours to look after the girls, and with the fallout over Skye, I need to be extra careful. Our next-door neighbours are an older couple, and Mrs Farraday was invaluable after Sacha died. Isla, in particular, isn't keen on her, because the woman doesn't stand for any nonsense. I know Isla won't be happy that Mrs Farraday is going to babysit, because she thinks she's much too old for a sitter, but under current circumstances, I disagree.

So here I am at the soup kitchen. It's busy this evening, and our army of helpers have everything well under control. I'm not even needed to dole out any food. We have volunteers from all walks of life, but the three who have been here since we started are Amy, our head chef, who, before retiring, managed a restaurant in a garden centre; Ian, who is a journalist for the local news-paper, and Fayola, who does all the admin and the rotas and is the chief mama of the sanctuary.

The place is buzzing, with people seated at all the tables, heads down, eating. I spot Jim, who was our very first visitor to Sacha's Sanctuary. He is wearing a thread-bare sweater with a gilet over the top, a black beanie, and trousers that swamp him. He is shuffling towards a table, carrying a tray.

'Jim, how are you? Let me help you.' I take the tray from him and place it at the end of a long table. I'm happy to see him, although the fact he is still homeless doesn't speak well about our services. Unfortunately, alcohol continues to be his best friend.

'Alright, mate. And you?' he asks as he eases into a chair.

I sit down next to him. I've learned not to recoil from the stench of stale vodka, beer or body odour. Although he looks twice his age, Jim is in his late forties, and he's never had a proper home. I think the idea of living in one place and taking on the responsibilities of everyday life are so overwhelming, he doesn't want to countenance it, even with all the help we offer. I've come to respect his life choices, but I pray he'll get help with his addictions, because I like the man and don't want to see him in an early grave.

'Things are going well for you these days, aren't they?' Jim asks, nudging me with his elbow.

'What do you mean?'

'All that stuff about you and Skye.'

'I didn't think you'd be into social media,' I say, surprised.

'I know how to use the computer and all, and people talk.'

'People have got the wrong end of the stick.'

'That's good.' He munches on a bread roll.

'Why do you say that?'

There's a shout from another table, and I glance up.

'Something not right about that girl,' Jim says. 'She claims to have been homeless, but her story don't stack up.'

'Why?'

There's the clatter of broken plates. Two men pounce on each other, and it looks as if everyone else at the table is piling in. Arms and legs flail, chairs topple, and there are shouts and screams. I jump up, and see that Ian and a couple of the other helpers are dragging two men apart.

'Do you want me to call the police?' I holler. We have all sorts of procedures and contingency plans if there's any trouble, but it's rare we have to involve the police. As normal, the mêlée is over as quickly as it began, no call to emergency services necessary. One of the men, a young guy I don't recognise, has got a bloodied nose. I lead him to the side of the room, sit him down, get him a cup of tea and stand over him as Fayola, who has all sorts of first aid training, gives him the once-over.

When the fracas has been dealt with, I look around to resume my conversation with Jim. But, frustratingly, he's gone. His words stick in my head. *Skye's story doesn't stack up.* I want to know what he means by that. It was such a strange thing to say. But then I rationalise. Skye is so famous, if her story didn't stack up, I'm sure she would have been found out by now.

I'm tired, and I want to get home in good time to relieve Mrs Farraday. After tidying away a few trays and wiping down a table, I say my goodbye and thank you to Ian and Fayola, then grab my coat from the back office and leave through the staff door at the rear of the building. It's drizzling with rain, and it's cold, so I hunch my shoulders and keep my head down low as I walk back towards the car park. The town is empty at this time of night, and I listen to my footsteps as I walk along the silent street. And then, out of nowhere, something, someone, hits me.

I see stars. Then blackness.

· · ·

WHEN I COME TO, there is a massive thudding in my head. The pain makes me want to throw up, and my eyelids are so heavy, I struggle to open them.

'It's okay, Nathan. The police and ambulance are on their way.'

I force my eyes open. It's dark and Ian is leaning over me. I'm lying on the pavement, and it's freezing. I turn my head slightly, and pain sears through my skull and down my neck.

'What's happened?' My voice is a croaky whisper.

'Looks like someone jumped you. Gave me the fright of my life. I think you've been out of it for a few minutes.'

And then I hear a siren, and the sound feels as if it's ripping my brain in two. There are blue flashing lights and male voices and doors slamming, and I shut my eyes and hope I can drift back into darkness.

The next time I awake, I'm in the back of an ambulance, being shaken from side to side, a mask over my face.

'You've had a concussion and a nasty blow to the head,' the paramedic says, 'but hopefully, there's nothing to worry about. All your vitals are fine. We'll be at the hospital in two minutes.'

'The girls,' I murmur.

We may get to the hospital quickly, but it takes hours for me to be processed. I'm wheeled into a cubicle in Accident and Emergency, the blue curtains pulled around me. Although my head hurts, that overwhelming tiredness dissipates. Ian is still with me whilst I'm checked over by a nurse.

'Go home, Ian. I'm fine now, and I could be here all night.'

'You will be here all night,' the nurse says as the blood pressure machine pumps up.

'If you're sure,' Ian says.

'Can you pass me my phone? It should be in the inside pocket of my coat.'

Ian finds it and hands it to me. 'What about your wallet and car keys?' he asks.

'Can you check?'

He riffles through all the pockets, and although my keys are still in the inside pocket of my coat, where my phone was, my wallet has gone.

Ian sighs. 'Guess you got fleeced for your wallet.'

'Could have been worse,' I say, trying to smile through the pounding headache.

When the nurse has finished her checks, Ian waves goodbye and then I call home. When I tell Mrs Farraday I've been in accident but there's nothing to worry about, she chokes up.

'As if you haven't been through enough, my dear,' she says. 'I'll hop next door and get my overnight things. Don't you worry, I'll stay with your girls until you're home.'

I smile grimly to myself. Isla will be livid.

A few minutes later, Isla calls me. I speak to both her and Chloe, reassuring them that I'm going to be fine and that there's nothing to worry about. But I've told them that before, after Sacha got diagnosed. They have every right not to believe me.

A doctor examines me, shining lights into my eyes, and organises for my head to be stitched up. Then a policeman arrives and takes a statement, which is a useless exercise, as I have zero recollection of what happened. And finally, shortly after 3 a.m., the doctor confirms that I will have to stay in the hospital for the night, due to the concussion, and I'm wheeled to a bed in a ward. Despite assuming sleep would be impossible, I drop off immediately, and the next thing I know is a nurse is leaning over me, taking my blood pressure.

'After you've had breakfast, we want you to get up and have a walk around. If you're feeling alright, I think the doctor will give you the okay to go home.'

'Thanks,' I say, feeling deeply relieved.

IT'S MID-MORNING. I'm fully dressed in yesterday's clothes, which are remarkably clean, as my coat took the most battering. I ring up the bank and cancel my credit and debit cards, feeling grateful that I had very little cash on me. I want to leave the hospital, but there are procedures in place, and I have to wait. I wonder if I should message Marie and tell her what's happened. I feel sure she'd come back, but I decide against it. It would make her pity me, and that's the last thing I want. If she is going to return, I want it to be because she loves and misses me, just as I love and miss her.

'Is there anyone who can come and collect you?' one of the nurses asks.

I bite the inside of my cheek. 'I'll just get a taxi,' I say. 'I assume one will be waiting downstairs.'

The nurse doesn't seem very impressed by my answer, but what can I do? I don't want to disturb any friends or work colleagues. It's not like I'm at death's door.

Twenty minutes later, there is a flurry of activity in the corridor outside my ward. I hear multiple voices and footsteps, and then a moment later a massive bouquet of flowers appears, with Skye emerging from behind it.

'Nathan, I am so sorry to hear what happened!' she gushes, thrusting the flowers at me. One of the nurses looks on, her eyes widening in recognition of Skye. I stand up and put the flowers on the table next to the bed. A mistake. There is now space for her to rush forwards and kiss me on the cheek.

'What are you doing here?' I whisper.

'As soon as I heard that you got attacked, I made my way to the hospital. You poor thing. Did one of your homeless people beat you up?'

'What?' I can't think straight. 'No. It didn't happen at the Sanctuary. It happened on my way back to the car. How did you find out I was here?'

We're interrupted by a nurse, an older woman who doesn't seem in the slightest bit impressed by Skye. I warm to her immediately, 'Right, Mr Edwards. You can go home now. Take it easy over the next few days, and if your headache gets worse or you feel unusually drowsy, you call 999 immediately.'

'I'll take you home,' Skye says.

'It's fine. I'll get a taxi.' I turn around to pick up my filthy coat.

'Absolutely not.'

We're interrupted by a young girl. 'Skye, can I have a selfie with you?'

'Of course.' She bends down and smiles at the girl's phone. When the selfie is done, the girl skips away with an expression of sheer delight.

As I walk out of the ward, I see Skye has gathered quite a little crowd of onlookers. It must be awful, never having any privacy, always needing to be on your best behaviour, looking well dressed, worrying what people think of you. But that doesn't mean I'm feeling any warmth to this woman.

'Please don't be angry with me, Nathan,' Skye says, holding the huge bouquet of white flowers in her right hand and briefly touching my arm with her left hand. 'I just want to be your friend. That's all. Can we push the reset button?'

I don't answer, but I do know that I cannot make a scene here. As we come out of the front door of the hospital, a TV cameraman and a journalist holding a microphone come running up to us. 'Skye! Nathan!' I freeze. Did she set this up? It must have been Skye; otherwise how would they know she was here? It's not like I'm newsworthy. I think of Ian, who works for the local paper, but I can't see him having anything to do with notifying a television crew. Undoubtedly this is one of Skye's publicity stunts, and she has me cornered. It's not as if I can bolt now.

'How are you feeling, Nathan?'

'I'm fine,' I say curtly, wondering why my attack is of any public interest.

'Skye, what did you think when you heard that your friend here was beaten up?'

Skye thrusts the bouquet of flowers at me, and I hold them awkwardly.

'Horrified. As you might know, Nathan Edwards runs Sacha's Sanctuary, the charity that helps reduce homelessness.'

I note how Skye swallows the word Sacha's, or did I just imagine that?

'Last night, when he was returning from helping out in the soup kitchen, he was brutally attacked. Look at this man who puts himself in danger every Thursday night.' She links her arm through mine and pulls me towards her. I frown. What the hell does she mean? Working at Sacha's Sanctuary most certainly doesn't put me in any danger.

'Nathan Edwards is a public hero and my personal hero. We're working together on a programme to prevent lawlessness amongst the homeless and get them off the streets once and for all. Please help by donating to Sacha's Sanctuary. It would mean so much to all of us.'

'Were you attacked by a homeless person, Mr Edwards?'

A microphone is thrust in front of my face.

Before I can answer, Skye butts in. 'No further questions.' She pulls me away from the camera. 'Try to keep up with me,' Skye whispers urgently.

We walk briskly towards the car park. The cellophane that wraps around the ostentatious bouquet of flowers crackles as we walk. When we reach her car, Skye releases my arm and opens her BMW. I pause. I really don't want to get in her car, but then I see that the television cameraman is still pointing his camera in our direction, so I climb into the passenger seat.

'Did you tell the media about this?'

Skye purses her lips. 'It was posted on the news section of the local newspaper that the head of a local homeless charity had been mugged last night. I was immediately concerned it might be you, so I rang up the hospital, and they confirmed it was you. Naturally, I was, and still am, worried about you and the girls. Once I found out that you were hurt but all was well, and that you were due to come out of hospital this morning, I may have happened to tell a contact at the local newsroom. But I can assure you, being featured with me on the local lunchtime and evening news will do wonders for the profile of the Sanctuary.'

'Sacha's Sanctuary,' I say, stressing Sacha's name. 'And am I meant to thank you for that?' I ask.

Skye's fingers grip the steering wheel, and she inhales. 'I don't expect a thank you for anything, Nathan. Look. I made a mistake. I read you wrongly.

Can we please move on from that and be cordial friends and colleagues?'

What choice do I have? I need her help. 'Yes.' I sigh.

We don't speak any more during the journey home.

As Skye turns her car into Rectory Road, I catch sight of something flapping at the entrance to our driveway. As we get closer, I realise that it's a ragged banner attached haphazardly to a tree. It reads, 'Get Better Soon, Nathan!'

Who put that there? Was it Mrs Farraday? Surely not. She's the sort of woman who complains if you don't bring your bin in within an hour of the rubbish lorry emptying it. I remember the fuss she kicked up last year when the neighbours two houses down parked their new camper van in the driveway. An eyesore, she called it. The sign could have been made by one of the girls, but it really isn't their sort of thing, and they wouldn't have had much time before being taken to school by Ellie first thing this morning. Besides, they call me Dad, not Nathan.

'That was done by some of your homeless people,' Skye says, glancing at me.

I don't ask how she knows. I don't ask whether it was she who told them where I live, because no one else would have done. I just sigh, relieved to be home; my heart empty, longing for Marie. I am so tired, my bones ache heavily with exhaustion. All I want to do is collapse onto my bed and sleep.

'Will you manage all alone?' Skye asks as she switches the engine off.

'Yes. I'm fine. Thank you for bringing me home.'

Slowly, I climb out of the car and then turn and swivel around to face her. I can sense her dilemma: whether to remain in the car or get out of the vehicle.

'Thanks again, Skye.' I move to close the door.

'Don't forget your flowers!' she says.

WHEN I AWAKE, it's dark outside, and I can hear voices downstairs. I lift my head and it pounds, the effects of the painkillers having worn off. I switch on the bedside light.

'Dad!' Chloe rushes into the bedroom and throws her arms around my neck.

'Easy, tiger,' I say, trying to keep her away from the gash at the side of my head.

'I was so worried about you,' she says, climbing up onto the bed.

Isla strolls into the room. She hesitates, but then she does the same, throwing her arms around me, sitting on the side of the bed. I'm relieved. Isla hasn't wanted to show her emotions for some time.

'Are you alright?' she asks.

'Yes. It was a bit of a fuss about nothing.'

'I'm so sorry, Dad,' Isla says.

'What are you sorry about?'

'Being mean about Marie. Being horrible to you. I wish Marie would come back. I guess I resented her because she's not Mum, but now she's gone, I miss her.'

'So do I, darling.'

The three of us stay huddled together for some long moments, and then I hear a clatter downstairs.

'It's only Ellie,' Isla says. 'She's brought us food for supper.'

'That's so kind of her. Let me get dressed, and I'll come downstairs.'

FIVE MINUTES LATER, I'm in the kitchen. Ellie has put the oven on and is slipping a pie inside.

'How are you feeling?' she asks as she turns around and throws me a warm smile.

'Sore, but alright. Thank you so much for all of this.'

'It's no problem.' It isn't the first time Ellie has come to my rescue, and no doubt won't be the last. She was amazing after Sacha died, so amazing that she knows where everything lives in our kitchen and what our food preferences are.

'Who put up the Welcome Home banner?' she asks.

I grimace. 'Some of the people from the shelter. I need to find out who, because they shouldn't know where I live.'

'Quick work.'

Too quick, I think to myself. Who did Skye organise to do that? I am feeling extremely uncomfortable about all of this.

'Dad,' Chloe says, 'it's all over social media that one of the homeless people you helped beat you up. Is that true?'

'I don't know, but I doubt it. The police don't know who attacked me.'

'Do you think they'll come here and hurt us?' Chloe asks, edging closer to me.

'No, little one,' I say, pulling her into a hug. 'No, I am sure they won't. The people I help like us and our family. I was just in the wrong place at the wrong time. Whoever did it stole my wallet. I'm sure he didn't mean to hurt me.' I turn away from the girls so they can't see the doubtful expression on my face.

Damn Skye. What the hell is she trying to achieve putting out rumours like that? She may think she's doing us a favour by increasing our fundraising, but she is simultaneously doing us a huge amount of harm by suggesting that the very people we are helping are dangerous. All our work is based on trust, and if our clients think we're untrustworthy, they will no longer seek out our help. She was homeless herself, so she should know better. But then I recall Jim's words. How her story doesn't stack up. Could Jim be right?

After supper, when the girls are doing their homework, I ring the shelter. Fortunately, Amy, our chef, answers the phone.

'Goodness, am I happy to hear your voice!' she exclaims. 'How are you, hon?'

'I'm fine, sort of. Do you know who put up a banner outside my home?'

'Um, no. None of our clients know where you live.'

It is one of our rules that we never give out staff's personal contact details. I am utterly confident that no one on our team would ever breach that rule.

'But there's a lot of indignation. Everyone loves you here, Nathan. The word is that they're one hundred percent sure that no one from this community would hurt you, and they don't like that they're being blamed.'

That's exactly what I thought. It may come across as conceited to assume that everyone associated with Sacha's Sanctuary loves me. Of course they don't, but the people we help are grateful, and the thought of any of them beating me up is highly unlikely. The more I think about it, the more I am convinced that Skye had something to do with this. She either orchestrated for me to be attacked to get publicity, which seems extreme, even for Skye, or she is taking advantage of a very unfortunate situation. Either way I am appalled by her; dismayed that she is milking my personal misfortune for her personal benefit. How the hell I'm meant to stop her, I have no idea.

21

After dropping off Nathan, I return home. It has not been a good twenty-four hours. Once again, I seem to have misjudged Nathan's propensity to gratitude. I thought he would appreciate me collecting him from the hospital, but he isn't like most other men. His reaction, combined with Monica crawling out of the woodwork, has wrong-footed me.

In fact, it's worse than that. Thanks to Monica, for the very first time, I have been backed into a corner. Perhaps I was naive not to consider the possibility of her appearing, but how could I have pre-empted it? I assumed she was dead. A merciful death after the pain of a lifetime hooked on devastating drugs. She might look like a shrivelled-up old prune, but she's much too alive for my liking.

I make myself a black coffee and pace the house, trying to work out what might be the best course of action. Dealing with Monica has to be my priority, and I can't sit back and wait. I need to go on the attack. It's always worked for me before, and there's no reason to think it won't work this time.

I walk into my bathroom. Above the bath, I have one of those mirrors with words printed across the front. You can get them personalised, selecting your own words or phrases, and I treated myself to an extra-large version three years ago. The words remind me that I am strong, I am beautiful, I am successful, and that the world loves me. I smile at myself, and then, flicking my hair over my shoulder, I reach for my mobile and I telephone that journalist, Martin Rodriguez. Unsurprisingly, the woman on the switchboard puts me straight through to him. As I wait for him to answer, I smile at myself in the mirror. It gives me confidence to watch myself when I am speaking.

'Good morning, Skye, I was wondering when I would be hearing from you,' he says. The smug bastard.

He continues: 'I wanted to be there when you had your first reunion with Monica, but she was adamant that it was a private matter, and she would only talk to me once you were on board. Hats off to her. She would have made a lot more money if we could have recorded that initial meeting. How did it go?'

'Fine,' I say curtly. 'What are you paying her for the scoop?'

'A few grand. But she wants it all to go to that charity you support, Sacha's Sanctuary.'

That's a surprise. I had thought Monica was just after the money. And it's not a good surprise. If she only wanted money, I could buy her off.

'When are you free to be interviewed?' Martin asks. 'If we can interview you both in the next forty-eight hours, it'll go into the women's section on Thursday, and I can allocate you a double-page spread. It'll be good for you, Skye. Good for your profile.'

'If you're free, I'll clear my diary, and we can do it

this afternoon. You can tell Monica.' Hopefully the stupid cow will be busy this afternoon.

'We'll come to your house, then.'

I turn away from the mirror. 'No. Absolutely not. Somewhere neutral and local.'

'Alright,' Martin says, but there's hesitation in his voice. 'I'll get back to you.'

WHEN MARTIN SENDS me a text message to say the interview will be held this afternoon at the Belleview Hotel near Gatwick Airport, I ring my hairdresser, whom I have on speed dial. I pay him handsomely, and on the rare occasion I need an emergency blow-dry, he is well-rewarded for dumping pre-booked clients in favour of me.

By 2 p.m., I am ready: coiffured and make-up carefully applied, because the camera always needs it. I wriggle into a figure-hugging, short black dress with high-heeled boots that come up and over the knee. I accessorise the outfit with a simple gold chain and gold hoop earrings. I look classy and in control. I need to remember that. I am classy and in control.

When I enter the reception area of the hotel, I recognise Martin immediately. Hacks have a certain look about them, like ferrets, eager to dig and dig, uncaring what the final kill might be. I suppose I recognise hacks in the way that criminals can spot a copper. He turns to me and puts out his hand. That's one of the worst things about my job. Having to shake hands with strangers. I grit my teeth, smile and pump his sweaty palm.

'Monica is already here. She's with Paul, my photographer, in a corner of the lounge. I hope you don't mind dogs. The hotel is hosting a Dog Party. They're in a private room, but we've already had a mutt in the lounge almost knocking over Paul's tripod.'

Good heavens. Who knew that people spent good money on hosting a canine party? I wonder whether they'll be an opportunity there for me. Perhaps I could gatecrash the pooch party, get a few snaps and pitch for dog food advertising. It's a market sector I've never considered.

Martin is speaking to me, and I've zoned out.

'Sorry?' I say as we walk together down the corridor towards the bright public lounge.

'I said I would have got a private room, but with the amount we're paying to Monica for the charity, the paper is out of budget.'

He stands to one side to let me enter the lounge first. It has three large patio doors leading onto a wide terrace, windows facing south and west hung with pale blue-and-grey tartan wool curtains. There are five sets of sofas and armchairs, a large stone fireplace and big watercolour paintings hanging on the walls, mainly of the Sussex countryside. Monica jumps up as soon as she sees me, arms outstretched as if she's coming in for a hug. Dear God. Paul the photographer has his camera at the ready, so I need to prepare myself. I pretend it's Nathan whom I am about to embrace.

'Skye, my darling,' Monica purrs, wrapping her scrawny arms around me, bony fingers digging into my flesh. She kisses me on each cheek, dry, papery lips making me want to recoil, the smell of stale cigarette smoke and a cheap perfume curdling the air.

'Hello, Monica,' I say tightly, quickly pulling away. The cheap acrylic in her mauve jumper pings with static. I glance at her as I sit down. The woman looks a fright. Hair undyed and unruly, cheap clothes and make-up so badly applied, her eyelashes have clumps of mascara that scatter black splatters on her cheeks. Talk about beauty and the beast.

'Good afternoon, ladies, and thanks for doing this interview. We'll have a chat first, and Paul will take snaps as we're talking, and then will do some posed shots at the end. Is that alright?'

I nod. Monica stares, her eyeballs bulging like a rabbit with myxomatosis.

'Skye, if we can begin with you. When was the last time you saw your mother?'

'Goodness, a lifetime ago. How old was I? Five or six?' I turn to Monica.

'You were taken into care aged five.'

'Yes. Not happy times,' I say, looking at the floor.

Monica squirms in her chair.

'Have you ever tried to look for Monica?' Martin asks.

'No,' I say flatly.

'So how was it when she turned up at your door?'

'To be frank, I was angry. This is the woman who left me in care as a young child, who was never part of my life, who, for all I knew, was dead. And then she just turns up one day, and here we are. I wouldn't have recognised her if we passed in the street.'

'That's perfectly understandable. You must have gone through a lot of grief as a child growing up, knowing you had a mother, but she wasn't able to care for you.'

'It wasn't easy. Although some of my foster mums were lovely, no child should be without a mother.'

'And what do you say to that?' Martin asks, leaning towards Monica. Paul has the camera ready and is clicking away.

The stupid cow is trembling. 'I'm sorry, Skye. It broke my heart, too, when they took you away from me.

I've always loved you. But the drugs loved me, and when they took hold, well, I was sick. What could I do? I tried time and time again to get off them and be the mother you deserved. And then, a few weeks ago, when I found out that you were my Skye, it felt like I'd been given a second chance. I know I don't deserve you, but all I ask is for you to allow me to say sorry. I will never forgive myself, and I know I don't deserve your forgiveness, but please, my darling Skye, will you let me be part of your life again?'

If we weren't in public, I'd slap the woman. She is so needy and desperate. Tragic, really. I pause and look up to the left, as if I'm considering my answer, digging earnestly for the compassion that I know my followers want. I take a deep breath and lean towards her, reaching for those scrawny hands.

'Mum, we can never get back all of those lost years, but of course I'm happy to see you again. I've dreamed of this moment every single day, praying before I go to sleep and thinking of you when I wake up in the morning. I thought about looking for you, but I simply couldn't face rejection a second time. Once I got over the shock of seeing you, and when I realised that your emotions for me were pure, that was the happiest moment of my life. Thank you for coming to find me.'

Tears are pouring down Monica's cheeks, streams of mascara dripping onto her cheap, shiny trousers. Just as well they're black.

Martin passes Monica a tissue. He turns towards me. 'From my conversations with Monica, I know she's eager to find out if you will accept her apology.'

I pause. 'Yes, I do. I don't suppose I'll ever truly understand, but what I do know is that looking backwards is never helpful. As everyone who follows me on social media knows, my programme is all about living for today. There is nothing we can do to change what went before.'

'Bubbles, Bubbles! Come here.'

A woman, probably in her fifties, dressed all in white, presumably to match her white West Highland terrier, totters into the lounge, manically trying to chase the small dog that runs around the chairs and then appears right in front of us.

'Hey, sweetie,' I say, leaning down to let the dog sniff my hand.

'Gosh, I'm terribly sorry!' the woman exclaims. 'Bubbles is such a naughty boy.'

I stroke the dog's head and hold his collar.

'He escaped from the room when one of the waitresses came in. You're such a little rascal, aren't you, Bubbles?' The woman leans down and scoops the dog up into her arms. 'I don't think the hotel would have allowed us to bring in dogs if it weren't for a charity event. At least Bubbles hasn't cocked his leg against the curtains, like one of his naughty friends did.' She laughs.

It's only then that she looks at me properly and does a double take.

'Good heavens! Are you Skye?'

I smile at her. 'Yes.'

'Oh my, I'm dreadfully sorry for interrupting.'

'What's the charity event?' I ask.

'It's to celebrate the first-year birthday of the Poor Pretty Paws Animal Sanctuary in West Chiltington. Gosh, it would be marvellous if you could pop in to say hello when you're finished here. I know it's awfully cheeky of me to ask, but do you think that might be possible?'

'With pleasure,' I say. I hope that Martin notes in his article how charming I am to any charitable cause.

When the woman has gone, Monica turns to look at me, a strange expression on her face.

'I'm so proud of you, Skye. You really have overcome all your fears, haven't you?'

I smile and shift in my chair, a flicker of unease in my abdomen. I'm glad that Martin asks another question.

'Skye, your life has been well documented, but Monica, we know very little about you. Perhaps you could tell us what life has been like during the past twenty years, and in particular, how you managed to overcome your drugs habit.'

'Of course,' she says, shifting to the edge of her seat. 'I've been clean for three years, eight months and twenty-seven days.'

'Congratulations,' Martin says.

And then I zone out as Monica drones on about her life on and off drugs, and how sorry she was for not fighting harder to keep me. After about ten minutes, the interview is wrapped up, and then it's time for photos. There is no way that I can allow myself to be photographed with Monica looking the way she is, so I suggest she go to the ladies' to clean herself up. I rummage in my Prada bag and hand her a stick of mascara.

'Thanks, love,' she murmurs before hurrying off.

'We'll take a few pics of you whilst we're waiting,' Martin says. I check my face in my little mirror, apply a fresh coat of lipstick and pose for the photographer. Monica reappears, looking only marginally better. She stands awkwardly beside me, half a head shorter.

'Let's have Monica seated and Skye lean forwards over the head of the chair and place your arms around Monica's neck,' the photographer says. I try not to shudder. After a few more poses of us sitting next to each other on the sofa, me trying not to inhale Monica's repugnant stale cigarette smell, I'm relieved when Martin and the photographer say it's a wrap.

'Can you send the photos and the draft article to Tiana, my agent, so we can approve them?' I hand Martin one of Tiana's business cards.

'That wasn't part of the deal, but I'll see what we can do,' Martin says. 'Thanks, ladies.'

And then they're gone. I wait a beat, stand up and turn towards Monica.

'See you,' I say as I pick up my bag and sling my coat over my arm. I walk out of the lounge and into the hall, Monica trailing behind me.

A waiter passes us, dressed in the obligatory black-and-white and carrying a tray with coffee cups on it.

'Excuse me, but where is the dog party being held?' I ask.

'Second door down on the left, ma'am.'

As we walk towards it, there's a racket of barking and raised voices.

'Wait, Skye.'

'What is it?' I have no intention of being nice to Monica now that the journos have left.

'I can't believe that you're brave enough to go into a room full of dogs,' Monica says.

I pause for a second, wondering what the hell she's on about.

'Did you get plastic surgery?'

'Of course I bloody didn't!' I hiss. 'I'm in my prime. Are you going to start criticising my looks? Perhaps you should look in the mirror first.'

'I don't mean that sort of plastic surgery. Did they fix you up after you were mauled? You know, I've never forgiven myself for that,' Monica says. I freeze with my hand on the doorknob. 'It was the final nail that broke the camel's back.'

'Mixed metaphor.' I roll my eyes. 'It's the straw that broke the camel's back and the final nail in the coffin.'

'Whatever. But when you were savaged like that, I couldn't stop crying for months.'

I can't listen to any more of Monica's nonsense, so I knock on the door and ease it open. The woman in white sees me and rushes forwards, her hands extended.

Monica slips in behind me. I wish she would go away, but I can't risk her making a scene.

'Is there anything I can do to support your charity?' I ask, bending down to stroke a brown mutt's ears. It snarls at me, and I step backwards, treading on Monica's foot.

'A few photos would be lovely. Perhaps we could auction off something you sign? One of our brochures, maybe?'

'Sure, no problem.' I glance around the room, enjoying the stares.

The woman hands me a pen and a brochure headed up Poor Pretty Paws Animal Sanctuary. I write my signature across the bottom half of the page. I've perfected it over the years. It's large and curvy and difficult to copy with all the additional squiggles I add to underline my name. I glance up and see Monica frowning. What is it with this damn woman?

'And a photo with our founding trustee, perhaps?' Bubbles' owner suggests.

I pose with a woman wearing a brown tweed jacket and matching skirt.

'Best of luck with everything,' I say as I bend down and snap a few photos of myself with all the dogs scarpering around me. Hopefully, I can get some leverage from this with organic dog food manufacturers or designer canine accessory retailers. I wave goodbye and leave the room, making sure none of the dogs follow me.

'You were mauled by that dog. Is there something you're not telling me, Skye?' Monica asks, hurrying to keep up with my quick pace.

'You know what,' I say, coming to an abrupt halt and crossing my arms. 'I've done what you asked of me, and now I want you to leave me alone. Do you understand?'

She shakes her head very slowly. 'No, Skye. I don't understand. Not one little bit. You've turned out very differently to how I imagined.'

22

NATHAN – NOW

'I don't want to go to school, Daddy,' Chloe says.

'Why not?'

'In case something bad happens to you.'

I pull her into a hug. 'Nothing is going to happen to me. It was a one-off, and look, I may have a black eye and a sore head, but I'm perfectly alright.'

'Still, I'm scared.'

'Have you seen what they're saying about Skye on social media?' Isla asks, interrupting our conversation. She walks into the room, her school uniform skirt rolled over several times at the waist to make it almost indecently short. She never did that when Marie was here.

'As you know, I don't look at social media,' I say as I loosen my grip on Chloe.

'Skye's mother has reappeared after twenty years.' Isla stands next to me and shows me her phone. 'Apparently she has shared her story about being addicted to drugs and having to give up her daughter, and now they've been reunited.'

I wonder what Skye thinks of that. It must be hard on her despite those beaming smiles in the photographs.

And then the doorbell rings. It's just before 8 a.m., and I jump but try not to show my concern to the girls. I chivvy them upstairs, telling them to hurry to get ready for school. I walk to the front door, peer through the peephole, and see it's a UPS delivery driver.

'Good morning. I have some parcels for you.'

There is one huge and very heavy box along with two smaller boxes. I sign for the delivery and take them inside. The big box is addressed to me, and the two smaller ones are for each of the girls. My heart sinks. More gifts from Skye, I suppose. Cautiously, I open the big box. It is a fabulous hamper of foods from Fortnum & Mason, presented in a big wicker basket with the initials F & M printed on the front. Inside, there are all sorts of delicacies from jams and preserves to biscuits and tea. The gift tag says, *Dear Nathan, Wishing you a very speedy recovery, With love, Skye.*

Isla comes clattering down the stairs, dragging her heavy school bag behind her.

'What's that?'

'A present from Skye.'

'Why are you looking so glum? It's amazing.'

'I don't think we should accept all these–'

'There are boxes for Chloe and me too!' She grabs the small box with her name on the front and rips it open. 'OMG!' she exclaims. 'It's the latest iPhone.'

'No.' I am seething. 'I'm sorry, but you can't keep that.'

'If you want to give yours back, then do, but you're not taking away Chloe's and my presents.' She grabs Chloe's box and races back up the stairs.

My shoulders sag. This is getting too much. Why is Skye so eager to buy our affection? It just seems wrong.

. . .

I'M at a loss as to how to handle Skye. I want her to remain part of the business, but to butt out of my private life, and I'm not sure how to facilitate that. I need to speak to someone about her, and as there's no one else, I decide Ash will have to do.

'I've got something I need to discuss with you. Can we have a private chat in the meeting room?' I grab us both a cup of tea and shut the door. He unfurls himself into a chair and looks at me, one bushy eyebrow raised.

'What's up?'

I sigh. 'It's an awkward one, and I need you to promise not to breathe a word of this to anyone else.'

'Of course,' Ash says.

I'm not worried about that. Ash never indulges in gossip.

'The problem I have is that Skye seems to be interested in me as much as the charity. She's coming on to me personally.'

He sniggers and then apologises. 'Most men would be falling over backwards for that.'

'The thing is, I'm engaged. Or I was until my fiancée left me last week.'

'Shit, Nathan. I can't believe you didn't tell us this.'

I shrug my shoulders. 'I don't like to bring my personal life to work.'

Ash chuckles. 'Me neither. If we're opening up to each other, I might as well tell you that I'm also getting married. My fiancé is called Konrad.'

'Congratulations,' I say, trying to keep the expression of surprise off my face. I'm thrilled he's happy, as he's a lovely guy. But it does make me realise that the people we spend the most time with shouldn't be strangers. I need to make more of an effort to get to know my team. It's not like there are many of us. Sacha used to be so good at that. She'd remember all of the staff's birthdays and organise annual jollies.

'So how has Skye taken your rejection, assuming you have actually rejected her?' Ash asks.

'That's the problem. It hasn't gone down well. Everywhere I go, she pops up, normally with a photographer in tow. She's sending inappropriately lavish gifts to the girls and me, and she's not even being subtle about threatening to hurt the charity if I don't yield to her advances.'

'Shit,' Ash says, letting out a whistle. 'At the end of the day, you and your kids' well-being are more important than the charity. If we need to dump Skye, then so be it.'

'Thanks, Ash, but it's likely that could be disastrous.'

'The only event that you've actually committed to is the charity sailing race this coming weekend. After that, let's pull back. I'll speak to Tiana and come up with some story to keep you away from her. I shouldn't worry too much. The worst that will happen is you'll dent her pride and she'll sulk for a bit.'

If Skye was a normal woman, then perhaps Ash would be right. But there is nothing normal about her, and I can't possibly tell Ash the true extent of my involvement. Nevertheless, it's a relief that I've shared part of the problem that is Skye.

We get up to leave the meeting room.

'I'll keep an eye out for you, mate,' Ash says.

ABOUT AN HOUR LATER, my phone rings.

'Good morning, Mr Edwards. It's Martin Rodriguez speaking. I gather that the social media influencer Skye is supporting your charity.'

'Yes,' I say hesitantly. I've never met Martin

Rodriguez, but we've spoken on the phone a few times. He wrote a great article on Sacha's Sanctuary for one of the weekend supplements, using our charity as the main example on a piece about the rise of charities plugging the gap due to cuts in government funding.

'I've got a feature coming out tomorrow about the reconciliation between Skye and her mother, although with the typical zeal of the influencer generation, that news is already dispersed across the internet. I just wanted to know how you feel about Skye's mother donating her fee for the story to Sacha's Sanctuary?'

'I had no idea she was doing that.'

'Yes. Monica Walker specifically asked for the fee to go to your charity. I suppose she wants to be seen to support the charity that her daughter is throwing her weight behind.'

'That's very generous of her and much appreciated.' I realise that if I speak to this woman, I'll have the opportunity to find out more about Skye. 'Do you have her contact details so I can thank her personally?'

'I do.' Martin gives me Monica's phone number. 'So is Skye's support of real financial value, or a lot of hot air?'

'Our donations have tripled in the past three weeks. The effect is solid,' I say, with some reservation, because despite the money rolling in, I feel sure the detrimental cost to me will continue to increase.

'And what's the story about you and Skye being an item?'

'There is no story,' I say, rather too sharply. 'The pictures lied.'

'That's what they all say.' Martin chuckles. 'Anyway, keep a look out for the article, and you'll be receiving a payment from the paper shortly.'

· · ·

I AM glad to have an opportunity to make contact with Skye's mother. Hopefully she will give me some insight into her daughter, insight that will let me disentangle myself without jeopardising the charity. I dial Monica Walker's number.

'How wonderful to hear from you,' she effuses.

'It's me who has to thank you for your generosity. Is there any possibility of us meeting for a coffee?'

'I'd love that, and you can tell me all about your charity.'

LATER IN THE AFTERNOON, I make my way to a small, independent coffee shop with a handful of tables. The setting is intimate and "olde worlde", with black low-hanging beams and the scent of freshly ground coffee. I am five minutes early for my meeting with Monica, so I find a table in the corner of the room and sit down.

'Is it Nathan?'

She looks nothing like Skye and much too old to be Skye's mother. Her face is deeply lined, and she has the yellow, rotting teeth of a heavy smoker and a rasping speaking voice. I know well what the aging effects are of drugs and alcohol. I stand up and shake Monica's hand.

'It's so lovely to meet you.' She shrugs off an old anorak and sits down opposite me. When she leans forwards to speak, her eyes light up and she exudes a surprising warmth.

'What can I get you?' I ask.

'Oh, no. I'm buying the drinks. You work for a charity.'

I laugh. 'And it's a business expense. You're about to donate a large sum of money to us; it's the least I can do.'

'A milky tea, if you insist,' she says.

I walk up to the counter and place an order for Monica's tea and an espresso for myself, then I return and sit down.

'It must be very emotional reconnecting with Skye after so long,' I say.

'Yes, it was for me. Less emotional for her.'

'Oh, really?' I tilt my head to one side.

'She's done amazingly well for herself, but she's nothing like I imagined she would be. It's the strangest feeling meeting your child after all this time and them being a stranger.'

'I can't begin to imagine,' I say.

'I wish I could go back and have my chance all over again,' Monica muses. 'Do you have children?'

'Yes, two girls.' I don't mention that my daughters are motherless.

'If you don't mind me asking – how serious are you and Skye?'

'Serious?'

'You know. The relationship.'

'Has she said anything to you?' I ask.

'She hasn't said very much about anything, but I saw the photos of the two of you together. You are a good-looking couple.'

'We're not a couple,' I say, shifting backwards in my chair.

'Oh, sorry.' She spills a little of her tea.

'No need to apologise. I think Skye is the sort of woman who always gets what she wants. She's showering us with gifts at the moment.'

She chuckles. 'That's certainly not the way I would have brought her up, but I've been absent from her life for so long, I wouldn't know. People change when they grow up, don't they?'

'She's been very generous towards our charity.'

'I'm proud of how Skye has turned out. She saw what she wanted, and she grabbed it with both hands, and to hell with everyone else.'

I smile, but I don't agree with Monica. I don't like her "to hell with everyone else" attitude. I sense a brutal hardness to Skye. It could be dismissed as being the result of her tough childhood, having to fight for everything herself, but I don't buy that. I know plenty of people who have had the roughest time when they were young, yet have turned into sensitive, empathetic individuals. It seems to me that Skye is single-minded in her pursuit of her goals.

The problems I have are several. I don't know what her goal is. Yes, it must benefit her by being associated with Sacha's Sanctuary, but why does she want to be part of my family life? I'm a reasonably attractive man, but nothing that special, and I have no doubt that she could find someone of her age without two teenage daughters as appendages. And for that matter, I don't like the way that she is buying the girls' affection. Once again, I long for the uncomplicated love of Marie.

'Why don't you tell me about yourself, Nathan? You must be a lovely man to have set up a charity.'

'I did it in my late wife's name.'

'Oh, blimey,' Monica exclaims, her hand rushing to her mouth. 'I didn't realise.'

'Please don't feel awkward.' It's bizarre, but I feel remarkably relaxed with this woman; so very different to how I feel around her daughter. It's unusual for me to volunteer that I am a widower. Such a sad word. I see Marie's face in my mind's eye. She was never Sacha's replacement. No, she was too different to her. Marie brought me joy. I take a sip of coffee and snap out of my introspection.

'Skye is a good person, too. She's doing a huge amount for charity,' I say.

'Yes, but–'

I sense that Monica is about to say something, but then she changes tack.

'It's funny to think that if Sacha's Sanctuary had existed ten years ago, we might have met,' she says. And the moment is gone.

We make small talk for a few more minutes, but I'm disappointed. I had hoped to get further information out of Monica, but it's clear that she knows little about the daughter she gave up all those years ago. Nevertheless, I like the woman. She's open and unashamedly apologetic for all the mistakes she made in the past. I've seen enough people addicted to drugs to be confident that this woman has, against all odds, reclaimed her life. I just wish she'd share a little more of her thoughts about her daughter. I am positive that she is holding things back.

'You know, now I'm clean, I think it's time for me to help others. My way of saying thank you.'

'But you are; you're donating the money that the newspaper is giving you for your interview with Skye.'

'It's easy to give away money when you've got some!' she chortles. 'No, I want to give my time. Do you think I could volunteer for your charity?'

'I don't see why not,' I say. 'I can put you in touch with Sophie in the office, who does all the volunteer checks and puts together the rotas. We can always do with an extra pair of hands.'

'Can I come in and meet her?'

'Of course. When were you thinking?'

'I wash up at an old people's home, but I'm free by 4 p.m. most afternoons. I could pop over tomorrow if that's convenient?'

'I'm sure it will be. Come to the office at 4 p.m. unless you hear from me to the contrary.'

'That's cracking!' She beams. She pulls out a pen from her bag and scribbles on the back of a receipt. 'This is my address and phone number, so your Sophie can do her checks on me. They'll give me a nice reference from Sunnyside Care Home, and I haven't got a police record. Just bits of petty thieving when I was in the depths of the drugs, but nothing bad for years now. It'll be lovely to give something back. I've had help from so many kind people like you over the years, and it's only now that I realise if it weren't for charities like Sacha's Sanctuary, I'd have been dead in a ditch decades ago.'

We say our goodbyes, but as I'm walking away, her words, "dead in a ditch" ring in my head. I turn to look for her, but Monica has vanished.

23

SKYE – NOW

Something awakens me. I turn over to look at my alarm clock and realise I forgot to turn it on. Damn. It's gone 9 a.m. I rub my eyes and sit up too quickly. I curse. There's someone knocking on the door, so I pick up my phone, and as normal, the doorbell battery is flat, so I can't see who is there. Why can't I remember to add that to my weekly schedule of "must do checks"?

Groaning, I haul myself out of bed, pull on my silk dressing gown and glance out of the window in the spare bedroom to see who it is. Bloody Monica. I ignore her, but the stupid cow isn't giving up. She's hammering on the front door now. I stomp downstairs. She lifts the letterbox flap and speaks through it.

'Are you alright, Skye, hon? I can see your car is here, and I wanted a quick word with you.'

'I'm fine. What do you want?'

'Any chance I can come in for a cuppa? I don't want to disturb you, but I was passing.'

Like hell she was. This is what I feared; that Monica might become a hanger-on. Try to be part of my life.

'I'm rather busy at the moment.'

'I had a coffee with that lovely friend of yours, Nathan.'

Shit.

I unlock the door and open it. She stumbles inside.

'Oh,' she says, looking at me all wide-eyed. I suppose I look a fright, with bed hair and no make-up. I can count on one hand how many people have seen me like this, but if we're doing the pretend-that-you-are-my-mummy thing, then why not?

'Would you like me to make you some breakfast, love?'

'I'm not your love, Monica. You will never be a mother to me. Do you understand?'

She shrinks backwards, her shoulders curling inwards, her jaw slack. The woman repulses me with her cheap clothes, weathered face and utter lack of self-care.

I swivel away from her and walk down the hall towards the kitchen. 'I'll put the coffee machine on. I was working late last night.'

Her plastic boots make a squeaking sound on my wooden floor. 'I had such a lovely time with Nathan. I see why you like him. He's a charming man.'

I turn around to face her. 'You know nothing! My relationship with Nathan is none of your business, and you're to stay out of my life. That was the deal. In fact, why don't you leave right now? I can't be doing with any of this!' I wave my hands at her.

She takes one step backwards and then something changes in her demeanour, and for a fleeting moment, I glimpse a hardness in her – that hardness that helped her survive years of ravaging her body with drugs and alcohol, that helped her get clean. Perhaps we're more alike than I had thought.

'All I'm trying to do is be friendly, Skye. I know that little show you put on for the journalists was all a pretence, that you have no feelings for me. And that got me thinking, Skye. People change so much from when they are children, but there are so many things about you that I simply don't recognise. Not just the way you look, but the way you act.'

She has the audacity to squeeze past me and walk into the kitchen.

'What are you doing? Get out of my house!' I say as I follow her into the room. 'How could you know me, anyway? You were a drug-addled waste of space who couldn't get her shit together enough to look after me. You ruined my life.'

'Yes, yes,' she says, waving her hand, as if it's nothing, standing in the middle of my kitchen, her back to the table. 'I've been thinking. When you were in that room full of dogs at the hotel, you didn't show a flicker of fear. How is that possible?'

'Because I'm a strong woman and I overcame my fears. If you bothered to look into my programme, view all the videos I've posted on YouTube, you'll find out about all the steps I took to become a better person. So I could make sure I never turned into you.'

She shakes her head scornfully, and I'm having to dig deep to stop my temper from erupting.

'It's that fear of dogs,' Monica says, stepping closer towards me. 'You were mauled by that pit bull terrier, stuck in hospital for days, without any one to love you. Every time you look in the mirror, you must be reminded of it. In fact, I'd like to see the scar.'

Monica lunges forwards and grabs the belt of my silk dressing gown.

'Stop it, you pervert!' I screech as I try to keep the gown tied up. But she dances behind me and lifts up the hem of the gown, exposing my thighs and buttocks.

'I knew it,' she says, an edge of steel to her voice. She lets go of the gown and steps backwards. I tie the gown up tightly.

'No scar. You're not my Skye! Who are you?' She bares her rotten teeth at me.

And now it's me stumbling backwards. I grab the edge of the marble countertop, stars flickering in my vision, my stomach heaving. This cannot be happening. My world is about to unravel. Not after all these years of hard work, single-mindedness and determination. She cannot do this to me.

'I had plastic surgery,' I say quickly.

'And how come you write so easily with your right hand? I saw you writing when you were in the room with those dogs. When you were a child, Skye, you were left-handed.'

I need to think quickly. 'They taught me to write with my right hand. I had a horrible foster mum who hit the back of my hand every time I wrote or drew with my left hand.'

'Liar. Teachers stopped doing that long before you were a child.'

'How do you know? You weren't there! You were the one who failed as a mother.'

'I gave birth to Skye. Don't you think a mother would know her own child? I feel it here.' She clasps a hand to her chest. 'Stop with the lies.' Monica steps forwards so she's just a foot away. 'Who are you?'

I need to pull myself together. Quickly. Think. React. Show strength.

'Of course I'm Skye, you stupid woman.'

'You're not! You think I wouldn't recognise my own daughter. Yes, I admit I was taken in by you at first. I was desperate to reconnect with you, and imagine my joy when I discovered who you were. My daughter, a celebrity. My daughter, earning all this money, living in splendour. But you conned me, just like you've conned everyone else.'

'Get away from me,' I hiss. 'Get out of my house.'

'Not until you tell me the truth. Who are you?'

'What do you want?' I ask. 'I'll give you money. How much?'

'You think bribery is going to make me go away? You are wrong, Skye, or whoever you are.'

'I'll pay you whatever you want, enough to go and live in Australia or America, wherever you choose.'

She lets out a short laugh; then she steps backwards and starts pacing the room. 'I want my daughter. And it's not you.' She swivels around, hands on hips, her chin jutting forwards. 'I'm going to ask you once more, who are you?'

'Your daughter,' I say, but I know it sounds weak. This woman is holding all the cards, and she knows it.

'Stop with the lying! Just tell me where my daughter is.'

'It doesn't matter!'

'It matters to me. It matters a helluva lot!'

She steps to me and grabs my arms, her foul, bony fingers digging into me.

I try to shake her off. 'It doesn't matter, because she's dead!' I enjoy the way the blood drains from her walnut-shaped face.

'You're lying,' she whispers. 'You just want to hurt me.'

'I am telling the truth. We need to focus on the here and now. I can make things right for you. I can help you, Monica. What do you need? A house, a car? I'll support you for the rest of your life if you want.'

'I don't want stuff! I want my daughter.'

'Look, I can't bring back someone from the dead, but I can make your life pleasant in the here and now. Let's discuss that.'

'I'll talk to Martin, and when the journalists get onto this, they'll dig and dig until they uncover the truth. That's what you're worried about, isn't it?'

I stop myself from nodding, but she's absolutely right. I'm terrified. So terrified, I feel as if my heart is going to stop beating.

'If my Skye is dead, who are you? And why did you take on her identity?'

I need to get a grip, remember that I am in control, that I've survived far worse. I take a deep breath. 'I've tried to protect you, Monica, because the truth will hurt.'

'Tell me,' she says. She sinks into one of my kitchen chairs.

'Skye was a drug addict, just like you. I tried to help her, I tried to be her friend because she had no one in this world. Not a soul cared about her. All because you deserted your daughter when she was a helpless child.' I jab my finger at Monica. 'She died of a drugs overdose years ago.'

'Why did you take on her identity?'

'I wanted to honour her. I saw something special in her. Something that she evidently got from you.'

I thought that would appease Monica, but for some reason it angers her. She jumps up from the chair. 'You're a liar, and I'm going to get to the bottom of this! I don't believe a word you're saying. I'm going to tell the world that you're a fraud, Skye, or whatever your real name is!'

'Go ahead!' I shout. 'Who do you think people are going to believe? Me, or you? A shrivelled up, money-seeking, fame-grabbing, delusional ex-heroin addict. You won't stand a chance! Just get out of my house.'

And she does. She races out of the room, and I hear the front door slam behind her, the walls in my solid house reverberating.

I wait a few seconds, and then I scream. I am totally screwed. Totally and utterly.

Bile rushes up into my throat, and I make it to the sink just in time to throw up. I turn the tap on full and gulp down a glass of cold water. I have to struggle to keep that down. I'm trembling uncontrollably, and in my moment of weakness, I long for strong arms to wrap around me. I see Nathan's face. And that reminds me, Monica told me that she had spoken to Nathan, but our conversation went so off track, I never asked her what they talked about.

I go upstairs and take a burning hot shower. I need to pull myself together. To work out what my next plan of action will be.

An hour later, I am back in control. I open the safe installed at the back of my wardrobe and take out one of the three burner phones. I dial the only number in the address book.

'Hello.' The voice is gruff and heavily accented.

'I've got another job for you.'

'Yes.'

'I hope you're not squeamish, because this one's a woman.'

'No problem.'

'And I don't want her beaten up. I want her dead. By the end of the day.'

'Today?' He sounds surprised.

'Yes.'

24

The next day, I'm at work trying to concentrate on editing a press release that Sophie dropped on my desk. Mid-morning, I get a text message from Monica.

'Looking forward to seeing you later. Got some important things to tell you about our Skye.'

I wonder what she means, but I don't have much time to contemplate, because I have back-to-back meetings, hastily finishing up in time for Monica's arrival at 4 p.m.

But four o'clock comes and goes, and Monica doesn't arrive. I'm not overly concerned, as reliability isn't commonplace in our sector, but by 4.30 p.m. I have a sense of unease. The girls have messaged me to tell me they're both at home, so I don't need to worry about them. But Monica seemed so eager to come and see me. I find the scrap of paper she wrote on and call the number. It rings and rings and eventually goes to voice-mail. I leave a short message.

By 5 p.m., the team is packing up to go home. I try

Monica again, and still there is no answer. I look up the telephone number for Sunnyside Care Home, where Monica said she works.

'Good afternoon. My name is Nathan Edwards, and I run a charity for the homeless called Sacha's Sanctuary. I understand that Monica Walker works for you in your kitchens. She has applied to do voluntary work with us. Please can I speak to a manager?'

'Hold on one moment and I'll put you through to Mrs George.'

I listen to a mechanised version of "Lovely Day", and then a woman says hello. Once again, I explain who I am.

'I'm looking for a reference for Monica Walker, and I'm also wondering, was she in work today?'

'No, she wasn't. She dumped us in it. I was one down in the kitchens anyway, and I could have done with Monica. It's a shame, because she's been reliable up 'til now.'

'Thank you,' I say.

'Don't you want a reference?'

'Yes, I do, but I'll get back to you, if that's alright?' Hurriedly, I hang up the phone. I switch off my computer, grab my coat and briefcase, wave goodnight to Ash and rush to the car. I look up Monica's address on my satnav. It's only fifteen minutes out of my way. I ring Isla from the car.

'I'm going to be half an hour late. Will you girls be alright? If you're hungry, heat up the pie in the fridge.'

'It's cool, Dad. No hurry.'

MONICA LIVES in a low-rise brick building, a council-owned property, divided up into small flats. It looks modern, and although the exterior is stark and there are no gardens or parks anywhere nearby, it's within walking distance of the centre of town. 12A is on the second floor, so I walk up the external staircase and along the corridor on the upper level. I knock on the front door. There is no answer. I try again. Still no answer. I try to peer into the window, but the lights are off, and I can't see anything. On a whim, I try the door handle, and to my surprise, the door is unlocked. I step in cautiously.

'Hello!' I say. 'Monica!'

I step inside, switching on the hall light. There is a short, narrow corridor, and I notice Monica's anorak hanging on a hook on the wall, her trainers neatly lined up on the floor underneath. I take a few more steps forwards, my heart pumping hard. Why is the front door unlocked, and why isn't she answering? Cautiously, I walk into the living room, which is a modest-sized room with a small kitchenette on the back wall. There is an old sofa covered in a stained brown chenille fabric, and a white plastic table and two plastic chairs. A small television, one of those old-fashioned ones, box-like, sits on the floor. I back out of the room and walk along the short corridor. I can see that there is a bathroom at the end, with its door open and a door to the left. 'Hello,' I say again. The door is ajar, but I knock first anyway.

'Monica?' I repeat. I step inside and immediately stagger backwards, trying not to gag, stumbling against the wall. Monica is lying flat on her back, her arms spread out to the side, a needle sticking out of the artery of her right arm. Her eyes are open, glazed, unseeing; her skin paper white. I take a moment to steady myself, and then I rush towards her, placing my hand on her forehead, trying to find a pulse on her wrist. But I know it's futile. Monica is cold. Dead.

I think I'm going to throw up. I rush out of the flat, gulping in fresh air, trying to steady myself by leaning against the wall. She told me that she was off the drugs; she was so proud of it. And she seemed totally coherent yesterday, loving life, embracing her new start. It doesn't make sense. But then addiction defies logic; I've learned that over the past few years. Perhaps she was doing one last shot as a celebration of reuniting with her daughter. I jab 999 into my phone, but my fingers are shaking too much, and I have to try again.

'Emergency. Which service do you require? Police, ambulance or fire?'

'Ambulance and police.'

'Connecting you now.'

'What is the phone number you're calling from?'

'This one. My mobile.'

The control assistant recites my number back to me.

'What is the exact location of the incident?'

I give Monica's address.

'And what has happened?'

'She's dead. There's a heroin needle sticking out of her arm. I think she overdosed.'

'Is the person breathing?'

'No,' I say too loudly, 'she's dead!'

And then things move quickly, although in the moment it seems to take for ever. Me waiting outside the building, pacing backwards and forwards, wringing my hands, realising that my girls are at home waiting for me, and once again I'm letting them down. I call Isla.

'Darling, something has happened, and I'm going to be late home. Are you okay alone?'

'Yes. Are you alright?' She must sense the unease in

my voice, so I have to reassure her, tell her that I'm perfectly okay, just helping some people in need.

'Don't worry about us,' Isla says. But I do. I worry that Skye is going to turn up at our house again. I can't help wondering whether she had something to do with Monica's death. It's a stretch, but I'm so uncomfortable around the woman, and still suspicious that she drugged me. Would she have gone so far as to give her mother an overdose of heroin?

'In the unlikely event that Skye turns up, don't let her in,' I say.

'What?' Isla's voice is questioning. 'Why? She's alright.'

'Just do as I say, please; otherwise I'll have to ask Mrs Farraday to come over.'

That does the trick. Isla promises to lock the doors and not let anyone in.

The police arrive first, followed by an ambulance, but the paramedics are wasting their time. Monica is long dead. And then, time slows down. The building becomes a crime scene; more cars arrive; tape gets put up; neighbours gather in little huddles in doorways, and I just want to go home. Poor Monica. The woman didn't deserve this.

And then I think of Skye. How will she feel about the mother she has only just reconnected with dying in such circumstances? I suppose the press will have a field day, and even Skye won't be able to control that.

'Mr Edwards, we just need to take your statement.'

'Yes, of course.' And so I repeat exactly what I have already told two policemen previously; how I was concerned that Monica didn't turn up at our offices; how she hadn't been at work today and why none of this makes any sense because she was clean. I looked straight into her eyes. I know she was.

'And how exactly do you know Monica Walker?' the policeman asks.

'Through Skye. Monica Walker is Skye's mother, and they were only recently reunited. I don't think they had a good relationship.'

I practice in front of the mirror. Over and over again, just like an actress, as I have done so many times before. I assess my facial expressions, my tone of voice, my phraseology. I have even studied micro-expressions, those tiny little facial tics that no one except a keenly trained expert would pick up on, those minis-cule giveaways. An extra blink. The involuntary snarl of a lip or upward movement of an eyebrow. Your body talks whether you want it to or not. I've worked hard on that over the years, and it's paid off. Often, I record myself and play it back, but not today. That would be stupid.

Such attention to detail is a necessary tool for success when so much of your life is played out in front of the camera. Some influencers cake their faces in make-up in the hope that it will cover those little giveaways, or they use Botox and fillers. Not me. I've learned the hard way, with no shortcuts, and I'm good at it.

The doorbell rings shortly before 9 p.m. I'm in the living room, my feet on the sofa, curtains pulled, watching the television. Half a glass of wine stands on the coffee table, the rim lined with my pale pink lipstick. Not that I have actually drunk any wine. I charged the doorbell earlier today in anticipation. It's playing out exactly as I thought.

Wearing thick socks and no shoes, I walk to the front door and open it slightly, keeping the chain on.

'Hello,' I say, my eyes wide. 'Can I help you?'

It's a policeman and woman, neither dressed in uniform. Thank goodness it's dark outside and that they're driving an unmarked car. At least the neighbours won't spot them. Tomorrow, I'll start househunting properly. Somewhere with land and at the end of a long drive, far away from any prying eyes.

'Skye Walker?' the woman asks.

'Yes,' I say, making my eyes even bigger.

Both of them flash their police badges, but I barely glance at them. 'What's happened?' I can feel the blood draining from my face as I unhook the chain.

'Can we come in?'

'Yes, of course. Of course.' I stumble slightly as I stand back from the door, letting them pass me. I lead them through to the living room and turn the television off.

'Please sit down,' I say, but I remain standing, totally still.

'Is there anyone else in the house?'

'No.'

'Is there anyone you can call to be with you?'

I shake my head. 'What's happened?'

'I'm afraid we have bad news. Your mother, Monica Walker, has been found dead.'

I sink backwards and collapse onto my armchair, my mouth a neat little circle, my body trembling ever so slightly.

'No!' My hand rushes to cover my mouth. 'No,' I whisper.

'We're very sorry. We believe she died from a drugs overdose. She was found in her flat a few hours ago.'

I turn away from them, shaking my head. Slowly I swivel around to face them, sitting forwards in the chair, my hands on my knees and tears welling in my eyes.

'She promised me she was off the drugs, that she hasn't touched them in years. I can't believe she did that, just when we were reunited.' I let out a little sob. 'I'm sorry,' I whisper. 'It's such a shock.' I let the silence settle for a moment, and then speak. 'Is it common for people to have a relapse?'

'It can be,' the policewoman says. 'We would like to ask you a few questions about your mother, if we may.'

'Yes, of course. Anything I can do to help.'

'When did you last see Monica?'

'It must have been on Monday afternoon. Oh goodness, the article in the papers comes out tomorrow. It's probably going to print right now! I have to ring that journalist!' I jump up from the chair.

There is no way that I am telling the police that Monica was here this morning, and I just have to pray that she wasn't caught on a security camera anywhere. But there is no reason for them to be looking at footage. An overdose is an overdose.

'Please sit down, Skye. We need to talk first. I realise this must be a terrible shock to you.'

I sit down slowly. 'Yes, it is. But in some ways, I'm not surprised, just saddened. Monica has been a junkie her whole life. That's why I was taken into care in the first place, bounced from one foster home to another. But I believed her this time; I really believed her. We did an interview together on Monday afternoon at the Belleview Hotel near Gatwick. She seemed fine then, jovial even. The journalist, Martin Rodriguez, will confirm that. The article he's written is going in the papers tomorrow, all about our reunion and how I've forgiven Monica and welcomed her back into my life.' I let out another little whimper. 'It seems so cruel. Just when I thought I had got my mother back, just when Monica thought she had her daughter back, for it all to be ripped away. But no. I'm not surprised. She's a weak person, and I suppose all the publicity must have taken its toll. She said she wanted it; she came to find me, but it must have been too much. I feel like it's my fault. If she hadn't found me, maybe the fame wouldn't have gotten to her.'

'No need to blame yourself,' the policewoman says, although I don't see any sympathy in her face. I need to rein the words in. She carries on with the questions. 'Have you visited Monica's home?'

I shake my head. 'No. I don't even know where she lives. She came here a couple of times, and then we met in the hotel. We've only been reunited for less than a week. What's going to happen now? Can I organise a funeral?'

'Not yet. There will be a post-mortem, and if it's confirmed that Monica died as a result of drugs, then the coroner will hold an inquest. Unfortunately, this can take time – months in some cases.'

'Will you be able to find out who supplied Monica with the drugs and prosecute them?' I ask.

'We will do our best, but please don't raise your hopes.'

I let the tears flow then. 'I'm sorry,' I sniff. 'This has affected me more than I would have expected. It seems so cruel, just when Mum returned...' I let my words fade away.

'Does Monica have any other next of kin?'

I shake my head. 'I don't think so. In fact, I know she doesn't; otherwise I wouldn't have been palmed off to foster care.'

'In which case, we will be passing your details on to the coroner, and we will keep you posted with progress on the post-mortem and inquest. We may need to talk to you again.'

'Of course, that's no problem. If I can't organise a funeral yet, can I at least have a memorial service? I want to do something to honour her life and remember these few special days.'

'You can do whatever you like, but unfortunately it will be without her body.'

We all stand up, and I accompany them to the door. I watch as they get into their car and drive away. I then walk back into the house and telephone Martin. I need to get all of these things out of the way before I celebrate. Old Monica deserves a toast to her sad life.

Martin answers on the second ring, as most people do when my name flashes up on their screens.

'I've had some terrible news,' I say as I pace around the living room. 'Monica was found dead this afternoon. The police think it's an overdose. Is it too late to pull the article?' I keep my fingers firmly crossed that the answer is no.

'Bloody hell,' Martin says. 'I'm sorry to hear that, Skye. You must be devastated.'

'Yes,' I say, trying to keep my face straight.

'There's no way the editor will let me pull the article, but we might be able to add something to it, in her memory and all that. Are the police alright with this being in the public domain?'

I don't know, and I don't care. 'Yes, it's not a problem. Monica would have become famous by association;

she probably already is. And just when I thought I got my mother back.'

'Tragic,' Martin says. 'I'm very sorry for your loss. Are you up to giving a statement?'

'Just say that I'm devastated to lose my mother within a week of reuniting with her. That it appears she overdosed, and the police are investigating. Although this is a personal tragedy, I won't let it get in the way of my work. I will grieve in private, Martin,' I say. 'My work has to come first, and particularly my charitable commitments. I am due to take part in the Piranha charity sailing race at the weekend.'

'And you'll still do it?'

'The show must go on.'

'Really?' There is an uncomfortable pause, but then he says, 'Thanks for letting me know, Skye. And again, condolences.' He hangs up.

I open a bottle of champagne and laugh hysterically when the cork pops right out and hits the ceiling.

I only drink one glass, because this is a private celebration and I have work to do. I pop a spoon into the top of the bottle and place it back into the fridge. I then go upstairs and fling open my wardrobe. I remove a black polo neck jumper that makes me look pale and shrug it on. I remove any traces of lipstick and put on a pair of designer sunglasses. Then I ruffle up my duvet and pillows and sit on the bed, legs crossed. I perch my phone on a mini tripod and press record. I know it's a risk doing a Facebook and Instagram Live, but I think I'll come across as more authentic if I stumble over my words.

'Hello, everyone.' I pause and sniff. 'I've had some terrible news, and I wanted to share it with you first, so you hear it from me and not the media. As some of you will know, I reconnected with my mother last week.' I turn my head away from the camera and swallow a sob. I take a tissue and blow my nose. 'I am totally devastated to let you know that she passed away today. I can't say any more at the moment, but as you will appreciate, I am distraught. It seems so cruel that I only had my mother again for less than a week, and now she's gone for ever. Please give me a few hours to process this and regroup. With love to you all.' I sniff loudly and lean forwards to switch off my phone.

That should do it.

As I watch the hundreds of thousands of condolence messages pouring in, I realise I need to plan the next few days very carefully. If we can't have a funeral for Monica, I need to organise some public memorial and do it quickly so that I can get on with my life and put everything else into place. The charity sailing race is too high profile an event to bail out of at short notice, and it also gives me some more time to get closer to Nathan.

THE NEXT MORNING, I am awake early. I read Martin's article online, and true to his word, he has written an emotional piece about my reunion with "tragic" Monica. There is an addendum to the article, one sentence saying that Monica was found dead yesterday. I am the story of the day, with even the broadsheets running short pieces about Monica's death just days after our reunion. Social media is awash with comments, the vast majority sending me their sympathies. I am very loved this morning.

You would think that I should feel that love, but I don't. The problem is that even though I have that warm, tingling feeling inside, that knowledge that whole swathes of the population know who I am, and they care deeply about my life, it is a one-way relationship. I don't know or care about them. My only concern is that I look good in their eyes, and I achieve that with aplomb. It's strange how at moments like this, when my public recognition and adoration is at its highest, I feel the loneliest. I don't have friends. Everyone wants a piece of me, but they don't know who I really am. I have to erect walls to protect myself, so they only see the shiny facade and don't get to know the imperfect centre.

The same goes for lovers. Holden served his purpose, but we both knew it was a relationship of convenience, to mutually raise each other's profiles. It allowed me to jet around the world and be seen on the arm of a handsome, successful athlete. For him, I was a pretty face who allowed him to shag girls and boys in every port whilst retaining an air of respectability. Such a relationship works for a while, but it's not satisfactory. And now, after all of these hard years, I crave more than satisfactory.

I dress carefully in a demure, long-sleeved black dress. When I have done my hair and make-up, I set up the camera and record myself once again.

'I can't thank you enough for all of your condolence messages regarding the sudden loss of my mother. These are extremely hard and emotional days. I hope the police won't mind me telling you that my mother was found with a heroin needle in her arm. I believed her when she told me she was clean, but it appears that wasn't the case. I have told you before about the perils of drug-taking, and now I have first-hand experience. Drugs have taken my mother.' I blink hard and sniff, then take a deep breath as if to compose myself. 'I have decided that the best way to commemorate my mother is to carry on with my work. This Sunday sees the annual Piranha Sailing Regatta, which, as many of you know, is the UK's biggest charity yacht race. Last year, I sailed with the DJ Purple Dollarz, and although we didn't win, we jointly raised over a million pounds for charity. This year, my partner will be Nathan Edwards, the inspirational founder of Sacha's Sanctuary, a leading charity for the homeless. I will not let my personal tragedy get in the way of my work. I intend to raise a million pounds for Sacha's Sanctuary, and I hope that you will support me in making that dream come true. Remember, if I can reach for the sky, you can too. Be true to you.'

I CHECK and double-check all of my messages and emails, but there is nothing from Nathan. That's strange. I assumed he of all people would have sent me a condolence note. I hope he isn't getting cold feet about the boat race, or perhaps he has been in a media vacuum for the past hours and genuinely doesn't know about Monica's death. I decide to call him, but his mobile goes to voicemail. I then try his office number.

A woman answers. 'I'm sorry, but Nathan isn't in today. Can anyone else help you?'

'No,' I say, hanging up. I am tempted to drive around to his house, but I restrain myself. If I come across as too pushy now, I might sabotage my own plans, and I certainly can't risk that. Instead, I send him a text message.

'*You might have heard that my mother died. I'm in shock, but it's important we still do the race, for the sake of Sacha's Sanctuary and my fans. I'm sure you know better than most the need to put on a positive front to the world. Can't wait until Sunday when we can celebrate after winning the race! Together we will conquer the world! With love to you and the girls, Sx*'

My next call is to a relocation agent, a woman called

Camilla Steading, recommended to me by Tiana when I briefly mentioned I was looking to move to a new house.

'You can't use an estate agent,' Tiana said, horror in her voice. 'You're too high profile. You'll need to use a specialist who will do everything for you and keep your name and house private. Camilla is the epitome of discretion. Everyone who's anyone uses her.'

I telephone Camilla and introduce myself. I don't get the same reaction of stuttering or awe, and I actually wonder if she knows who I am. It's only when I mention that Tiana is my agent that she perks up.

'What exactly are you looking for?' she asks, in a nasally, cut-glass accent.

'A big family home, with considerable grounds.'

'What family do you have?' she asks.

'Two girls. Two gorgeous teenage girls.'

26

A letter to my truest friend, Skye:

D*earest Skye,*
This is to say sorry. I know you will never read this letter, but I need to write it. You deserve an explanation, and I want to tell you everything that has happened since you've been gone. And I want to share with you all the plans I have for the future. I think you'd be proud of me.

We need to go back to that day, well, the evening before, actually.

D*INNER with my cousins was unbearable. Dad was going on and on about 'our little charity case'. You. 'The bigwigs from the supermarket were so impressed with Skye,' Dad gushed. 'You should have seen her, making up all those cardboard boxes, never complaining. And my foreman said she's the fastest worker he's ever had on the team. I have to admit I* *wasn't too keen on having Skye in the house, but I don't think she's nicked anything yet!'*

I wanted to shout at Dad, tell him what a hypocrite he was. It was Dad who forgot you at work that afternoon. He sickened me, and I could tell that you felt the same way about him. You used to throw him scornful looks when you thought no one was looking. All he ever did was boast how clever and rich he was, what a successful compassionate businessman he was. That evening, as normal, he was flashing the cash, ordering two bottles of Bollinger just to make Uncle Jan and Aunt Tereza look inferior. Even Mum looked a bit uncomfortable.

'It's amazing how Skye has adapted to living with us,' Mum said. *'She's a bit rough around the edges, but she always says thank you, and she helps around the house. Not like our Tiffany.'*

'Yes, you could learn a few things from Skye,' Dad scowled at me.

I wanted to scream. They were all forgetting that it was me who found you, me who brought you home, me who gave you my money.

'Can you believe it! The girl has never been on an airplane, not even a commercial flight.' Mum laughed. *'We're taking her with us tomorrow when we fly to Jersey for the weekend. She's beside herself with excitement.'*

Uncle Jan and Aunt Tereza smiled awkwardly. I almost felt sorry for them, having all our excessive wealth rubbed in their faces when they still lived in a communist era-built apartment in a tower block on the outskirts of Prague.

'It's good for Tiffany to have someone of her own age living in the house,' Dad said. *'She's become very self-centred and lazy. It's always the worry with having an only child, isn't it? They think they're the centre of everyone's universe, never having to share anything. At least you don't have to worry about spoiling your two.'*

I stood up then, scraping my chair backwards and grabbing my purse. My parents were talking about me as if I weren't there, so I might as well not be.

'Tiffany, darling, where are you going?' Mum asked. My aunt and uncle glanced from side to side with embarrassment.

'The loo,' I said through gritted teeth.

I did go to the toilets initially, but then I grabbed my coat and I walked straight out of the restaurant. Mum and Dad didn't see me leaving, which was perfect. I booked a taxi, but while I was waiting, an idea came to me.

The cab pulled up. 'Changed my mind. I won't be needing a lift after all.'

'You'll be charged a cancellation fee,' he said.

'No problem.' He threw me a strange look, but turned the car around and drove off.

'I was getting worried about you,' Mum said when I returned to the table and sat down. They were onto their main courses, and my food was getting cold.

'Sorry, wasn't feeling great, so I stepped outside for some fresh air.'

Dad ignored me, as he normally did, and during the rest of the meal, I zoned out. I had a plan to formulate, and in order to execute it properly, I needed to act normally and keep my head down.

THE NEXT MORNING, I got up at 6 a.m., pulled on some warm clothes and crept out of the house and into the hangar. I ran my hands over the Cessna, a feeling of sadness sweeping through my body. It seemed a shame to be saying goodbye to this lovely little plane, but then I reminded myself. Soon, I'd be able to get a bigger and better one. It's funny how sometimes everything aligns perfectly. My plan wouldn't have stood a chance of working if it had been mid-summer, but luckily for me, it was unseasonably cold outside and would be *even colder up there in the sky. I knew Dad would switch on the heating system immediately, because Mum feels the cold. I located where the exhaust attaches to the engine and gently loosened the V band clamp. I had no idea how quickly the exhaust gases would leak into the heating system, or even if they would, but hopefully sufficient carbon monoxide would waft through before they touched down in Jersey. I didn't want my parents to suffer; I'm not that cruel. No, it was far better if they fell asleep and were unconscious when the plane went down.*

Shortly after 7 a.m., you and my parents were in the kitchen, munching your breakfast. You couldn't sit still; you were that excited about flying in a private plane. Normally, I couldn't bear the sound of chewing, it made me want to scream, but that morning, I barely noticed it.

'I've filed the flight plan and did the preflight checks,' I said nonchalantly. Just because I didn't enjoy my A levels and didn't want to study engineering didn't mean I hadn't studied how an aeroplane worked. I had a good teacher who was vigilant in teaching me about preflight checks. The thing is, if you know what to look for to ensure things don't go wrong, you know exactly what to do if you want things to go wrong.

'Shame you don't show the same diligence towards your schoolwork,' Dad said. His typically sarcastic comment only added to the certainty of what I was doing.

'That's where you're wrong!' I raised my voice, feeling a rush of empowerment. 'I got a last-minute interview at Bristol University this afternoon. The email came through yesterday.'

'Why didn't you tell us, love?' Mum asks. 'That's wonderful news!'

You looked up at me, surprise on your face, but I ignored you.

'Because I wasn't sure if I wanted to go,' I said.

'Of course you need to go!' Dad exclaimed.

'I want to come to Jersey with you. I like it there.'

'Don't be so stupid! You can go to Jersey any time. An interview at a good university could change the course of your life. You are going to attend that interview whether you like it or not! Book yourself on a commercial flight from Bristol to Jersey and come and join us this evening.'

Dad was so predictable. 'Are you sure?' I said, my back turned towards you all just in case my flaming cheeks gave me away. If there was one person who might see through my lies, it was you.

'Of course I'm bloody sure!' Dad said.

'I'll amend the flight plan, then.' I strode out of the room, a massive smile on my face. You all fell for that one: hook, line and sinker. I didn't have an interview. I hadn't even applied for any universities. All I needed to do was change the flight plan number of passengers from four to three.

Then I paused. Why not use this opportunity to get rid of you, too? I couldn't decide. Should I, or shouldn't I? You were getting on my nerves. Not only did you get all those likes when you did that video on my YouTube channel, but Mum and Dad seemed to prefer you to me. But if I was to spare you, I'd have to persuade you not to get on the plane, and you'd seemed so pathetically excited at the chance to fly in a private jet. And then I thought about how you snubbed me and threw me those looks of pity, and I thought, what the hell. It would be much easier to keep to the original plan and let you get on the plane, wiping away all traces of you. I changed the number of passengers from four to two. No one would miss poor little orphan Skye.

I didn't even say goodbye to you. How can one say goodbye to people when you know it might be the last time you'll ever see them? I needed to be resolute and not allow Mum to be nice and potentially change my mind. But then again, I had no idea if it really would be the last time I saw you. Perhaps the loosening of that clamp wouldn't do *anything. Perhaps life would go on, and I really would be joining you and my parents in Jersey for the weekend.*

I LEFT the house in a taxi before you all left for Jersey. I would have liked to have watched the Cessna speed along the grass runway and take off, but I had to disappear for a couple of hours and pretend I was on my way to Bristol. When I was sure you had gone, I got a taxi and returned home. It wasn't until late afternoon that I allowed myself to feel. I tried ringing Mum's and Dad's mobiles over and over. There was no answer. Eventually, it was on the news. That's how I found out that my parents' plane had disappeared off radar and come down in the sea. That's when I knew that the plane would have filled up with carbon monoxide. I knew I should have felt guilt and devastation that my parents were dead, or even worry that I might be found out. But I didn't. I felt a heady rush and the lightest feeling I've ever sensed. I was free. I had money. I could do whatever the hell I wanted, and it certainly wouldn't be anything to do with studying engineering or running a salad business. I barely thought about you.

For the first couple of weeks, everything went to plan. Uncle Jan and Aunt Tereza tipped up to comfort me, but they couldn't stay long. My cousins were younger than me and being looked after by their grandmother in Prague. They invited me to go back to the Czech Republic with them, but I insisted on staying at home. I couldn't think of anything worse than being shacked up in a tiny grey apartment in a country where I didn't speak the language. I wanted to enjoy my freedom.

It wasn't until the day of the funeral (minus the bodies, because fortunately for me, they were never found) that I discovered the catastrophe my parents had left behind.

I was standing outside the church, wearing dark glasses, accepting the condolences from my parents' friends and colleagues, most of whom I didn't know, when a man in a dark suit and a heavy black overcoat came up to me. He had a rim of white hair circling a bald head and thick white bushy eyebrows. 'Tiffany, dear, you don't know me, but my name is Arthur Wilson.' He pumped my hand up and down. 'I am your father's solicitor and executor. We need to have a conversation. I realise it's a difficult time for you, but perhaps I could come to your house at 6 p.m. this evening?'

I shrugged. What did I know about legalities and wills? My bank account was running low, and I desperately needed to get access to my parents' funds, so I eagerly agreed to his visit.

'Sit down, dear,' Arthur Wilson said a few hours later when I led him into the living room. I almost retorted, you don't have the right to tell me what to do in my own home, but there was something about his expression that stilled me.

'I'm afraid it's not good news,' he said as he settled into Dad's armchair. 'Tomorrow, King Salads will be put into bankruptcy. It has been wobbling on the brink for some time, but the sudden demise of its owner and principal shareholder has sent the banks into panic mode.'

'I couldn't care less,' I said. How naive I was aged seventeen. 'I don't intend on working there anyway.'

'The thing is, my dear, this house and everything your parents owned is mortgaged to the hilt. You are going to have to sell all their assets. The houses, the boat, their cars. The banks own everything.'

'What do you mean?' I couldn't process what he was trying to say.

'Your parents borrowed everything. I tried to warn Jeffrey, but he didn't… Anyway, I'm afraid that the burden now falls on you. Everything will need to be repaid, and I fear that their borrowing was such that there will be nothing left. In fact, you will be inheriting debts.'

'What do you mean, nothing?' I jumped up. It didn't make sense to me.

'Look, Tiffany, why don't you come to my offices tomorrow and we can have a chat through everything. I'll explain the situation in detail.'

The implications of what Mr Wilson said didn't truly hit me until the following afternoon when I answered the doorbell to two burly men.

'We're here to take repossession of one Rolls-Royce, one Porsche and one Mini.'

'Sorry, my parents aren't here,' I said, trying to shut the door on them.

'We know, love. Your parents died. We've come to collect the cars. Now don't make it difficult for us. We don't want any unpleasant business, do we?'

They showed me the court documents where it listed the registration details of the three cars. They showed me various other official-looking documents, and although I couldn't tell whether they were legitimate or not, based on what Mr Wilson had told me, I assumed they were. I was scared, and what seventeen-year-old, recently orphaned and living alone, wouldn't be? They took the Porsche and the Rolls.

'I'll be back for the Mini,' the smaller of the two men said. But there was no way that I was going to let them take my car. I ran upstairs and dragged two large suitcases from the loft. I jammed as many of my belongings in them as I could and lugged them downstairs to the garage. I heaved them into the boot of my car, and I drove away. How stupid I was. How very ignorant. It wasn't until a few months later that I realised how much you could have helped me. You would have told me to forget my teddy bears and fill the car up with mother's jewellery and all the valuables I could fit in. But I didn't have you, and I followed my childish heart.

I stayed that night in a Travel Lodge. I thought I was all grown up, checking in by myself, lying spreadeagled on the bed in that soulless hotel room. But I didn't sleep well. I missed the security of my own bed, surrounded by my childhood possessions and all those teddy bears and dolls that creeped you out. So the next morning, I drove back home. I would have driven straight into the drive, but I saw a lorry with the words Fast Transit Removals on it waiting at our gates, so I parked up a little further down the road, and I walked along the side of the lane and hopped over the stile where the public footpath ran along the field behind our house. And then I realised that it was all real. Strangers were emptying out our house, taking everything. Literally everything. And Mr Wilson was standing there talking to a man with a clipboard. I watched as container after container was filled up, and then an estate agent came along with one of those big signs and put it next to the gates. It said 'For Sale'.

I knew in that moment that I had no life here. Everything I had taken for granted had gone. I destroyed my parents for no reason, because they had already destroyed themselves, and me. I had nothing. Just the contents of those two suitcases and, for now, my car. If I didn't disappear, they would take those too and still come back for more. And you. You were just collateral damage. I tried to imagine what you would do if you were in my position, and thinking about your resilience gave me strength. If you could survive with nothing, so could I.

I drove and I drove, heading further and further north. I had never been to Scotland, but that's where I ended up. Edinburgh. I tried to sell the car through a reputable garage, but when the salesmen frowned and disappeared around the back for too long, I legged it. In the end I sold the Mini for cash, far below it's worth, I'm sure, to a dodgy back-street garage. But at least I had some money to keep me going for a while. All that time I took inspiration from you, Skye, my one and only friend. Now I had the chance to be the person I really wanted to be, and how ironic it was that I got the authenticity that I desperately craved. I became Skye Walker on my second day *in Edinburgh, and Tiffany Larkin was gone for ever. I am your legacy, and I think you'd like that. I don't know if anyone tried to look for me, but if they did, I never found out about it. I scrimped and saved for a nose job, and with a change of hairstyle and clever make-up contouring, even I didn't recognise myself in the mirror. It wasn't long before I got traction as a social media star. With single-minded dedication, it's possible to make it work. Yes, I owe a lot to you, to poor homeless Skye, whom no one cared about when she disappeared.*

ALL THESE YEARS ON, *I rarely think about Tiffany. I am Skye. I talk like her, I look like her, I act like her. I have become her. I have fully morphed into you. I'm sorry about your mum. Actually, I'm not really sorry, and I don't think you would be either. Monica deserved what she got. She was never there for you, was she? I think you'd approve of me giving her those five minutes of fame. I'm glad you never got to meet her again. You deserved a better mother than her.*

And here we are. My life is almost perfect. I say almost, because I'm missing love. True love. Not that phony adoration from millions of people who don't really know you, but the honest, simple love that defines the core of a family. Although I despised both of them, I think Mum and Dad had it. I've no idea what Mum saw in Dad, but there must have been something. I reckon she would have laid her life down for Dad. I want someone to do that for me. But I've never let anyone get close enough.

I've thought long and hard about my life and my success. I've got the fame and the recognition. Everyone knows my (our, I suppose) name. The link-up with Sacha's Sanctuary was inspired, because it makes me appear kind and compassionate, and it lends credibility to my backstory of homelessness. And now there's only one thing missing. A husband.

You would love Nathan. He is perfect. I'm sorry you won't be there to be my maid of honour, but I'll think of you on our wedding day. I promise.

Why Nathan? I hear you ask. I suppose it was just serendipity that helped me find him. Tiana, my agent, suggested I get involved with a charity, so I did some online searches on local charities. There's a lot written up about Nathan, but it was his profile picture on his website that was the clincher. He's mature, attractive but not ridiculously handsome, older, and in the flesh, he's even sexier than his photos suggest, yet he doesn't realise it. In fact, he reminds me a little of my flying instructor. You remember him? And best of all, Nathan has a ready-made family with a vacancy.

I don't want children. What if I made the same mistakes that my parents did? What if my child tried – or even worse – succeeded in killing me? No, my genes have to stop with me. That's why a ready-made family is perfect. Teenagers who will shortly be fleeing the nest, fledglings who will adore me and help disseminate my brand. And girls, they had to be girls.

Tomorrow, Nathan and I are going on a yacht race, just me and him out on the sea. I'm going to let you into a secret, Skye. Nathan's and my futures are inextricably tied together. It won't surprise you to know that I have two plans. I'm hoping that plan A is the one that works out. But don't worry, I have a plan B. I always have a plan B.

But that's enough of my ramblings for tonight. Now I must hurry and prepare for tomorrow's race.

Dearest Skye. You were my only friend, and you still are. I just wish I had realised it at the time.

'I don't want to do the charity sailing race,' I say to Ash. It's Friday afternoon, and we are holed up in the meeting room, which seems to be our new home.

'No choice, mate,' Ash says. 'There's going to be national press coverage. BBC, ITV, Sky and all the papers. Sacha's Sanctuary will get unprecedented news coverage. It will propel us into the stratosphere.'

'I don't want to go out on a boat with Skye. She makes me uneasy.'

'Oh, come on. That's a bit dramatic. She's got a crush on you, and you should be flattered.'

'I'm serious, Ash. I have a bad feeling about all of this. How devastating do you think it would be if I pull out last minute?'

He shrugs his shoulders and looks away from me. 'At the end of the day, this is your charity, and if you don't want to go, then don't.' He stands up and grabs his notebook. 'I've got a few emails to finish up.' Ash leaves the room.

I groan. Ash isn't the demonstrative type, but it's

obvious he's disappointed and thinks it's a mistake for me not to go, but needs must. I have to put my family above the charity. I walk back to my desk and take a long time to compose an email to Skye, but eventually decide the shorter, the better.

Dear Skye,

My apologies for letting you down at the last minute. Unfortunately, I won't be able to make the sailing race tomorrow. I wish you the very best of luck with it and hope you can find someone to replace me.

Best,

Nathan.

THE MOMENT I walk through the door at home, Chloe pounces on me. 'Skye has invited us to go to the yacht race with you tomorrow, and we're going to be in the VIP lounge with all the stars and the press, and afterwards she's booked us into a suite in this luxury hotel! And she's sending a car for us tomorrow morning.' Chloe dances around the kitchen, fizzing with excitement.

Didn't Skye get my email? 'I'm sorry, darling, but–'

Chloe cuts through my words. 'Skye came into school this morning, and she spoke at assembly, and she told the whole school that Isla and me are her VIP guests, and she's going to raise money so we can have a photography studio at school. Mr Withers, our headmaster, came up to Isla afterwards and thanked her for introducing Skye to the school.'

I have to turn away from Chloe so she doesn't see the dismay on my face. Skye is very clever. She knows exactly how to get to me: through my children. The girls will be gutted if I say we're not going, but I can't let them change my mind. I run my fingers through my hair and grind my teeth. I try to rationalise why I don't want to do the sailing race, and other than having a bad gut feeling about it, I have no valid reasons. Yes, Skye is pushy. Yes, she has come onto me and made it very obvious she wants more than a business relationship. Yes, Monica has just died, but the police seem to think it was a drugs overdose. Yes, Skye manipulates people and the media to get the results she wants. Yes, Skye thinks she can buy affection.

But none of those reasons add up to anything more than me disliking the woman. I wish I could talk this over with someone. Not just someone, but Marie.

'Go and do your homework, darling,' I say to Chloe, 'Otherwise, you'll be going nowhere tomorrow.'

I walk upstairs to my bathroom, shut the door and pull out my mobile phone. My fingers hesitate over the call button. Marie left me over Skye, and here I am wanting to ask her advice about the woman. But mostly, I just want to talk to her. I press the call button, and to my surprise and relief, Marie answers.

'I miss you. I miss you so much,' I say, my throat choking with emotion. It's true. How I wish she were here with me right now.

'I miss you too,' Marie says quietly.

And then we talk. Really talk. She tells me everything she's been doing these past days, and I do the same. I tell her about how I was beaten up, and how I found Monica dead, and she's horrified that she wasn't here for me. And then I tell her that I'm bailing out of the charity yacht race tomorrow because I really don't want to go.

'No, Nathan. You cannot cancel. Think of the good it will do for the charity, and your girls have had enough disappointments and unhappiness over the past few years. They deserve a treat. I can't stand that Skye woman, but I think you're overreacting.'

'Really?' I say with surprise. 'I'll go if you will come home.'

'Don't do it for me. Do it for Sacha's Sanctuary and your daughters.'

I sigh. I know she's right. 'I still want you to come home.'

'Call me tomorrow after the race,' Marie says.

'I love you,' I say.

She sighs. '*Á demain.*'

I walk back into the bedroom and sink onto the bed. At least Marie is talking to me now, and if she thinks I should go, I suppose I should. Hopefully it'll be too late, and Skye will have found a replacement for me. I send her a text message.

'Further to my earlier email, have you found a replacement for me?'

A text pings back almost instantly. 'What email? What replacement? Everything is organised! The car will be at your house at 7 a.m. to collect you and the girls.'

I DON'T EVEN HAVE to wake Isla and Chloe. They are up before me, and we are all ready when the doorbell rings at 7 a.m. When I see the black limousine, I have a sinking feeling, wondering whether Skye is in the car, ready to further ingratiate herself to my children. I lock the house and follow the girls. To my relief, she isn't inside, and the driver reassures me that we are his only passengers.

The journey takes just under two hours. For most of that time, I doze and try not to think about lurching up and down on waves in the company of a woman I distrust. We are dropped off at the harbour entrance. I stare at all of the yachts, in their different shapes and sizes, and breathe in the tangy, salty air. It sounds like lots of little bells are ringing, as hooks bang into aluminium masts, creating a gentle cacophony in the wind.

I've never had a yearning to sail, probably because the sea has always felt like an uncontrollable, seething mass. I am rational enough to realise that my apprehension is one hundred percent down to the drowning of my little cousin and my consequent weakness at swimming. It's the mountains that call me, much to Marie's delight. I am a strong skier and a proficient rock climber. I make a promise to myself. Next week, I will palm the girls off to friends for a couple of nights and fly out to Switzerland, to tell Marie that I can't live without her.

My thoughts are tugged back to the here and now when I see Skye jogging towards us, her hair tied back in a ponytail. She's wearing a baseball cap, a thick navy jacket and waterproof trousers, which, somehow, she's made to look stylish.

'Hi, everyone!' she says. My girls beam at her. 'Hey,' she says to me, standing on tiptoes to give me a kiss on the cheek. 'Are you ready for this?'

I smile, but it feels fake. I decide to level with her. 'Honestly, no. I'm not a sea lover, and the whole thing terrifies me.'

She prods her elbow into my ribs. 'You big wuss. No need to worry. I know exactly what I'm doing, and so long as one of us is in charge, we'll be fine. First of all, I want to introduce you to Clara, who is going to look after Chloe and Isla for the day.'

A young woman steps forward. I hadn't even noticed her standing behind Skye. She is plump, with rosy cheeks, and looks as if she's only a couple of years older than Isla.

'Clara is a trainee at So She & All. She'll take you girls to watch the race on big screens in the Club House, and you'll meet the celebrities, and you can eat and drink as much as you can manage. Right, Nathan. We've got work to do.' Skye turns around.

'Will you be alright?' I ask Chloe and Isla.

'I'll make sure they have a great day.' Clara beams at me. 'Would you like my mobile number, just in case?'

'Yes, that would be great. I assume caretaking teenagers isn't part of your job description?'

She laughs. 'It'll be fun. I've got five younger siblings. No need to worry about Isla and Chloe. We'll have a great day.'

'Can we go sailing, too?' Chloe asks.

Clara chuckles. 'Not today. We only get to watch today, but don't worry. You won't be bored.'

'Thanks,' I say. 'Be good!' Clara's contact details ping through onto my phone. I turn and hurry after Skye, waving at the girls.

'Come on, Nathan,' Skye shouts. 'We need to hurry. I've got the boat ready, but I need to show you the ropes, literally and metaphorically.'

It isn't until I've nearly caught up with Skye that I realise she has Sacha's Sanctuary's logo embroidered on the back of her jacket. Ash was right. It would have been really bad of me to pull out at such late notice. We stride past scores of yachts, many with people busy on board, tugging at lines, scrubbing decks and goodness knows what else.

'Right, this is my boat. It's a Hans Christian 43.' She jumps up onto a white yacht. It has the words *Reach For The Skye* emblazoned in red on the side. It is much bigger than I anticipated, and the nerves kick in as I wonder how it's possible to sail this with just two people, one of them being a complete novice.

She holds out her hand to help me on board, and I have little choice but to take it. Once on deck, she reaches down for a bag and pulls out a navy jacket and trousers identical to her own with the logo on the back. 'Pop those on over your clothes. It'll be chilly out there today.'

I am pulling on the overtrousers when a man appears on the pontoon, a camera around his neck.

'Hello, Skye!' he shouts. 'Can I get a photo?'

'Of course.'

She whispers to me in a low voice, 'He's from a leading news agency. It's a great photo opportunity.'

I pull on the jacket and follow Skye to the side of the boat.

'Stand close together, please,' the photographer says as he lifts his camera up to his eye.

Skye puts her arm around my waist and looks up at me, her eyes wide and soft focused, her lips slightly apart. I glance at the photographer and notice to my dismay that he has been joined by a gaggle of photographers, all snapping away.

'Are you an item, Skye?' a woman shouts.

Skye giggles and pulls me in even tighter, briefly laying her head on my shoulder.

I am utterly horrified. What the hell is she doing, pretending that we're in a relationship? I knew she was delusional. And I knew I shouldn't have come.

'Keep smiling,' she whispers. 'It's for the camera.'

'Are you going to win the race, Skye?'

'As you may or may not know, this yacht is a long keel boat, so it's not the fastest, and we won't be the first across the line, but with our handicap we could win on points. We've got a very good chance, so place your bets!'

'Are you a strong sailor, Nathan?'

But I don't get the chance to answer, as Skye speaks first. 'That's enough, guys. We need to get ready for the race.' She turns away, and I watch the little pack of photographers disperse, off to seek other celebrity prey.

'Right, I need to walk you through all the safety protocols,' she says.

'Why didn't you put the journalists right?' I ask. 'Why didn't you tell them we're not in a relationship?'

'I'll teach you how the VHF radio works, how to reef the sails, where all the safety equipment is.'

'Are you listening to me, Skye?'

She has her back to me and is crouched down winding some ropes.

'As much as I like and respect you, we will never be in a relationship, Skye. I hope you understand.'

'We have a lot of work to do today, Nathan, so I would appreciate if you could concentrate on the here and now. Kindly follow me around the boat.'

We go down the teak wood steps to below deck where Skye shows me where the hatches are, how the toilet works and where the stopcock is, where the fire extinguishers are and how the VHF radio works – and in the case of danger, where the emergency button is. I shiver. Her voice is toneless, and she barely looks at me. Although it's obvious she is upset by what I said, she is single-focused on issuing instructions. I gain some comfort from her showing me where all the emergency equipment is and giving me cursory instructions on what I should do in the unlikely event that we find ourselves in danger.

On deck, she points out how the boom works and how I need to perpetually duck my head. In all situations, I must always have one hand on the boat so I stay attached. She points out how the winches work, and how to hoist and reef the sails. There is so much information to absorb, and I'm far from sure I have grasped everything, and doubtful I will remember it in the heat of the race. It's a relief when she hands me a life jacket; at least I won't sink.

EVENTUALLY, it's time for us to leave. Skye switches on the motor, looks over the side to make sure that water is being pumped out, and then goes back to the helm.

'Release the mooring lines, Nathan,' she shouts. I pull the ropes in and put them in the boat. She is standing at the helm and slowly moves the boat away from the moorings and motors out of the harbour. I estimate we're travelling at less than five miles an hour.

'Coil up the lines, Nathan, and put them under the benches, then clip on your lifeline.' I do as I'm told and then walk carefully along the boat to stand near Skye.

'I'm really sorry about Monica,' I say to Skye. 'It must be devastating losing your mother so soon after finding her.'

'Yes,' she says, her face expressionless.

'It was a terrible shock to find her like that.'

Skye's head jerks back, and she stares at me. 'What?'

'Didn't the police tell you? I was the person who found her.'

Skye's face whitens, and her knuckles grip the helm so tightly, it looks as if the bones are going to pop through her skin. 'What were you doing at Monica's house?'

'She was due at our offices to discuss some voluntary work, but she didn't show up. I was concerned, so I went to her flat and found her.'

'What did she tell you about me?'

I pause before answering. It's an odd question and accompanies a tightening in my sternum. 'Nothing,' I say eventually. 'Although she was planning on telling me something about you that she said I should know. What was that, Skye?'

'She was a drug-addled, delusional woman,' Skye says. 'And right now I need to concentrate on sailing and not be distracted by her.'

FIVE MINUTES LATER, we've passed the harbour entrance, and then we're out on the grey open sea, the waves short and choppy. I keep my eyes on the horizon, but I feel seasick within a couple of minutes. It's that rocking motion up and down that makes my stomach slurp. I double-check that the anti-nausea wrist bands are pressing in the right place and take in some deep breaths. At least I feel safe clipped to the boat and wearing this chunky lifejacket.

Skye is constantly looking at her watch as she lines up our yacht alongside all of the others. There is a motorboat moored at the starter line, and Skye is staring at it.

A white flag with a red circle in it is raised from the motorboat along with a single horn sounding.

'Is it time to go?' I ask, my heart beating a little faster.

'Five minutes. That's the preparatory signal.'

There are at least twenty other boats alongside us. The next five minutes seem to stretch for an eternity. There is another horn sound and the raising of a blue flag, and then a long sounding of a horn, and both the flags are taken down. And we're away.

I am surprised that the other boats seem to speed off,

caught by the wind, racing towards an invisible horizon. We're the last, by some distance. I glance at Skye, but she's expressionless. I had imagined that she would be uber-competitive, aiming to be in amongst the first few yachts.

'Worried we're at the back?' She laughs at me. A strand of hair has come loose from her baseball hat and is streaming behind her head. 'The first will be last, and the last will be first. Everyone underestimates me, Nathan. This boat is slow, and the handicaps will work in our favour, because I know exactly what I'm doing.'

I watch as the motorboat speeds off towards the yachts at the front of the race. We seem to be sailing in a straight line, with the wind billowing through the sails. For a moment, I can see the attraction of this, the way the wind powers us forwards, as if we're in control of the sea, as opposed to the other way around. But then the wind picks up, and my stomach heaves.

'You need to reef the sail, Nathan!' Skye shouts. Her voice sounds reedlike on the wind.

'Reef?' I frown at her. Did she explain what that was earlier?

'Reduce the surface of the sail by folding it over the boom. Put the lines over it and secure it safely. Hurry up and walk to the front of the boat.'

I take a few steps forwards, but I'm restrained by the rope that's attaching me to the boat.

'Unclip the lifeline. Hold it in one hand and hold onto the rails with the other. Keep steady as you walk forward, and you'll be fine.'

I have never gripped a rail so tightly as I creep towards the front of the boat.

'Reach for the lines at the front!' she yells.

I let go of the side of the boat to reach for the ropes,

but as I do so, the boat swings to the right. I hear the roaring of the wind and the flapping of the sails.

And then nothing.

When I come to, I am half out of the boat, my legs soaking wet, being bashed by waves against the side of the boat, water streaming underneath me. I think I'm screaming, but I can't hear anything except the violent whooshing of water. I look up and see Skye hauling herself along the side of the boat, but her lifeline isn't long enough. She unclips it at her life vest. She grabs a long pole with a pointed end that looks like a hook to haul things out of the water.

'Help!' I scream.

She is nearly at my side.

'Can you reach me?' My heart is hammering, the air being pushed out of my chest. 'Take my hand!'

She steps forwards again. If she falls in, I'm as good as dead.

'Be careful, Skye! Be careful!'

'I'm always careful, Nathan.'

And then she smiles at me, but there's a frigidity to her smile that makes it look like a knowing grimace, and the terror magnifies one hundredfold. She stands just out of reach of me and slowly turns the pole around so that the handle rather than the hook is facing me.

'What are you doing?' I yell. 'Use the hook to grab me.'

'If I hit you with the hook side, it will leave identifiable marks. That's a risk I can't take.'

'What?' I struggle to free myself, because surely it will be better for me to fall into the waves than be hit with a stick like a sitting duck.

'Did you make the boom hit my head?' I ask.

She laughs.

'What do you want from me?'

'Here's the thing, Nathan. I have everything I want except the perfect home life. I fell in love with you. I would have cared for the girls as if they were mine.'

'You don't know what love is, what love means.'

'Oh, yes I do. And when I want something, I always get it. I can't force you down the aisle, but I can grieve at your funeral, holding your girls' hands. I can adopt them.'

I see that image in my head, and it horrifies me. My girls need me.

'I'll tell the world that I've lost my best friend, my soulmate and my lover. The man who was a true hero to so many. You don't have to worry about that. The world will mourn you alongside me.'

She raises the pole and brings it down toward my head, but I'm ready for her and stronger. I grab the pole with my right hand and pull it towards me, my hand firmly over the non-slip handle, just as the boat rolls. The hook goes over Skye's wrist and catches in her Rolex watch. She tries to balance herself, to get a better hold of the pole, but I pull it towards me again. Skye is unbalanced, rocking, and then a wave smashes into the side of the yacht, and she tumbles straight into the water. I strain to look for her, and the seconds seem to stretch for eternity.

Then her head breaks the surface just a few metres away from me, but the boat swings and her skull cracks against the hull. I watch with dismay as she and the pole disappear into the water.

'Skye!' I scream. But I hear nothing except the rushing of waves. I look around frantically. She will resurface. She must resurface. The cold water is sapping my strength, and I feel myself slipping, and I know that I have to save myself if I have any chance of saving her. The sail starts flapping, and the racing flow of water around my legs seems to calm down. I don't know where I muster the strength from, but I grab the rails and manage to swing a leg over the railing and haul myself onto the boat, my legs so heavy I'm not sure that they will work. The boom is lurching from side to side, so I crawl towards the helm. I haul myself upwards, trembling, my head throbbing, and grab the steering wheel.

But what am I doing? The waves are getting bigger, and I can't see her anywhere. Could she already have drowned? How stupid to wear navy clothes, which are invisible in the water.

I need to get help. What did she say I should do? I am shaking so much, but I need to be strong. I need to find the VHF radio. Where was it? What did Skye say I had to do? I grab the wooden rails and slip down the stairs into the cabin below. I find the radio and press the emergency button.

'Hello! Can you hear me?' I yell. 'There's someone overboard, and I can't see her. You need to help us!'

I expect to hear crackling static and someone responding, but there is silence. I jab the button again. Still there is nothing. Desperate, I haul myself back up to the deck. Perhaps another boat will see us, and I can wave at them. Perhaps I will be able to spot Skye in the water. But all I can see is grey water meeting grey sky, with crests of white where the waves crash into each other. I can't even see the shoreline and have no idea which way the boat is heading. I try to quell the panic. I need to think clearly. I grip my fingers onto the wheel, trying to keep the boat heading in a straight course.

And then I hear it. A horn. And again.

A motorboat comes flying over the waves, straight towards me.

NATHAN – NOW

I owe a lot to Clara. As soon as it became apparent that there was a man overboard from one of the competing yachts – or in this case, a woman – she distracted my girls and took them off for a drink and a muffin. At least they were spared the terror that it might have been me. The next twenty-four hours passed in a haze. I was brought to shore and checked over by paramedics. Skye's yacht was returned to the harbour and examined. The police were called, of course. The coastguard searched the sea, using boats and helicopters, until nightfall.

The girls and I were put up in a local hotel for a night, and I was questioned, but I never felt as if I was under any suspicion.

At 10 a.m. the next morning, they found Skye's body. Everyone was very kind to me, saying that as an experienced sailor Skye knew that she should never have unhooked her lifeline. Terrible accidents happen at sea, apparently. So I didn't tell anyone that Skye was trying to kill me. There seemed no point.

Another driver took us home. My heart pounded as

the car pulled up into our driveway and I saw there were lights on in the house, lights that I most definitely did not leave on when we left the previous day. As I got out of the car, the front door swung open, and I have to admit that I cried.

Marie came running towards me, her arms outstretched. The girls piled into our hug, and even my Isla, who pretends to be all grown up, gave Marie a big kiss and told her that she missed her.

'How did you know?' I asked as we walked hand in hand into the house.

'I rang Marie and told her everything,' Isla said. 'You need each other.'

'And thank goodness she did.' Marie put an arm around Isla's shoulders.

THE OUTPOURING of grief over Skye's death was over-whelming. I was caught at the epicentre of a media storm, with everyone wanting to know what happened, asking how I would cope, having witnessed the devastating death of my new lover. Donations came rushing into Sacha's Sanctuary, and those only increased after Martin Rodriguez wrote an obituary piece on Skye, stating how her memory could be preserved through the work of our charity.

Ash and the team put an embargo on any media contact. We stayed silent, which was difficult, because amongst the grief came death threats, people who thought that I was to blame for the untimely death of their everyday heroine, because I didn't try hard enough to save her. And perhaps they were right. But then again, if Skye hadn't tried to attack me, she would still be alive today. The initial pathology report suggested that Skye was unconscious when she fell into the sea, and she died from secondary drowning. At least she was spared the terror.

And yes, I feel terrible. Despite knowing that her demise was due to her own actions, I blame myself. Did I imagine that she was trying to kill me? Surely she wasn't that demented? But my dreams are haunted by Skye holding Isla's and Chloe's hands at my funeral, and I know that my dreams would have been her reality. I cling onto Marie tightly every night, and she soothes me when I awake, drenched in sweat and trembling from my nightmares.

THIS MORNING, I received a phone call from the police. They have asked me to go into the police station. I am, frankly, terrified. Have they found something that suggests I was responsible for Skye's death? Marie insists on coming with me, although she won't be allowed into the interview room. Just knowing that she is sitting in the car, waiting for me, gives me strength. I walk into the police station and say that I have a meeting with Detective Constable Dominic McCarthy.

Dressed in an open-neck shirt and dark trousers, McCarthy has a tanned and lined face, dark eyebrows and a bald head.

'Thanks for coming in to meet me,' he says as I follow him along the corridor of the police station. He pushes open a door to a small interview room.

'Please have a seat. Would you like a tea or coffee?'

'No, I'm fine, thanks,' I say as I sit down at the table.

'I want to discuss Skye Walker's death with you.'

I nod and try to keep my face impassive. But my heart is banging inside my chest.

'Please talk me through exactly what happened once again.'

I take a deep breath and try to banish the mental image of Marie and the girls visiting me in prison.

'Skye told me to go forwards and reef the sails. I forgot to duck, and the boom hit my head, and I was pushed over the side, but got caught on the railing. Skye walked towards me to try to help, but the same thing happened to her, and she was pushed over the side.'

'But she unclipped her line.'

'Yes. I was totally panicked and don't recall exactly what happened.'

I hold my breath and hold his gaze, reiterating the story that I have told repeatedly. How I wish I could tell him the truth, that Skye tried to kill me; how she told me that she would adopt my girls and pretend to grieve for me, all because I didn't want a relationship with her. But who would they believe? Me or the social media darling, the woman who could do no wrong?

There is a long pause as Dominic McCarthy holds my gaze. Then his pale grey eyes move away from mine and glance at the file on the desk.

'As you know, we are still investigating the death of Monica Walker. A notebook was found at Monica's flat in which she wrote a letter addressed to Martin Rodriguez, the journalist, detailing her suspicions that Skye was not her daughter, but had been impersonating her daughter. The pathologists have carried out a DNA test on both bodies and confirmed that the two are not related. They also found some post-mortem marks on Monica's body that suggest she was injected with heroin rather than taking it herself. We are treating her death as suspicious.'

I gasp. 'Did Skye do it?'

McCarthy narrows his eyes at me. 'Do you have any reason to believe Skye might have killed Monica?'

I sigh and glance around the room and then return

my gaze to McCarthy. 'No,' I say. And it's true. I can't imagine Skye getting her hands dirty like that.

'We have discovered that the woman we knew as Skye Walker is, in fact, Tiffany Larkin, who went missing ten years ago after her parents' private plane came down off the coast of Jersey. She disappeared shortly after her parents' funeral. We will be reopening the investigation into that plane crash.'

'You think Skye – I mean, Tiffany – somehow brought the plane down?'

'We don't know, but we do know that Tiffany's flying instructor said the plane was in excellent condition and that Tiffany was an accomplished pilot. The most probable cause of a plane ditching into the sea is carbon monoxide poisoning. According to family members, Tiffany vanished after discovering that her parents left her substantial debts. We also know that the family took in a girl called Skye Walker, who had been reported as a missing person by her social worker. Based on Monica Walker's letter, our working theory is that the real Skye Walker died on the plane with Mr and Mrs Larkin, and Tiffany, who we know wasn't on the plane, took on Skye's identity to avoid her parents' debts. Did you ever have any suspicions about Skye?'

'Yes,' I say, nodding my head. 'She was highly manipulative. She made it very clear that she wanted a relationship with me, but I rejected her advances. I even wondered whether she was behind me getting beaten up.'

'We have discovered two substantial payments from her account. One was made on the day that you were attacked, and the larger one was on the day that Monica Walker died. We suspect that Skye employed a hit man to do her dirty work.'

'Bloody hell,' I say, letting a whistle escape from my lips.

'We will, of course, try to keep as much of this information out of the public eye, but if it does get out, there will be a media storm, and you will be at the heart of it. We wanted you to have the heads-up, as Sacha's Sanctuary does so much for the local communities, and it would be a great shame if your work was negatively impacted by this.'

'Thank you,' I say, although I can hardly process everything I've been told.

I could tell Dominic McCarthy the truth, and now would be the time to do it. He would probably believe me, but what is the point? The woman we all knew as Skye is dead, and she can never be held to account. Would people really believe that their idol was a monster? Probably not. Will I be able to prove that what you see and read on social media may be just an illusion? Unlikely. And most importantly, do I really want to shatter the image that my girls have of Skye, to let them know that there is such evil in our world? No. They have suffered enough.

'How will the media find out that Skye was Tiffany?' I ask.

'I'm not saying they will. We have to wait and see. From my perspective, I'd like to blow this wide open, but with Tiffany Larkin dead, there's no one to charge. I'm not sure it's in anyone's interest for this to be in the public domain.'

'But they could find out anyway?'

He nods.

'The coroner will complete the inquests into both deaths, and the verdict records will be in the public domain. Depending upon what the coroner concludes, the truth may be revealed at that point. And then the cases will be closed. What are your plans for Sacha's Sanctuary?'

'Despite everything, Skye did a lot of good for us. Our income has dramatically increased, so we intend to carry on ramping up the services we already offer.'

'I'm glad to hear that.' McCarthy stands up and extends his hand.

I leave the police station with a sense of lightness. As I climb into the car, Marie looks at me expectantly.

'It's all over,' I say, and repeat what the policeman told me. 'Your gut instinct was correct.' I lean across the car to place a kiss on Marie's lips.

Dad and Marie aren't home when Chloe and I get back from school. I'm glad. At least I can have a few minutes of flopping on my bed and scrolling through Instagram without one or the other of them biting my head off for not doing my homework.

'Look, you've got a letter,' Chloe says, handing me a small padded envelope with my name and address typed on the front. I rip it open. A silver USB stick tumbles into my hand. It's weird, because there's no note inside and no return address on the envelope.

'What is it?' Chloe asks.

'None of your business.'

I drag my school bag up to my room, shut the door and switch my laptop on. I slide the USB stick into the slot. It takes a moment, and then a video starts up. I gulp when I see Skye's face. Shit. She's sitting on her bed, her white satin duvet pulled up to her chest. She's not wearing any make-up, and she looks knackered. This is creepy.

I hesitate and then press play.

'Hello, Isla. If you're watching this, it means I'm

dead. I've made this video because you need to know the truth. I've got something to tell you about your dad. I fell in love with your dad and with you and Chloe. We'd make a wonderful family. But your dad was having none of that. He used me, Isla. He slept with me, and then he rejected me. That's why Marie left. Your dad cheated on his fiancée. No one wants to hear this about their father, but I'm sorry to say his charity is just a front to persuade the world that he's a good person.

'I've recorded this video because I've got a bad feeling about the yacht race tomorrow. I think your dad intends to kill me, push me over the side of the boat perhaps. I'm an excellent sailor but a lousy swimmer, and he knows that. I can't cancel out, because too many people are depending upon me, and hopefully, I'm worrying about nothing.

'I'm really worried about you, Isla – Chloe as well, but you the most, because it's always hardest for the eldest child. I've given a lot of thought as to how you can stay safe. This is what you need to do. You're sixteen next month, aren't you? On your birthday, you'll get a load of money transferred to your bank account. Use that money to go far away from your father, somewhere he'll never find you. You're going to be my legacy, and one day you'll be as famous as me, more so, even. I want you to take on my social media and be my successor. You'll be amazing at it. My agent, Tiana, will show you the ropes.

'You'll get more information on your sixteenth birthday, so you're just going to have to stay strong and brave until that day. Smash up this USB stick and toss it into a fire. And never tell anyone about this. Most importantly, never tell your dad what you know. Never. Because if you do, your life will be in danger, too. Remember, my lovely, that I'll be watching you from the sky. Be brave, Isla. You know what you've got to do. I reached for the sky, and you must too. Be true to you.'

The screen goes black at the exact moment I hear footsteps in the corridor. I slam the lid down on my laptop.

There's a knock, and my bedroom door swings open.

'Hi, darling, Marie and I are home. What are you up to?'

I turn my back to Dad so he can't see my face. 'Homework. Only boring homework.'

———

A LETTER FROM MIRANDA

Thank you so much for reading *The Influencer*. Like many during this year of lockdown, I have spent too much time on social media. I've been fascinated by how much we are influenced by what we see on these platforms, and I have wondered what is real and what is make-believe. However, the roots of this book go back further, to the real case of an Australian woman who pretended she had overcome cancer through natural remedies. She became a natural health guru and launched a hugely successful career off the back of her 'story', with a global following, book and app deals, until the truth was discovered. Everything was false. I was going through chemotherapy when she was at the height of her success and could have so easily been inspired by her erroneous advice. Fictional Skye's story is almost tame in comparison!

I am very lucky to live in such a friendly location. When I posted a research question for this book on our local community Facebook group, I received so many offers of help. In particular, I would like to thank Sandra Matthews and Sarah Spoard. Thank you as well to my close friends Sophia Mason and Cris, and my niece, Samantha Scott, for their advice. Huge thanks, as always, to my husband Harmen, who is my biggest supporter and conveniently a Yachtmaster – rather beneficial for this book! All mistakes are my own.

It's the wonderful team at Inkubator Books that makes my writing possible. I am so grateful to Brian Lynch and Garret Ryan. Thank you too to Jan Smith – it's been such fun having a partner in crime! My thanks as well to Jodi who edits all of my books.

I have had massive support from the book blogging community who do such a stellar job in telling the reading world about new books. Thank you to everyone who has reviewed my books, and a special thank you to book blogger, Carrie Shields.

Lastly but most importantly, thank *you* for reading my books. Without you and the reviews left on Amazon and GoodReads, I wouldn't be living my dream life as a full-time author. Reviews help other people discover my novels, so if you could spend a moment writing an honest review on Amazon, no matter how short it is, I would be massively grateful.

My warmest wishes,

Miranda

www.mirandarijks.com

Published by Inkubator Books
www.inkubatorbooks.com

Printed in Great Britain
by Amazon

79399320R00181